THE FOURTH
ELEPHANT'S EGG

THE FOURTH ELEPHANT'S EGG

THE HYPATOMANCER'S TALE
BOOK THREE

BEING THE TWELFTH ROMANCE OF NOVA EUROPA

ROBERT REGINALD

THE BORGO PRESS

MMXI

THE FOURTH ELEPHANT'S EGG

FIRST EDITION

Published by Wildside Press LLC

www.wildsidebooks.com

DEDICATION

To the memory of my friend and collaborator,

Jeffrey M. Elliot

(June 14, 1947 - December 12, 2009)

and for

Bill Bamberger

"O brave new world, that has such people in't"

CONTENTS

PROLOGUE

"I'LL NEVER TRAVEL TO THE OTHERWORLDS"

My late friend, Willíe Shaking-Spear, and I were sharing a couple of brews at Les Épines Noires, a backwater tavern in the equally backwater town of Sabbedelle, Neustria, one fall day in '08, when he suddenly turned to me and said: "Now is the summer of our discontent made glorious autumn by popping this cork"—and then he opened another bottle of champagne with a great whoosh of bubbly exaltation. He spewed a little into my cup, and placed the spout directly to his lips, guzzling down a quarter of the quaff before relenting. His belch would have awakened the kraken itself—if Sabbedelle had abutted on the sea.

I was returning overland from a period of study in the Grand Duchy of Hildesheim in Germania, making a tour of the northern Papal States, and Willíe…well, he'd just decided that he'd cross the Channel and spend a few days drinking with an old buddy about seriously old times. That was Goodfellow Shaking-Spear for you—he never passed up an opportunity to booze and muse.

"Why such dissatisfaction, my old friend?" I asked.

"I've decided that I'll never be King," he said in his deep voice, burping again.

"But you never *wanted* to be King," I said.

"That has nothing to do with it, Morphy. I'll never be the Holy Roman Cæsar, either."

"Well, that's probably true." I sipped a little of my drink—it was a particularly frothy, fruity vintage that was actually quite enjoyable—in small amounts. "But, why would you?"

"I wouldn't, of course. And…and…."

"Yes?" I asked.

Then his eyes cleared, and he put the bottle down very deliberately with a loud "clunk." He looked at me across the table, and said in his determined way: "I…will…never…travel…to…the…Otherworlds, Morphy." The frown that accompanied his statement told me that this particular pronouncement came straight from what amounted to his chilly little heart.

"I probably won't, either," I said.

He shook his bald head sadly, and said: "But you will, my friend. You *will*."

I just laughed. "Why would I want to?" I asked. "The notion's just absurd, Willíe."

"Laugh all you want, Morphy," Shaking-Spear said, "but I've seen it in my globe. You're going out *there* someday"—he waved his hand at the dirt-encrusted ceiling of the shabby inn—"and you're going to do *great things*. And I'm…I'm just a purveyor of pettifoggery."

"Of *what*? I said.

"Of…of petits-fours in prose, of petite pollywogs of perambulating phrases, of…."

"I get the picture," I said, although I didn't have the vaguest notion of what he was talking about. Sometimes he got lost in a storm of syntax when he was sailing his cup through the Brewski Straits. "You've done great work, Willíe. You're going to be remembered as a spell-maker and wordsmith who towered far above his contemporaries. You have a talent…."

"I have nothing!" he almost shouted, drawing the attention of the tavern keeper. *"I've done nothing!* I'm just another hack. And after I'm dead, you'll be soaring out there through the stars, transiting the vasty spheres of the æther, where no man from Nova Europa has ever gone before. You'll be remembered for all time."

"No, not a chance," I said. "People believe the stories that you tell, Willíe. They immerse themselves in your fantasy worlds for a few hours or days, and you give them something that no one else ever can, save maybe a priest or a showman. You lend them hope! You show them a vision of some other place or time or person who's living a life that's exciting and stimulating and real—at least to them, those sad little people.

"Even if what you say about me is accurate—that I have some glorious destiny to experience in my future years (which I don't think is true for an instant)—who would ever lend it credence? No one believes in *real* marvels. They just don't. Even if I accomplished all that you say, I'd still be a nobody— and *you'd* still be Willíe Shaking-Spear, the greatest writer of our time, perhaps of all time."

"But I'll never travel to the Otherworlds," he whispered, reaching up to brush a tear scurrying down his cheek. "Never!"

"But you travel there every day in your dreams," I said. "So, which is the better reality, my old friend? Answer me that."

He drank the rest of his champagne then, and promptly asked for another, and gradually sank down into that spell of moroseness that would eventually claim his great spirit.

And now, so many years later, I suddenly recalled that moment from my past, and wondered if, indeed, anyone would ever remember me. Willíe's reputation was secure; mine was still in play.

* * * * * * *

I'm called Morpheús the Mage, former Scanner Prime of the Kingdom of Kórynthia on Nova Europa, who was once also known as Oridión son of Kallíkratês, a hypatomancer (a foreseer of the future) of great potency and power.

Perhaps Willíe influenced me after all, because although I advanced steadily from position to position in the government of Kórynthia, I gradually became dissatisfied with my station, to the point where I started looking for other possibilities. And then, one day, I heard this voice calling to me from the æther.

"Help me!" she said—for it was definitely female—"Help me!" How could I resist?

So, I set out from Nova Europa to rescue a Lady imprisoned halfway across the universe, on a world that no one but me had ever even heard of, somewhere out in the Fifth Circle. The distance was so vast, the energy required to reach that point so large, that even the Overseers, the human-like inhabitants of the planet at the very center of the Spheres, who wanted to control everything, rarely transited there.

But I found a way to use the network of transit mirrors created by the Overworlders to further my ends, as well as theirs—until finally I traveled beyond the limits of their time and space, and penetrated the boundary of the Sixth Circle.

To rescue the Lady Niobë and to heal the looming breach in the cosmos, I also had to find and retrieve the four Elephant's Eggs. Even now, I have no idea, really, of what the Eggs are or how they can be manipulated.

I and my compatriots eventually reached the planet of the Pachyderms, those strange creatures that either had created the Eggs—or at least were acting currently as their guardians.

With great difficulty, I found and identified the first three Eggs, and managed to get my team building a primitive transit device that would take us off-world again—because the elephantine creatures possessed no technology of their own, and would only give us a minimum of assistance. With me I had my faithful bodyguards, Sergeant Hawk and his vagabonds; my wherret familiar, Scooter; Mistress Zalmanna of the Overseers; the canine Finder, Arrgruffruff; and my "wife" in name only— Shah'rah the exotic dancer.

I didn't know what the future would bring, or whether my quest to locate the "Lady" would succeed or fail. I didn't know why I was doing what I was doing, save that it seemed a necessary act if I was ever to grow inside, and learn enough about myself and the universe to make a difference.

I had to go forward—with my friends. I had to find what was out there. I had to believe that my life was worth living. I had to keep trying.

And then the machine we were building was finally ready.

"Prepare to transit," I said—and I smiled…smiled at everyone, both to give my friends heart and to give myself strength, as I shepherded them through our makeshift transit-mirror.

"To the stars—through difficulties!"

CHAPTER ONE
"WHAT THE FRUITY FARTS...?"

Anno Domini 1625-1627
Anno Juliani 1265-1267

I was the last one through the gate, preceded by Scooter, my "wife," Hawk and his men, Boupho, Arrgruffruff, and then the Tyro. I shut down the link as soon as everyone had "landed." But where exactly *was* this?

We were literally embedded within a fog, unable to see anything around us. I also couldn't feel the device or mirror that had facilitated our journey through ætherspace.

"Take each other's hand," I ordered, grabbing those of Zalmanna and Shah'rah. The wherret ran up my body to my shoulder.

"This is very strange, Master," it said. "I sense nothing out there."

I decided to wait until the bank lifted, but after many hours of lingering, wondered if the condition was somehow permanent. Finally, however, as the dark began to fall, the stars started to come out, one by one, as the mist gradually dissipated.

We were standing on the surface of what appeared to be, so far as I could tell, a great butte perched on a hill or small mountaintop. Just behind us loomed a huge oval object that I assumed was the transit-mirror or –machine that had allowed us to reach this world.

Suddenly the side of the structure lit up as the device activated, shining a brilliant emerald glare over the landscape. We instinctively backed away as a tall man abruptly appeared before us, materializing out of space and time.

He yelled at us in some lingo that no one understood.

"We come in peace," I said in Tyrosian.

"Who the bloody hell *are* you?" he exclaimed in a heavily-accented retort. All I could see was his black outline shadowed against the glare.

"The same could be asked in return," I said.

"This is Meremptah territory," he said. "I repeat: who are you? What are you doing here?"

"No, that cannot be," Mistress Zalmanna said. "It is just an old tale...."

"What is?" I asked the Tyro.

"That another great power lies in or beyond the Sixth Circle," she said. "But there is only one real power in the universe—Tyrotarichos."

"Believe that if you will," the man said. "I am what I claim to be."

"We're just explorers of the void," I said. "We only ask to be allowed to transit to another way station."

"That's not possible," he said. "You've infringed upon our private network of transportation stations. You'll have to account for yourselves before the authorities."

He pulled out a weapon of some kind, a stubby piece of metal that he held in his right hand, and then pointed it at us. It reminded me of the belchers that had been issued to Hawk and his men back on the Tyrosian homeworld.

I saw Eagle sidling slowly over to one side, preparatory to making a move on the stranger, but the latter just raised his arm and aimed it right at my heart. "You try anything, and that one dies," he said.

Then he spoke something again in his own tongue. The color of the transit-device changed from green to orange, and its power level, judging by the ambient humming that revved up the scale, obviously increased. The man stepped to one side, and motioned us towards the aperture.

"Enter one at a time," he ordered—and then indicated to me, "You go last!"

When I entered the mirror, I felt a pull unlike any I'd ever experienced before, and an abrupt jump that sent me to a second address—and then immediately to a third, and a fourth, and a fifth. Somehow the machines were linked to each other in a way that I'd never imagined possible.

I literally fell through the final gap in ætherspace onto a hardwood floor, rolling over as I hit. I was grabbed by a pair of armed guards, and hauled back away from the opening. Our captor appeared within seconds thereafter, emerging right on the same spot where I'd been initially deposited.

I quickly scanned the room: every member of our group was present and accounted for, thank the Lord.

I finally got a glimpse of the stranger: he was taller than me by almost a foot, and looked very much like the humans from the First Circle, except that he had no ears as such—just openings on either side of his head that obviously served the same purpose. He was dressed in some kind of formal uniform striped with black-and-white crosshatching.

"I am Cor-Cornéggiyan the Evaluator," our captor said, "the Great and the Mighty. And who are you?"

"Morpheús of Kórynthia," I said, "and my traveling companions: Mistress Zalmanna, Lady Shah'rah, Hawk, Warbler, Bird, Roc, Raven, Eagle, Boupho, Arrgruffruff, and Scooter."

"What are you doing in Meremptah territory?"

"We seek new life and new civilizations," I said.

"Yes, we boldly go where no wherret has gone before," Scooter added.

"Uh, huh," the Evaluator said to the creature. "I've encountered one of your species before. He was very tasty when roasted over an open fire. However, I've never seen *your* kind before"— he nodded at the Yowler.

We were each being methodically stripped of all our belongings as we stood there.

"Look at what I found, Sir," one of the alien guards said, reaching into my pouch and handing something over to Cornéggiyan—it was the First Egg. He didn't find the Hand of Morlock, the Pathfinder, or the two books, which I now always tucked away in a pocket of ætherspace before traveling. I don't know why I hadn't done the same with the Egg—and I wondered later if the artifact itself had blocked my usual cautionary urge.

"What's this?" our captor asked.

"A crystalline orb," I said. "I don't know exactly how to use it, or for what purpose it's employed"—which was entirely true as spoken.

Suddenly the thing zapped him, and he abruptly dropped it on his foot. He yelled in pain and then pointed his weapon at the thing. The Evaluator fired a mighty blast of sound, but the pellet—or whatever it was—just ricocheted off the Egg, and drilled a hole through the base of the transit-device, which immediately shut down.

"What the fruity farts...?" he said. He swiveled around and again pointed his belcher at me. *"Tell me what this is!"*

"It's just an old artifact," I said. "It was discovered on Erésvepe by a colleague of mine, Master Melanchthon the Merciless."

He tried to pick it up, but it dinged him again.

"Ye gods!" he shouted.

He tried to stomp on it, but it somehow threw him halfway across the room. Several of his men sniggered.

"Damn you!" he exclaimed, and then ordered: "Scoop it up and put it in a box. Imprison them all."

"Yes, Sir," two of the guards, and a squad of the gendarmes grabbed us by the arms. They took us to a suite of rooms somewhere underground, and bolted the door on the other side.

"This place cannot exist," Mistress Zalmanna said, still looking shell-shocked. "It was a fable, a legend, just a story that travelers told. No one believed them."

"What is Meremptah supposed to be?" I asked.

"According to the rumors, it was another large empire

located somewhere out beyond the Fifth Circle—and was, perhaps, the counterbalance to Tyrotarichos, either in political authority or at least in the psychic sphere. Several philosophers believed that Meremptah, or something like it, was necessary to explain certain anomalies that had been observed in long-ætherial transit. No one has ever been able to develop a theory that fully answers the questions regarding the chaotic swirls that are known to occur out beyond real space and time. Supposedly, the existence of Meremptah might satisfy some of those variances.

"But if that is the case, where have they been all these millennia? Why have none of our own explorers ever encountered them in their many travels?"

"More to the point, where exactly *is* this place?" I asked. "If it's far off the known transit routes, that might provide a possible explanation for their anonymity."

There was a knock on our door. I motioned everyone to step away from the entrance. We could hear the bolt draw back, and a lone guard stood there in the doorway.

"Yes?" I said.

"This is for you, Sir," the man said, his voice almost slurring, like he was drugged or not quite awake. He held out his hand: on his palm was the pulsing presence of The First Elephant's Egg.

I walked over to him and took the crystal. He turned and shut the door again. I looked down at the artifact.

"Well, I'll be damned," I said.

CHAPTER TWO
"EVERY LAST STICKER AND PRICKER"

It was obvious to me that the Egg had "persuaded" the guard, unbeknownst to himself, to return the artifact to the individual it preferred, for whatever reason. I wondered if the crystal had some kind of consciousness in and of itself, or if it was connected to the other Eggs or to another entity somewhere "out there." What exactly were the Eggs, and what were they intended to accomplish?

I needed to spend some additional time exploring the orb's potential, in order to uncover the answers to this and other questions, but right now I was more concerned with breaking out of our confinement, and zipping our way to a more pleasant—and perhaps more controllable—destination.

"Hawk," I said, "did you save anything?"

"No, Sir: they got it all, every last sticker and pricker."

"Any of the rest of you?"

But our captors had been quite thorough in divesting us of everything we carried—except for the Egg, of course, and the other three implements that I'd stashed in their ætherial hideaway. I carefully deposited the Egg in with the rest.

"Is there anything else here that we can use as a weapon?"

"Nothing, Sir," came the reply. "The beds, tables, and benches are all bolted to the floor."

"Then we'll have to use our wits," I said. "We have to find some way of determining how big this place is, and where we're located vis-à-vis the transit room and other important facilities.

"I can probably squeeze under the door, Master," Scooter said. But it turned out the creature couldn't, because it sat too snugly within its frame.

"What about the air vents?"

I knew that closed-in buildings such as this station required internal ventilation, although I didn't understand the physical mechanisms needed to produce the effect. On Nova Europa, we used blow-imps on those rare occasions when the natural circulation of air wasn't possible.

But here again the Meremptahs had planned well. We located the openings, but they were covered with a firmly-attached set of fine wire meshes.

"I can't attenuate myself to that extent, Sir," the wherret said, "without risking damage to my internal organs."

There was one other possibility.

"The garde-robe!" I said. After all, the effluent had to go somewhere!

"Oh, no, Master, not that," Scooter said. "I have to draw the line here. It's just not…."

"Well, let's take a look anyway," I said, and led our group into the alcove that served as our communal commode. But as with certain other societies that we'd encountered, including the Tyrosians, the Meremptahs employed a much more sophisticated type of plumbing than anything we had available on the homeworld.

I saw a round, smooth bowl partially filled with water, and a hole right in the middle—and I didn't know what kept the fluid from just draining away. These things were always mysteries to me.

"There!" I said, pointing down at the thing. I pressed the lever to activate the machine, and the liquid swirled 'round and 'round several times before just flushing away through the gap in the center. "You can go there!"

"Uh, I don't think so, Master," Scooter said. "I could easily drown down there. I have no idea where this goes, or what it merges into. If there's a processing facility, I could be ground up or dissolved or anything like that. Not to mention the ordure! Why, it would foul my coat!"

"Why don't you ask the Egg?" Shah'rah suddenly suggested.

"What do you mean?" I said.

"Well, you've told us that you think it has the ability to communicate with you. If it wants to move on, if it wants to find its companion Eggs, wouldn't it help us achieve that? Just ask it, Morpheús."

I hated to be put in the position where such a reasonable suggestion—something that hadn't even occurred to me—was offered by a *woman*. At the same time, however, the fact of the matter was that I didn't quite know *how* to contact the artifact, even if I'd already done so once before.

I'd posted Eagle at the door to listen for possible interruptions, and when he whistled low beneath his breath, I quickly pocketed the orb that I'd just retrieved again, and turned towards the door.

But it was just the attendants bringing us something to eat—carefully guarded, of course, by a squad of the gendarmerie. They lugged in a steaming pot filled with some kind of stew—mystery meat interspersed with equally mysterious vegetables, in a green sauce—plus several jugs of sweetly-flavored water. I asked Scooter, whose digestion system was almost indestructible, to sample both wares, and the creature pronounced them "fit to eat, if a bit bland."

Of course, "bland" to a wherret is the same thing as hotter than the fires of Hell to the rest of us, so when I dipped a wooden spoon into the mess and took a big slurp—a grave error of judgment, I now admit—I thought my tongue was going to roll up, shrivel away, and be seared straight off. I grabbed the nearest container of liquid and drank several pints right down the old gullet. Then I began to hiccup, and couldn't stop until Hawk slammed me on the back a couple of times.

Thereafter, we all sampled the victuals more carefully. One could actually reach a point after a dozen bites or so where the pangs of hunger overrode any concern for the surface of one's palate!

Although our suite consisted of several interlocking rooms—none of them with windows or other doors, of course—the only private space was the garde-robe. The Meremptahs had left a set of bedrolls and blankets lined up along the wall. All of our spare clothes and personal items had been confiscated. There was one tap providing clean water next to the facilities.

Not long after "dinner," the lights began to dim, and we understood this as a signal to prepare for bed. I grasped the crystal in my hands as I slid beneath one of the covers, and tried to focus on whatever was inside.

When I'd been ill, I'd easily drifted into the wake of its consciousness—or whatever it was—but now I seemed to be blocked from attaining that easy familiarity again. It was the same damn problem that I'd experienced with Lady Niobë on occasion. Either I found myself interfacing with her as if we were old compatriots in a longstanding relationship—or I felt like a complete stranger when butting up against her mores and prejudices. What was the matter with me, that I was so unable to come readily to terms with other beings? I'd had many relationships over the years, of course, but now that I really thought about them, none had ever been close, at least not in the way described by so many others.

Master Melanchthon, by all accounts, had spoken directly to the thing, and had apparently received some kind of understandable response.

"Please!" I begged, "I need your help."

There was a twinge of—something—deep within my soul, but no direct response, not that I could identify anyway. What did it want of me?

They *all* wanted something, every last one of them. They wanted me to tell their fortunes, to make them come true, to assure them that everything would be all right in their lives, that they'd be happy and content and rich and famous—or whatever else it was that they desired. But life wasn't like that, it really wasn't, and I was tired of lying to everyone.

Or they wanted me to lead them—but to where? I wasn't sure myself anymore.

Or they wanted me to save them—but for what? I couldn't even answer my *own* questions, much less find solutions to those posed by others.

I just wanted them all to go away and leave me alone!

Suddenly I was appalled by what I'd just admitted. It wasn't true, not really. In reality, I was lonely and sad and utterly terrified of spending the rest of my days isolated from anyone who really gave a fig about my existence.

"Master!" the soft voice whispered in my ear.

"What?" I said. The room was completely dark by now.

"You called, Master. Is something wrong?"

"Would you"—I gulped at my temerity—"could you just hold me for a while?" I asked Shah'rah.

She didn't reply, but unfolded the bedroll and slipped in next to me, her warm body cozying up next to mine. I should have been aroused—*would* have been, under any normal circumstance—but I was so depressed right then that I just needed the touch of someone, anyone, to get me past myself. She wrapped her slim arms tight around me and gently moved my head to her chest, and I lay there just drifting, drifting, and, gradually, finally edging over the abyss into a deep sleep.

Somewhere in the depths of the night I felt the touch of the entity that I sought.

Yes, it said, *we will help.*

CHAPTER THREE
"WE MAY NOT HAVE THE TIME"

When I awoke the next morning, Shah'rah was gone, and my memory of the previous evening seemed almost a dream—gray and rather hazy around the edges. But I could detect the faint odor of her body yet lingering on the blankets, and I knew that everything had happened as I'd imagined—including the communication that I'd received from the Egg!

Then the door to our prison was thrown open, and Cor-Cornéggiyan the Evaluator rushed in with a squad of guards, rousing everyone who wasn't already up.

"Someone has stolen the crystalline weapon!" he shouted.

Then: "Search them!" he ordered his men.

And so we were lined up and frisked very thoroughly—but the Egg wasn't there! The Meremptahs did the same with our bedding, but again, nothing was found.

"Harrumph!" was all the man could say as he stomped out of our suite.

"Where is it?" Mistress Zalmanna asked, as everyone gathered around.

"Safe," I said—and then I reached into one of my pockets and pulled the thing out where they could see it.

"Ooh," they said, as the orb began its rhythmic pulsing.

"How…?" Shah'rah asked, but I didn't answer.

Scooter ran up my leg to my shoulder and whispered in my right ear: "I know what you did last night!"

"Oh, shush!" I said.

"Can this device facilitate our escape?" the Tyro asked.

"Perhaps," I said, "but I still need more time to determine how it works."

"We may not have the time," she said. "I feel that our captors may proceed to torture or imprison us—or even sentence us to death."

"Why should they?" I asked. "We're no threat to them."

"Yes, but...."

"What haven't you told us, Mistress?"

"It is true what I said previously, that we have no direct knowledge of these people. But what I failed to say was that we have sent several large expeditions deep into the Sixth Circle, seeking to expand our control of the worlds there by establishing a series of key transit bases, just as we have in the other Spheres. All of these were unsuccessful.

"We never received word back from several of these ventures, once they had reached a certain point in their travels. Another one sent us a garbled message that they were under attack from an unknown foe, before communications were completely lost. Only one expedition experienced a different outcome.

"About twenty years ago, we mounted a new exploration of this particular sector of the Sixth Circle, and once again lost contact with our people several weeks after they departed. Just one member of that group returned, and the only thing that he was ever able to say was, 'Stay out of this space'.

"And so we have, at least thus far."

"So you now think that the Meremptahs were responsible?"

"That appears to be one possible answer. They do not seem to be much limited here, although we have never seen them in the Fifth Sphere."

"But what we've seen, they could cross that boundary at any time."

"Then why haven't they, Master?" Scooter asked. "It doesn't make any sense."

"I just wonder what's holding them back," I said. "Perhaps they've tried in the same way you have, and been defeated."

"If so, we have not been the agent," Mistress Zalmanna said. "Then who was?"

But we had no information on which to base our speculations, and I was left with the sense that any answer—to the question of our escape, at least—must derive from *The First Elephant's Egg*.

Why were these artifacts made, and by whom? What was their purpose? How did they function?

The crystal itself remained silent, despite my best efforts to access it that afternoon and evening. I finally decided to give it a rest, and to attempt contacting the Lady Niobë again through the sky-orb that the Tyros had given me.

"How do you fare?" she asked, when the connection was finally established after several attempts on my part.

I told her about our situation, of my illness, and how we'd escaped from Pachydermia. When I mentioned the odd uniforms of the Meremptahs, she said: "They sound very familiar. I think we've had dealings with these people in the past, although they called themselves by some other name. This was before the Bird-Men invaded our world."

"What happened then?"

"Well, the Volúcris wouldn't have anything to do with them. They said they were their 'enemies' or something like that— that wasn't the word they used, but a term more subtle, indicating someone who'd betrayed a trust. They just didn't like them. On the other hand, I don't think there are many humans whom the Bird-Men *do* like!"

"Probably not. What about your situation?"

"Amazingly, it continues to improve in small ways. I distrust all of it, however. My son wants something, but he hasn't told me yet what it is. I know I won't like it whenever it rears its pointed head."

"I don't know what to do, Lady," I said. "Every step that I take seems blocked or obfuscated. My whole life has gone that way. I can't seem to make any progress—towards rescuing you or finding the Eggs or anything else."

"Perhaps you're thinking about it in the wrong way."

"What do you mean?" I asked.

"Well, it seems to me that you've made tremendous advances—just not in the ways that you thought. You don't have the control that you wanted. But really, none of us do. It's all an illusion."

"But...." And then it suddenly seemed to me that she was right, after all, and that I was being too timid in my aspirations. Maybe the answer was right there in front of me.

"We'll try it your way," I said.

"Then I'll see you soon," the Lady said.

CHAPTER FOUR
"SO, LITTLE ONE, LET'S SEE WHAT YOU CAN DO"

"So, Little One," I said to the Egg, holding it up to the light, "let's see what you can do." It seemed to flicker in response, but perhaps I was just "seeing" things.

I called our group of adventurers together, and told them what I intended to do. "Follow me," I said.

Scooter ran up my body to my right shoulder, and we walked over to the door. I pressed the crystal against the metal (for such seemed to be its composition), and saw a muted flash. Then I reached down and...slowly turned the knob!

I peered through the slight gap thus created. I could see the backsides of two guards, one to either side of the opening. I willed myself into the orb, and whispered, "Sedate them!"

One of the men yawned quite loudly, and then leaned back against the wall to the right of the doorframe.

"What's the matter, Robb?" his companion asked, before half-stifling a groan himself. Then he sat down on the floor, setting his spear under his left arm, and went to sleep.

Hawk and his crew poured past me and stripped the guards of their weapons and armor.

But I was absorbed with trying to maintain my own consciousness while directing the energies contained within the thing throbbing on my hand. It was gradually heating up, and I wondered how long I could actually grasp it before getting seriously burnt.

"Where do we go?" I asked, and it tugged me forward, and then left down a long hallway. The others tagged behind, keeping an eye out for security teams.

We turned left again, and then moved gradually up a slow ramp that wound one full circle around itself before emerging into a greatroom of some type.

I stopped at the entranceway, because there were people coming and going at the far end, and I saw no way to traverse the space without attracting their attention.

"Find me another way!" I commanded, but the Egg just tugged me again towards the open room.

I sighed: I was being forced to trust the device, even though the thought made me nigh unto nauseous. This was far too dangerous, not just for me, but for Shah'rah and my other companions!

It pulled on me again. I stepped out from the shadow of the door, and started walking towards the exit on the far side. One by one my comrades trailed behind, peering constantly at the aliens scurrying by.

But, strange to tell, none of the Meremptahs appeared to notice us! In fact, they actually moved out of our way to avoid seemingly inevitable collisions. As I trod that very long path across the crowded space, holding The First Elephant's Egg out in front of me like some beacon lighting our way, the masses simply parted, as if I were a modern-day Moses dividing the Red Sea. I could hear them talking to each other—gabble, gabble, gabble—in the background, but instinctively, I and the others knew that we had to maintain our silence to avoid being noticed.

Suddenly we were through the door on the opposite side, and proceeded almost immediately into a side-passage that was little traveled.

As soon as we were out of sight of the controllers, Scooter whispered in my ear, "What just happened, Master?"

"I wish I knew," I said. "Now, keep quiet, everyone!" I hissed.

That slow, meticulous escape from our prison suite remains

embedded in my mind to this day as one of the most bizarre things that I've ever experienced. It was frightening in its intensity, particularly since I didn't have any idea of what was going to happen next. Perhaps that was just as well.

Then we approached a door that was closed to us, and I knew somehow that the transit-room was located just on the other side. I motioned for everyone to gather close.

"The Egg tells me that it can only control the Controllers until it begins working on the transit-machine," I said. "Then they'll notice us immediately, and take steps to stop us from departing. We have to be ready for them."

"Ask it, Sir, if we can grab some more weapons before it releases the buggers," Hawk said.

"Yes, it says," I said.

Then I slowly opened the door, and we again walked boldly out into the well-lit heptagonal room. The orb indicated that we wanted the sixth device, a great metallic object set into an alcove, with a complicated control console attached to its side. I motioned for everyone to stop and look carefully at what was going on around us.

There were perhaps twenty technicians and guards spread around the periphery of the area, flanking three entrances and seven machines, one to each inset. I noticed one man passing his hand over a bank of colored lights that changed hue as he apparently manipulated them. There was no way, I saw, that we could master the intricacies of this system without extensive training: it was so different from what we were accustomed to that I had no idea, really, how it worked. In this particular contest between the Egg and I, the Egg would surely win.

They were talking back and forth among themselves in their clicking lingo, when suddenly one of the alcoves—the fourth, I think—lit up as it was activated, and a party of three Meremptahs in fancy uniforms emerged from the space, and immediately departed through an adjoining exit.

I nudged Hawk, and pointed to one of the metal belchers carried by the guards. He nodded his head, and then motioned to his men, who very quietly and carefully tiptoed one at a time over to each of the guards, and stripped them of his weapons. There were too many for us to use, but we jammed the surplus pieces under the furniture, trying to wedge them there as tight as we could.

When we were about ready, I motioned again for the group to follow my lead, and we edged over to Console Number Six, where a lone worker was fiddling with the control mechanism. Then I held up the fingers of my right hand, and silently counted down from five to one.

Eagle slammed a fist into the technician's face, and he slumped to the ground. Suddenly we were the apple of everyone's eye, as all of the Meremptahs swiftly swiveled and focused on our little group of intruders.

"Dugless!" one of them yelled, and then did something to the console before him that set off a loud bleating noise that was obviously telling the world that things were seriously screwed up in Transit Control!

Behind me I heard the great metallic gate slowly rumble to life—although I didn't know who was operating the machine (it wasn't me!)—and then a bright amber light suddenly flashed, casting our sharp shadows nearly across the room. Even though the alien guards now lacked their weapons, they started to rush forward, counting on sheer numbers to overwhelm us. But Hawk and his men mowed down any of the Meremptahs who approached closer to us than twenty feet, and finally the rest stayed back, waiting for reinforcements.

These began appearing in ones and twos just as I received the thought that we should start leaving—and real soon now!

"Move out, folks!" I yelled over the din, as Hawk shot one of the well-armed newcomers.

I literally shoved Shah'rah through the opening, and the Yowler leaped after her, following by Mistress Zalmanna, and then Hawk's crew and Boupho, and finally me and Scooter last of all. Just before entering ætherspace, I saw one of the guards taking careful aim at my back, and knew that I was going to die right then and there—but the bolt, when it came, just bounced off, skewing into the device to my right. The Egg protected its own!

And then I was through, and felt again the bump-bump-bump of the series of linked transits that the Meremptahs seemed to favor with their machines, until finally I lost track of what was happening or where we were. Everything went black.

CHAPTER FIVE

"HELLO?"

The problem with transiting is that sometimes, just occasionally, you can lose control of the process. For example, in this case two very bad things happened right at the onset—someone or something other than myself activated the controls of the transmitter-device, and then all of us (apparently) lost consciousness in ætherspace.

So when I awoke, I had no idea where I was, except that I was tucked naked and warm and alone in a comfortable bed in a darkened room. I sat up slowly, created a cold-flame on the tips of the fingers of my right hand, and softly said, "Hello?"

But no one responded, and I saw nothing else in the room save a wooden hanger on which my clothes were carefully arrayed. When I walked over to them, I could sense that they'd been cleaned and pressed. I slowly put them on, as well as my polished boots, and then carefully opened the one door.

Some kind of artificial lighting—I couldn't fathom the source—illuminated the corridor outside. I turned to the right—it was as good a direction as any—and walked the fifty feet to where the passageway jogged to the left, then right, and then left again. The occasional doors were all locked. Finally I entered what appeared to be a large, open community room of some kind, with comfortable chairs scattered here and there in front of low tables. Something about the furniture intrigued me, and when I examined them more closely with my inner sight, I realized that they'd been fashioned of some type of artificial fabric and substances that I'd never encountered before.

"Ah," a voice spoke from behind one of the oversized seats, "Welcome, Master Morpheús." The language was slightly accented Tyrosian.

I jumped at the unexpected intrusion. A tall, very thin man of indeterminate middle age rose and walked towards me.

"Where are my companions, Sir?" I asked.

"Safe," he said. "They'll join us as soon as they rouse themselves."

As he slowly approached, I realized that my host was human, although his physical characteristics seemed odd to me. He might have been forty or fifty years old, except for the very deliberate, almost shuffling way in which he walked—a manner, I suddenly realized, that I'd seen employed only by the very infirm and the elderly. His hair was light brown, and he sported two long salt-and-pepper sideburns and just the touch of a goatee smudged beneath his lower lip.

I heard a noise behind me, and Shah'rah ambled half-asleep through another entrance to the room. She was followed in quick order by the rest of my weary group of travelers, all of whom gathered around me in a semi-circle, confronting our captor (for this is what I assumed he must be).

"Welcome to you-all," he said in a kind of Greek drawl. "Please be seated and enjoy the refreshments"—and then I realized that the tables were covered with drinks and trays of food (and they *hadn't* been when I arrived, just moments before!).

"What...?" I said, looking around me in amazement at the cornucopia spread before us. "How...?" And then: "Who *are* you, Sir?" I asked. The man somehow looked vaguely familiar to me.

"I've gone by many names in my life," he said, "But I think you know me best as Mathurin."

"Master Mathurin!" I exclaimed. "But...you'd be more than a thousand years old. You can't be him!"

"Actually, two millennia, my son," the mage said, "And, yes, I'm that very same person who's commemorated on the

Hand of Morlock that you carry in your pouch—well, actually, *this* one!" He reached into the open air, and plucked the silver sculpture and the amber stone that it grasped within its hands directly from the æther.

"But...." I didn't know what else to say or ask, although I was teeming with questions. It's just that I was so stunned by this turn of events, that I couldn't gather my thoughts together. To find the old mage *alive* after all this time....

"Please," he said, his voice suddenly echoing around the room, "please sit down and enjoy yourselves, ladies and gentlemen. The refreshments have been provided for you, to help replenish your energy after the long trip you made."

That comment prompted me to ask, as I followed the ancient Master and plopped myself into a comfortable chair next to his, "And where exactly are we, Sir?"

"The name of this place doesn't matter," Mathurin said. "You won't be here long enough to explore anything outside of these rooms in any case, since you must depart soon. Suffice it to say that it's not within the realm of your experience or possibility, and you cannot remain in this place for very long without being affected by its ambiance."

"Then, how did we get here, Sir?"

"Well, as to that," he said, chuckling to himself, "It wasn't an accident, of course. I sent my little friend to retrieve you." He opened his hand, and the First Egg that I'd taken from Master Melanchthon suddenly blazed out its radiant glory, illuminating the room to such a degree that I couldn't peer at it directly. I was rubbing my eyes to clear my vision when I heard a slight buzz that sounded almost like a purr.

"Reveal yourself, Essora," the magician ordered, and when my eyes could see again, I was stunned to find a beautiful woman in an amber wrap standing there beside his chair, her left hand draping idly on his shoulder. She wasn't entirely human, I think, but I could have fallen in love with her no matter what her origins. She bowed her head slightly in my direction.

I shook my head slightly to clear my thoughts. "Uh, that's not really one of the Elephant's Eggs, is it, Sir?"

"No, Master Morpheús, it isn't, and I apologize for my small deception. But time runs short, and I had to bring you here by any means possible.

"The universe as you and I know it has a fatal flaw," the great mage said. "Picture it, if you will, as a giant clockwork. Within the mechanism are a series of intricate weights and balances and gears that keep time moving forward—and mostly you and the rest of the beings who inhabit the Five Spheres never encounter such things, or have any knowledge of their existence.

"But over time—over a very long period of time—things gradually run down, and at some point the clock must be carefully rewound in order to function properly—or the chaos that makes up the Sixth Sphere and beyond will overwhelm it, and crack the æther in a such a way that our worlds as we know them will become irretrievable.

"We have now reached that point, and you yourself have seen the gradual fracturing of the structure that maintains time and space within this pocket entity.

"The Maker-and-Fixer-of-Things was one of the beings who brought order to chaos uncounted æons ago, and he/she created the Eggs to assist more ordinary intelligences to rewind the mechanism again. I was one such when I was young.

"But as you have already seen with your inner light, I am no longer what I was, and have not the power or energy to do what must be done to preserve all of the good things in life. That task now falls to you, Master Morpheús, my distant descendant."

"But...." I again didn't know what to say, and I'm rarely so speechless.

"I...I h-haven't the ability," I finally stammered out. "I don't know what to do or how to do it. There must be someone else who can help."

Mathurin reached down and picked up what looked like a large purple grape, and bit it halfway through, the juices squirting out to either side. One violet drop marred the blandness of his beige shirt.

"Life is good, isn't it, Morphy?" he said, popping the remaining piece into his mouth, and closing his eyes with pleasure. "It's sweet and tart and full of vigor. And I've never eaten a piece of fruit that tasted as good as this, because this is now."

Then his eyelids slowly opened again, and he looked directly at me, really *looked* at me, probing into my very soul. "But it's gone, just like that, and soon I'll be gone as well. My time here is nearly done.

"Sometimes there's just no one else who can do exactly what you can do. You and I are both Dream Weavers and hypatomancers, a very special breed indeed. But even *we* are not sufficient by ourselves to accomplish this task. It always takes another."

Suddenly I realized what he was saying. "Lady Niobë!" I exclaimed.

"Yes. The Yin and the Yang, the male and the female, the separate halves of the same soul, The Maker-and-Fixer-of-Things—call it what you will, but each of us needs that counterbalance in order to mend what is broken. She's the direct descendant of that woman with whom I partnered the last time that I undertook the recalibration of our universe; and she'll be a necessary adjunct to whatever you must refashion."

"But the Eggs...."

"The Eggs of the Great Elephant, the implements created by The Maker-and-Fixer-of-Things, are the tools that you will need in order to accomplish this working. It will be the grandest spell that you ever forge, and it will take from you all that you have and all that you've learned—and all that I can give you of my memories and knowledge. That's why you're here.

"And, in answer to your question, there's no one else. Not really. If you fail at this great task, the consequences could be utterly dire for all that you know and love and cherish and value."

The weight of the responsibility he was imposing on me was suddenly almost overwhelming.

"But the Eggs, at least according to, uh, Essora," I said,

"are scattered throughout the Five Circles. How can I possibly retrieve them? It would take a lifetime of travel."

"Ah, well," the Master said, "You don't need all of the Eggs, Morpheús, just one of each. You see, they're linked one to another psychically, and when put together, can be used to control *all* of their brethren, wherever they might be located. They *have* to be scattered to be employed properly, so that the working that you ultimately create will affect simultaneously all parts of the region of time and space that we inhabit. Otherwise...."

"Otherwise, things will fall apart," Mistress Zalmanna said.

"Yes, Madame, they will," the old man said.

"Why did you leave Tyrotarichos?" she asked. "Why did you abandon us?"

"Every father must allow his children to grow and mature at their own pace. Eventually, it became obvious to me that I was hindering that growth, that my presence was itself an obstacle to what you could eventually become. Alas, that you failed to take advantage of that opportunity. Now, I think, it's too late for you.

"Each civilization rises and falls with the music of the Spheres. Each has its day before the sun finally sets, and night draws its curtain over the remains. Even this pocket universe of ours will one day expire, only to be replaced by another, more vigorous entity.

"I left because there was no reason for me to stay any longer."

"But I don't have the Eggs," I blurted out. "And even if I did, I wouldn't understand how to use them."

Master Mathurin just smiled a wry grin, before saying: "What did my great-grandson Parakôdês tell you, my son?"

"Uh...." I was about to say that I didn't remember anything that was pertinent to this situation from our two conversations, but then I thought back again for several moments, before finally responding: "He said to me, 'Everything that you need to move to the next stage, you already have. What you lack is the vision to understand.'"

"And this is quite literally true," the mage said. He suddenly tossed me the Hand of Morlock. I caught it in my left hand on the fly, almost without thinking, and was jolted by the immediate surge of energy that it gave me.

The amber stone blazed its fury to the world, forming almost a halo over the head of the silver sculpture of Mathurin—and when I looked past the artifact to the man who'd given it to me, I saw the same golden glow emanating from around his brow.

"The Hand will point the Way," he said.

Then he reached into the air, and pulled the second composite artifact out of the pocket of ætherspace where I'd secreted it (I obviously could maintain no mysteries before the intent gaze of this seer). He opened his palm, and the Firedog walked across the open space into my waiting right hand.

"The Pathfinder will find the Way," he said.

He held up both of his hands and plucked the twin copies of *The Necropompeion* out of the air, and then layered one volume upside down over the other, where they appeared to meld together. He reached over and laid the merged tomes onto my lap.

"The Book will enable the Way," he said.

I looked down at the assembled implements that I held in my two hands and between my knees, and I realized suddenly that together they carried an enormous residue of sheer power and energy. I instinctively placed the Hand of Morlock upright on the left side of *The Necropompeion*, and the Pathfinder on the right, with my fingers grasping both, and they—and I—became a single entity.

"The torch is passed," Mathurin intoned. "May you know your Way, and may it be One."

CHAPTER SIX
"MY PET NAME FOR IT IS CHAOS"

"Then these three implements," I said to Master Mathurin, gazing down on them where they rested on my thighs, "These are the first three Elephant's Eggs?"

"Yes," he replied, "They're the tools that you'll need to heal the cosmos."

"But how?" I asked.

"That's something that you'll have to determine for yourself. I can't tell you exactly what you need to do or the way in which it can be accomplished, because this varies from Dream Weaver to Dream Weaver, and from æon to æon. You'll have to find that Way through your own efforts, Master Morpheús. Perhaps Lady Niobë can help—she seems to have a sensible head on her shoulders."

"Why can't *you* join us, Sir?"

"If I leave this place for very long, my son," the old man said, "I'll die, and life is still precious to me, even though the sands of my time are running short. There are medicines on this world that help address some of the insufficiencies of my body—gaps that I can no longer make up myself. They also implanted a machine—they call it a defibrillator—into my heart to keep it going. Now I'm dependent on it, and the treatments that accompany it."

I suddenly heard a wailing noise off in the distance somewhere. It gradually came closer and louder, and then faded away again.

"What's that?" I asked.

"An emergency vehicle to treat the sick—it just passed by my residence," he said.

Then he sighed, an exhalation almost of despair combined with exasperation. "You wouldn't understand, Morpheús. This place is unlike any world that you've visited. It relies solely on mechanical devices to sustain itself, artificial constructs that men have fashioned from metal and wire and substances that they've made themselves. Magic here is merely the stuff of fantasy stories—and although the people proclaim a belief in matters spiritual, in reality they scoff at real-life *magie* and the workings of the æther. As a result, their wonders entice no wonderment from their starving souls. Still, they have their virtues, and some of their treatments for the chronically ill address certain ailments that can't be cured by one of our physicians or healers.

"Now, I've become a prisoner of my own selfishness."

Then I heard another noise outside, a strange kind of rhythmic booming occurring at set intervals. It raised the hackles on my back with its incessant, raspy noise. I arched my eyebrows in query.

"Several of my neighbors are quite willing to share their musical tastes with others," he said.

"That's *music*?" Shah'rah asked. "It sounds terrible!"

"This world has not developed much beyond the most primitive stage in its arts. That's why my pet name for it is Chaos."

"Sir," I said, returning to the subject at hand, "I still lack the Fourth Elephant's Egg, and by all accounts I can't do anything to fix the problem that you've described without it."

"This is true," Mathurin said. "But you haven't completed your travels yet, Morpheús. My home is just one stop on a long journey. You must...."

The young man named Boupho who'd invited himself to join our group in Erésvepe had crept up behind us while we were talking, and now he pressed one of Hawk's weapons against the back of my head.

"Give me the implements!" he ordered.

"Ah, my old friend Karlin," the ancient mage said. "I was wondering when you'd finally reveal yourself."

"Have I met you under some other name, Sir?" I asked over my shoulder, wincing at the feel of the hard, cold metal cylinder pressed against my neck.

Mathurin just chuckled. "He's better known under his academic moniker, Doctor Scarabbaios."

"But…," I sputtered, "but, he's dead! We consumed his flesh during his memorial service!"

"Not quite dead yet, I think," my distant ancestor stated. "He faked his demise and altered his appearance so that you'd lead him to the Elephant's Eggs, which he's been coveting for hundreds of years. He thinks that they'll give him control over everyone else—and himself. Poor demented fool!"

"Never mind that, 'Matterin,'" Boupho (or Scarabbaios) said. "Hand over the three Eggs, Morpheús, or I'll kill you where you sit."

I thought about my options for a moment, and finally said, "No."

"What?"

"If Master Mathurin is right," I said, "having the Eggs will do you no good at all. If I'm dead, he says, there'll be no one to restore the balance of order among the Five Spheres. In the latter instance, I'd really prefer not to witness the disintegration of all I hold dear. So, kill me!"

I misjudged the level of the man's madness, however—Doctor S. abruptly pulled the trigger of his weapon. I could hear its empty click echo right next to my ear. Eagle, who was standing nearby, immediately tackled the mage, and together with Hawk, quickly subdued him.

"You mages are hopeless when it comes to modern arms," the Sergeant said, holding up the belcher in one hand. "You have to flip the safety off to make it work."

Then they tied him to a chair.

"What shall we do with him, Sir?" I asked Master Mathurin.

"Leave him with me. There's no way he can get off this world, and he'll spend the rest of his days doing wherever he wants to do here. I think he'll fit right in."

He suddenly rose from his padded seat. "And now, my son, it's time for you and yours to be on your way again. Where would you like to go?"

"Can you send us to Naprimér, Sir?"

"Alas, no, that's too far distant. How about Yelloweyen?"

"Yes, yes, yes!" Mistress Zalmanna said. "We can find our way from there. Take us to your transit-mirror, Master."

"There *are* no transit-mirrors on this world," Mathurin said. "That's why Doctor Scarabbaios will be unable to leave this place in the future. But, even with the restrictions under which I operate, I still have some of my talent remaining."

He walked to the center of the room, accompanied by his comely companion, Essora, and then bent slowly down to the floor, and with his right hand drew a large circle in the air, returning to the same place whence he'd started. "My dear," he said to the strange but beautiful lady by his side.

She reached over to his construct, her fingers splaying wide, and then slowly pulled back...a flap of nothingness. I could feel the aura of ætherspace trying to impinge itself on real space and time.

"How...?" I said, my mouth gaping wide in wonder. Yes, I'd heard the account of "Lord Matrin" that the Lady Niobë had read to me from *The Matrinology*, but I just thought of it as a fanciful tale from the past. It never had struck me as being real.

The old man laughed out loud. "A good magician never reveals his tricks!" he said, stepping backwards. "I can only hold this opening wide for a few moments (this world is not conducive to the exercise of my powers), so you must depart right away, my son. Be well, be wise, and be happy. I very much enjoyed meeting you. And don't worry: you'll do just fine."

Then he bowed to me, still smiling, and motioned me towards the unseen hole in space. I tucked away the Eggs into the pocket of the æther that I used to safely secure such things, and strode confidently into the emptiness. A new day was dawning, and I was ready now to face whatever might confront me in the future, my companions at my side.

CHAPTER SEVEN
"I NOT NOBODY!"

In just the blink of an eye, we were there, returned once again to the last great transit-station in the network that the Overseers maintained in the Fifth Circle.

"Home!" the Yowler Arrgruffruff growled as we emerged from the machine on the other side. "Home again, home again, jiggety-jig! But I didn't find my missing packmate!" The canine creature lived up to his name by raising his head and howling his disappointment—just once—and jumping 'round and 'round in obvious ecstasy at being back to his den.

Then he turned to me: "I stay herre now, Masterr."

I thanked him very kindly for his services as a Finderer, gave him some gold strips in payment, and wished him a full bowl of chow and a hundred healthy pups. He wagged his tail, and went bounding off to find his friends.

Mistress Zalmanna immediately secured lodgings for us again in the station apartment complex, using her connections to get us the best of everything. It felt absolutely wonderful to soak in a hot bath, and I stayed there for over an hour, working through all my concerns and aches.

When I disrobed, I noticed that the medallions that the Tyros had attached to my chest were missing. They'd been present, I knew, before we visited Mathurin's World, so he must have removed them after our initial transit there, while I was still unconscious. I wondered if he'd done the same with Z.'s disk. I didn't miss them.

After we cleaned ourselves and changed our clothes, we were led by the Tyro to The Brown Bone, an eatery near the station, where we feasted on "trits" and other delicacies prized by the Yowlers. Actually, the food there was generally very tasty, and all of the selections had been approved for human consumption. I particularly enjoyed a stew comprised of chunks of meat nestled in some kind of spicy gravy, interspersed with vegetables and what appeared to be a rice-like filling.

By then we were starting to get drowsy, so when we returned to the great Tyrosian transit-station, Mistress Zalmanna showed us to our sleeping quarters.

"I am sorry," she told us, "but there are not enough places available for each of you to have your own space. Most of you will have to share your rooms and beds with another. I have made the assignments based on my best judgment."

Of course, I was paired with Shah'rah, my "wife."

"But I need my privacy," I told Zalmanna, "in order to prepare for the next phase of our journey."

She looked at me completely without pity. "I have no choice in the matter, Master Morpheús. Our records show you as the legal husband of Lady Shah'rah. Therefore, you must be housed with her. I have explained all this to you before."

And so she had, but that didn't make me feel any better. Truth be told, however, I was so exhausted by this point that I would have slept with Arrgruffruff, if he hadn't returned to his pack.

I just dimmed the glowlight, turned my back to my "wife," and slept the sleep of the righteous (ha!).

Somewhere in the middle of the night, though, I needed to pee something desperately (too much of The Brown Bone ale!), and being stuck on the inside half of the bed—the half that was anchored against the wall—I had to try crawling over the recumbent body of Shah'rah without waking her.

"What, uh, is off?" she asked, sitting up and almost beaning me in the process. I hadn't meant to wake her.

"I, uh, I have to use the facilities," I said, raising the ambient illumination slightly.

She moved her legs so they hung off the bed, and I was then able to get around her.

When I returned, much relieved, she was still sitting in the same position.

"What it is?" I asked.

"Why do you say, 'not-wife,' *Maestro*?"

I really didn't want to have this conversation right now, but I foolishly responded: "Because you're *not* my wife. I didn't agree to the marriage in the first place."

"But you, uh, you put your name on form."

"I did so to keep us both from being imprisoned," I said, "which would have helped no one."

"You not nice to…*me*," she said, her eyes dribbling tears. She wiped them away with a swipe of her right hand. "You say 'not-wife' to everyone, all time. Make me feel, uh, like nobody. *I not nobody*! *Not*, Don Mórpheo!"

She was right, of course—I'd treated her abominably, and there was no excuse for it. It wasn't her fault that we'd been trapped into a random bonding that neither of us had deliberately chosen. But I'd been blaming her in my own mind ever since, and proclaiming my unhappiness far and wide to anyone who'd listen.

I sat down next to her, and took her damp fingers in mine, and said: "I will not deny our union in public again. I apologize for demeaning you in front of the others. It wasn't right or fair to you. If we live through this journey, then we can evaluate whether we wish to go forward together or not. OK?"

She turned her face to me, and kissed me lightly on the left cheek. I barely heard her whisper, "OK."

Then I crawled into bed again, pulled up the covers, and tried to go back to sleep. I was noticeably unsuccessful in doing so.

CHAPTER EIGHT
"HE'S STILL ALIVE?"

Being unable to find the sleep that my namesake, the god of Greek mythology, could so easily dispense to his followers, I finally arose a second time from my bed in the transit-station at Yelloweyen, threw a shift over my nightdress, and wandered into the common room. Even at the sixth hour of the night, an attendant was on duty.

"Yes, Sir?" she asked.

"I'd like something hot to drink," I said. "And, oh yes, I've lost my sky-orb. Could you find me a replacement?"

"I'll have to get authorization, Sir," she said. "Be back shortly."

When she returned, she had a mug of some kind of warm broth—not as strong as the concoction served in The Brown Bone—and a new communication device, identical to the one that the Meremptahs had stripped from me.

"Thank you," I said, making a mark of acknowledgment on the tablet she presented. Then she returned to her station, and I tried to link again with the Lady Niobë on Naprimér.

When I finally reached her, I noticed a red welt on her brow. When she saw my reaction, she grimaced slightly and said, "Yes, my dear son slapped me several times when I told him that I couldn't provide what he needed. Again! At some point, he may decide that I'm utterly dispensable."

Then she changed the subject: "So what's happened with you, Morpheús?"

I told her how we'd escaped from the Meremptahs, and our subsequent encounter with the mage Mathurin.

"He's still alive? I can't believe it!" she said. "He must be…."

"He admitted to having lived several thousand years," I said. "However, I have no doubt that it was he. He knew too many things about too many things. And the Eggs: I had them all along, and I never knew it. But he wouldn't tell me where the Fourth Egg was located, or even how to recognize it when it's found. So we're still feeling our way through the void, so to speak."

"Could you use the Firedog to lead you to the Egg?" she asked. She was smart, this Lady!

"I tried that, but I was told that the query was taboo, and could not be answered. Actually, I tried posing the question several different ways, and was turned back on each occasion."

"Well, I see several possibilities," Niobë said. "The other three Eggs came to you back on Nova Europa, without you even seeking them for yourself. Perhaps the Fourth is there as well.

"But I also wonder if the Fourth Egg isn't here on Naprimér. Remember, the legends that we have regarding the Great Teacher Matrin clearly indicate that *this* world was where he started the process of healing the void, and that he later (apparently) visited Nova Europa. He had to have had the Eggs, or something like them, to employ as his tools. Maybe the first Three Eggs were deposited on your planet, and the Fourth Egg was left some-where on mine."

"That doesn't make much sense either, though," I said, "because we've been told that multiple copies exist of versions One through Three, and two copies of Four. Mathurin indicated to me that I only needed to find one of each, that having all four would enable me to control the scattered clones as well— and that, in fact, healing the Circles would require me to gain mastery over *all* of the Eggs, wherever they were located.

"But to do that, I first have to find The Fourth Elephant's Egg."

"I still think the best idea is for you to travel to Naprimér.

If you can free me and my world, we can combine our powers and seek the Fourth Egg, wherever it might be. Surely we can do this together."

I couldn't think of anything better to do, so I told her that I agreed. About that time, Mistress Zalmanna appeared, and I quickly closed our link.

"I was informed," the Tyro said, "that you had requested a replacement sky-orb."

I showed her the implement resting on my right palm.

"Return it to me forthwith, Morpheús. We are now within the realm of the Overworld again, so you should not require the use of this device any further."

"Alas," I said, "but under the terms of our agreement, as ratified by your High Council, you're supposed to obey *me*, and not vice versa, until we locate The Fourth Elephant's Egg. We haven't found that artifact yet, so you must still abide the will of your superiors."

She got very orange in the face then, but I had her by the neck hairs, so to speak, and she knew it. She said nary a word, but stomped her foot twice, and then abruptly left the room. Somehow, I gained a great deal of satisfaction from the encounter.

I went back to bed, and *this* time, I was able to fall asleep with no problem at all!

CHAPTER NINE
"STIPULATED BY THE DOG"

The question, as it always seemed to be, was how to get from "here" to "there." The remnants of my group were seated around a beautifully polished wood table, discussing just that issue, but we weren't getting very far.

"Naprimér is not listed as such in any of our indices," Mistress Zalmanna said.

"I don't believe that it was ever on the transit routes," I said. "Judging by what the Lady Niobë has told me, their 'zip-ports' employ a primitive form of transit-technology that simply don't provide enough power to move very large objects outside the immediate vicinity of their own world."

"What about the Volúcris, Master?" Scooter asked.

"Their home world is known, but travel is strictly forbidden in that sector, because of their innate hostility," the Tyro said. "Our technology is greater than theirs, but we avoid them when possible."

"The Firedog gave me an address of sorts," I said. "According to what it told me, Niobë's planet is located in the 'Fifth Circle, Fourth Range, Sixty-First Inclination, between Delirant and Moucheron, not far from Zezament'."

Zalmanna wrote down the specifications and excused herself.

"I never realized," I told the others, "how difficult it would be to find one particular ætherplace. The number of worlds located here is almost uncountable. For all of their abilities, the Tyrosians don't know—can't know—everything about this area. There are evidently entire regions of space that remain uncharted by them—either because they feel that nothing there is worth exploring, or due to hostile natives whose impediment can easily be bypassed."

"Why must we go there...now?" Shah'rah asked.

"Because I can see no better option. We know that Mathurin made some kind of impact on the early history of Naprimér a very long time ago—that he changed society there. Maybe he left some traces of himself that we can use to track the Fourth Egg—or it might even be hidden somewhere on the planet."

"You not to know what...*El Huevo Cuarto del Elefante* is?" she said.

"It could be almost anything," I said. "I'll know it when we find it, because the other three artifacts will react to their sibling."

Then Mistress Zalmanna returned, her face downcast. "There is no record of these three worlds mentioned in the database at Yelloweyen. The address the Firedog mentioned is not specific enough to locate Naprimér."

She waved her hand at the far wall, and a schematic of the Five Circles appeared there, each of them being shaded with a slightly different pastel hue. "Here," she said, "you can see where we are"—a pulsing point of red light appeared near the boundary between the Fifth and Sixth Spheres on the top, right-hand part of the map—"and this is the section of space stipulated by the Dog"—a wedge of pale pink stood out against the darker red of the Fifth Circle, about a third of the way down the side from where we were now located.

"How far away is that in real terms?" I asked.

"Far," she said. "Very, *very* far. The region is not well mapped, and includes part of the Volúcri Predation, as noted here"—a green sector overlapped the pink, edging out into the Sixth Circle. "We can travel the long-transit routes established by my people as far as the inside boundary of the Bird-Men's empire"—she demonstrated the point on the wall screen—"but how we get inside that hegemony is the real problem."

Suddenly the door to the conference room burst open, and a contingent of guards filed in, with Tyro Brentinna, the manager of Yelloweyen Station, trailing the party. "Citizen Zalmanna!" she said, pointedly omitting the honorific of Mistress, "You are hereby arrested in the name of the High Council of Tyrotarichos, together with of all your co-conspirators"—clearly she meant the rest of us—"for acts of treason against the state."

"On whose authority?" Zalmanna asked.

"The High Master Kameïhameïhalonn," she said.

"But what about High Master Phenneïlonn?"

"Citizen Phenneïlonn has also been named in the indictment. Here is the document." Brentinna handed it to Zalmanna.

The former Tyro member of the High Council blanched when she read what was written there. "This warrant is in order," she finally said. "We are to be transported to the Homeworld, there to be tried for consorting with the 'Enemy'—who is unnamed."

"The Meremptahs," I said.

"Who?" Tyro Brentinna asked.

"People who are not supposed to exist," I said. "And now that you know about them, you'll undoubtedly be remanded with the rest of our party."

"No. I cannot…."

"Let us go!" I said. "What we're doing is far more important than petty politics."

"We are programmed to obey," Zalmanna interjected. "We cannot act otherwise, Master Morpheús." Then she turned to Brentinna: "These people are innocent. Let them proceed."

"No. I cannot…."

"Then we are doomed to repeat the same mistakes of the past," she finally said.

We were escorted back to our quarters, where we were given a few moments to gather our things; and then taken to a closed compound with no windows and only one entrance. The door was securely fastened, and guards posted outside. Food was brought at discreet intervals, but we weren't otherwise allowed to leave, even for a moment.

"How long will we have to wait?" I asked Zalmanna.

"I do not know," she said. "The traffic in this sector can be heavy at times, and Tyro Brentinna will have to obtain secure transportation up and down the line—not an easy or quick thing to do, even with the authority of the High Council. We have perhaps a week, give or take a few days."

"Then we must find a way out of here before then," I said.

But, try as we might, none of us could think of a practical escape plan. Even if we exited our rooms in safety, and managed to get to the main transit-room, overcoming the security personnel at every point, where would we go? The primary æthernetwork in this region was either run or supervised by the Tyrosians, and the independent stations all funneled through the main transportation links.

There were no alternatives without returning to the Sixth Circle, and it would take us forever to transit laterally through the chaotic border region. Most of the established channels there moved either away or towards specific Tyrosian crossroads stations, to further the trade between the two areas.

No, if we wanted to reach Naprimér within a reasonable period of time, we'd have to remain within this Sphere.

We adjourned to our cots and cubicles—for this is what we'd been left with—and once again I found myself sleepless with worry. Finally, I pulled out the sky-orb (the Tyros had never retrieved it), and dialed the Lady Niobë again.

Miraculously, I found a clear path almost immediately, and I explained our dilemma.

"You have the means," she said, after considering the matter for a moment. "You told me that Teacher Matrin was able to access ætherspace directly."

"Yes, but I don't have any notion how he accomplished it," I said.

"Figure it out!" she said. "You're smart and capable, Morpheús, and you carry within you some portion of his blood, however small. You have the talent, you have three of the Eggs, and you saw what he did—you were right there to obverse the phenomenon. Re-examine the picture more closely with the help of your familiar, and find a way.

"You need to develop this ability in any case to help shape the future of the Five Circles—if that's what you intend to do. Even with my assistance, you'd still have to undertake the main working yourself. Yes, I'd be watching your back, so to speak, and lending you additional stability and power; but you'd be the prime mover. Someone *has* to be.

"You can do this, I'm convinced of it. Matrin obviously showed it to you close-up for a reason."

Indeed. The Lady was right once again. There was no reason for my ancestor to demonstrate the technique so openly unless he intended for me to follow his example. But did I really have this talent? I knew of no description of this kind of procedure except in *The Matrinology*, the Naprimeran collection of fables and stories about the semi-mythical Teacher and Dream Weaver.

"I'll try," I said.

"Don't let Zalmanna see you do it," Niobë cautioned. "If she understands the technique well enough to duplicate the process, she'll barter it to the High Council to return to their favor. Don't ever trust her, Morpheús."

I thanked the Lady again for her help, and closed the link. I felt movement down at the end of my bed, and saw the wherret rolled up in a ball by the side of my calf, apparently asleep. But then I noticed that its eyes were wide open, watching me.

It was always watching.

CHAPTER TEN
"'THE HAND WILL POINT THE WAY'"

Creating a hole in ætherspace sounded easy enough, but doing so without losing oneself and one's immediate environs to the pervasive suctioning effect of the Great Nothingness was nigh unto impossible. Even with Scooter acting as a balance, I found myself so frightened of the possible consequences that I really couldn't concentrate properly. The thought of being marooned eternally in the void is enough to send any sane magician right over the edge.

One of the problems is that none of our philosophers had ever satisfactorily explained exactly what the æther constituted—a solid medium, a kind of fluid, a gas, whatever. It seemed in some ways to consist of all of those things—and none of them. We knew some of the rules governing access and transit through the æthersphere, but had no understanding, really, of *why* such techniques worked. And I knew that even the Overseers had no better grasp of the science behind transiting than we did.

I tried to remember exactly what Master Mathurin had done to open his gate. He'd reached out with his right hand and had drawn a large circle in the air, somehow breaching real space and time in the process, but without losing control of the access point. I knew instinctively, though, that I was missing something vital, that I didn't really understand what had happened there.

"Scooter," I said. "When Mathurin created the gateway

leading from his world to Yelloweyen, did he employ any implement?"

The wherret was silent for a long moment before replying. "I'm not sure, Master," it finally said. "It does seem to me that I saw a glint or flash of some small object in his right hand, but I don't know what it was. Yes, upon reflection, I'm sure that he was clutching something between his thumb and forefinger."

"Could it have been the jewel that we confused with the First Egg, the gem that became the Lady Essora?"

"I suppose," the creature said. "But Sir, she was standing right there the entire time."

"So she was," I said. "Still, I wonder...."

I reached into my pouch and pulled out the Hand of Morlock, the silver image of Mathurin (or so I thought) clutching a curious piece of amber littered with the remains of the insect life of the ancient world. I examined the artifact again very carefully, turning it over several times.

"Do you have any idea who Morlock was?" I finally asked my familiar.

"No, Sir."

I went out into the common room that fronted on our cubicles, and sought out Zalmanna. I showed her the object.

"Do you recognize this man?" I asked.

"No," she said.

"He's not Mathurin?"

"No."

"Describe him to me."

"I only know him from images," she said. She listed the physical attributes and facial features of the man that we'd met on the Place Without Magic, the one I called Mathurin's World.

Although the image on the statue could have been the same person as a young man, he actually more closely resembled my ancestor Parakôdês.

"I wonder if this implement is inscribed with Mathurin's name because it once belonged to him," I said, "And not because the image is intended to represent him. This may really be the individual named Morlock, whoever he was."

"Morlock, you say?" she asked.

"Yes—this is supposed to be the Hand of Morlock."

"I remember hearing of a world of that name somewhere in the Fifth Circle. It was a place where mankind had split into two species, one resembling us called the Wellsians, who devoted themselves to acting and producing melodramas and farces, and the other covered with fur. The latter, the Morlockai, were master craftsmen, creating objects of great beauty and utility. I would suggest that this man originated there."

"But who is he, really?" I asked.

That question went unanswered, so I returned with Scooter to the privacy of our roomette.

"This First Egg is the key," I told the wherret. "Remember what Mathurin told us: 'The Hand will point the Way'?"

"But what does it mean?" Scooter asked.

"I think it's meant to be taken literally." I placed the object in my right hand, with the top of the statue—the part that held the gem in its outstretched arms—grasped upright in my fingers, so that the top part of it extended upwards an inch or two. Then I impressed my will into the amber jewel, making it flash with a brilliant yellow-orange hue.

Taking control of the concentrated force within the gem, I used the Hand like a stylus, pushing it against the invisible wall separating real space from ætherspace, and cut a small, rectangular line in the fabric of reality. I left a flap still attached on one side so that I wouldn't lose complete control. Then I put the implement down, and very carefully pried back the opening that I'd thus created. I could sense the unreality pressing back at me, but I reached out with my will and twisted the leys, making a small hole from our quarters to the main transit-room on the Station. I felt the great mirror on the other end suddenly activate, and quickly shut the gate down before it could be traced.

"I did it!" I told the wherret, *"I did it!"* I wanted to shout and run and scream in triumph, but I knew that I had to keep this particular secret all to myself.

"With enough power, Master," Scooter said, "why, we could go anywhere!"

And so we could.

CHAPTER ELEVEN

"YE GODS! IT'S
THE MONKEY-MAN!"

While we were still working with the Hand of Morlock, I heard a commotion out in the Common Room, and quickly closed down the æthernet link I'd created, withdrawing my consciousness from the amber.

I rushed outside, the wherret on my shoulder, just in time to see the Station guards escorting Zalmanna towards the open doorway.

"What's going on?" I asked Tyro Brentinna, the facility manager, who was shooing out the rest of her people.

"I've been ordered to separate you people into individual quarters, starting with *her*"—she nodded in the direction of Zalmanna. "I'll be back for the rest of you later, as soon as I can make the proper arrangements for secure rooms."

Lady Shah'rah and Hawk both rushed over, and asked: "What do we do?" I could see the Sergeant's small squad hovering just behind him.

"Gather together your things, and bring them here right away," I ordered. "We're leaving this place."

While they were getting their packs, I went to the entrance, and sent a surge of energy into the locking mechanism, just enough to gum up the works.

Within moments, Warbler, Bird, Roc, Raven, Eagle, Hawk, Scooter, and Shah'rah—all that remained of our merry crew—had crowded around me, waiting for the magician to reach into his bag of tricks. Suddenly I heard a banging on the one door leading to our compound.

"Time to go, folks," I said.

I heard an exhalation of "oohs" when I duplicated Master Mathurin's trick of creating a gateway in front of them out of "thin air." I reached into ætherspace, and tried to link to the transit-machine on the ghost world of Festuca, the Station that had been abandoned by the Tyros some sixteen years earlier. Finally, after much travail, I was barely able to access the device, but the connection was weak at best, certainly not enough to rely on for transiting.

Now I could hear some serious thumps coming from the entranceway.

"Scooter!"

"Yes, Master," it whispered into my ear.

"I need your strength."

It quickly nipped me on the earlobe, and linked its energy to mine. It was just enough to firm up the tenuous link. I probably should have picked some place closer, instead of a site halfway around the Fifth Circle; but I wanted to reach an absolutely safe haven where the Overseers wouldn't immediately detain us for questioning.

I twisted the leys, enabled the receiver, felt the interdimensional hooks go home, and yelled at my friends, "Jump!"—almost literally pushing them one by one through the aperture. Just as I heard the main doorway into the Common Room giving way before the efforts of Brentinna's guards, I leapt into ætherspace myself, the last in line, with the wherret perched at its usual spot on my shoulder.

When we exited through the great transit-mirror on the other side, I shut down the opening that I'd created, and closed off all access. Without a physical device to examine on Yelloweyen, no technician would ever be able to determine where we'd gone.

I felt sorry about abandoning Zalmanna, but I had no choice. I didn't know where she'd been taken, and had no way of finding out. She wasn't aware of my new-found abilities, so she couldn't tip off the High Master back on Tyrotarichos, even if she wanted to. I would miss her broad-based knowledge of this Sphere; I wouldn't miss her imperiousness and general potential for unreliability. In her heart, she still served her masters back on the Overworld, and could never be trusted.

We were exhausted, as usual, by the effects of the long-jump, and would need to recuperate for several days at the minimum. Fortunately, we already knew where the abandoned Station's supplies were located within the confines of the facility, and I asked Hawk to re-establish our living quarters.

I gave Scooter a special assignment: to access the database embedded within the transit-device, and find anything that it could about Delirant, Moucheron, and Zezament, the worlds located nearest to the Lady Niobë's home on Naprimér. In theory, we were now much closer to those places than we had been on Yelloweyen, so our escape from that planet had bene-fited us in yet another fashion.

Outside, the wind moaned. I hated being stuck on this dead place for more than a day, but we had no choice. We had to regain our strength for the next transit.

I activated the several glowlights in the main room and the several back areas, which gave enough illumination to dispel the outside gloominess of this cloud-enshrouded globe. Meanwhile, Hawk and his men dusted off the beds again, and with Shah'rah, fixed us a warm meal.

I was just sitting down to eat when something began banging on the only door into the Station.

"What the hell could that be?" Eagle asked. "There's not supposed to be anyone here!"

Hawk had scrounged some basic Tyrosian weapons from the security container, and he immediately pulled one out, motioning us to hit the floor. He and his men surrounded the entranceway, and then opened the lock.

"Gobble, gobble," I heard, in a familiar-but-unfathomable dialect, and then a shaking furry head slowly peaked around the gap.

"'Please…help,'" Scooter whispered in my ear, translating the lingo.

The Sergeant motioned the cowering creature inside, keeping him under close guard.

"Ye gods!" he finally said. "It's the monkey-man, Sir!"

CHAPTER TWELVE

"'PATAPHYSICIAN, HEAL THYSELF!"

And so it was! The Mouchard ape-official, Yé-Yé-Za-Zou, who'd been accidentally transported with us to this godforsaken, abandoned world of gray, and then had run away from us and could not be found before our departure, had somehow survived the intervening months intact. Well…alive, perhaps, but gaunt almost to the point of starving, and utterly terrified. It was obvious from the poor creature's condition that he wouldn't have lived much longer.

Raven brought him a bowl of the standard Station rations, and the monkey-man just gobbled it down. Then he ran into the back of the facility, found himself a sheltered spot underneath one of the beds, and quickly went to sleep. We could hear the occasional whimperings of his disturbed dreams.

"Must help…him," Shah'rah said, looking me in the eyes. "Must, husband!"

"We will," I said. "I have the ability to send him back to his homeworld of Mouch, and I'll do so as soon as he's able to make the transit. Meanwhile, we need to get some rest ourselves."

Hawk's men agreed to stand watch on a rotating basis, with one of them awake at all times, while the rest of us headed for the beds and cots, thankful to have even the minimal comforts of home. At least the Festuca Station was secure, warm, lighted, and well-supplied with water and food.

Although I was beginning to feel the effects of long-transit travel myself, I wanted to check with Scooter before I went to sleep to see if it'd been able to find a secure route to Naprimér.

"No, Master," my familiar finally said, from where the wherret was sitting next to the transit-mirror. "This device only contains information on the local network of Tyrosian stations, nothing else. I suspect also that the database itself is obsolete, due to the inactive nature of this particular facility. It hasn't been updated since the place was shut down; and if I attempt to link it to the control-station for this sector to get more material, that will alert the authorities there immediately, and we'll have unwelcome visitors very quickly."

I sighed: it was pretty much as I'd expected. Then I went to another corner of the main room, and attempted to raise Niobë on the sky-orb, but I couldn't make the connection work. Finally I gave up, and decided to wait until morning.

Our crowded quarters—it contained just four beds—meant that I had to share a cot with Shah'rah again, but I was finding this little chore considerably less onerous as time went by. There's nothing like an armful of warm girl to get one's, uh, hopes up!

The next morning, Scooter came to me and said: "Master, there's something you need to know. I've been talking as best I can with Yé-Yé-Za-Zou, and he says that there are other people still living on this world."

"Impossible," I said. "We did a cursory survey of the place when we were here the first time, and failed to find any large animals of any type, including man."

"Nonetheless, Sir, he says that they're there, living off fungal vegetation, grubs, and small animals. They're gradually starving to death, of course, but some small groups yet survive at different locations. That's how he managed to stay alive all this time. He says that you must help them."

"How? We have to leave soon to reach Niobë's world. Without The Fourth Elephant's Egg, I have no way of fixing this planet. If we activate the transit-mirror to move these people off-world, an alarm will likely be sent to the main station up the line—and

I wouldn't know how to locate and corral them all in any case. Even if I could, I personally can't unzip and hold a gateway open long enough to accomplish the feat myself, even with the assistance of the two copies of *The Necropompeion*. I'm not a miracle-worker; I can't possibly save these people."

"Husband," Shah'rah said from right behind me, "*tú* must…do something. Not right that these…peoples…they die. Overseers did this. You must fix. Please. *Must fix!*"

I saw a shadow pass in front of the lone window in the main room. I walked out to the entrance, unfastened the lock, and opened the door.

They were a short people, averaging four-and-one-half-feet in height, with bushy, bright yellow heads and beards (even the women), dressed in tan or gray or brown shifts, huddled together in fear and despair, seeking whatever warmth they could generate against the damp chill. One of them stepped forward.

"Please, Sir," he said in Tyrosian, "please help us. Our people are dying. Please."

What could I do? If I had been brought into this world to make a difference, as I was constantly being told by the likes of Master Mathurin, I had to start somewhere. I possessed three of the four Eggs. I ought to be able to figure out something that would help restore the ecological balance on this world—a balance that had been destroyed by the experiments of the Tyrosians.

And this was when I started missing the analytical mind of Mistress Zalmanna, who had access to the databases maintained by the Overseers, who knew how to use them, and who could always think things through to their logical conclusions. I didn't even know what the Tyrosian scientists had done to so contaminate the atmosphere. It was way beyond my comprehension, and still seemed to me an almost hopeless task. I didn't even know where to begin.

"'Pataphysician, heal thyself,'" I muttered out loud.

CHAPTER THIRTEEN
"SUFFICIENT UNTO THE HAY IS THE WEEVIL THEREOF!"

I put my familiar to trolling the limited Station database again, looking for information on what had happened to this world, but Scooter soon reported back to me that it was having no luck accessing or understanding the data that were there.

I also began questioning some of the natives, using their elected spokesman, Nonnengagué, as my translator (he spoke understandable Tyrosian). Some sixteen years earlier, a group of Overseers had transited here from Tyrotarichos, the world at the heart of the Five Spheres, and erected a number of machines to direct (something) at the atmosphere—and that something had ruined this world. But the surviving local people knew very little about these devices, other than the fact that they existed.

I decided that I needed to see these constructions for myself, so I probed the one transit-device that we had at the Station, looking for any links to local *viridaurum* (green-gold) mirrors that might yet be active. I found three nodes still alive, and took Hawk and Scooter with me when I traveled through the æther to the first site.

This emplacement included the small office where we materialized, and a huge adjoining metal behemoth that had fallen over in some storm, and now lay on its side in the damp dirt, rusting away its girders. We'd get nothing from that facility.

The second location was more promising, in that everything seemed to be intact; but when I tried to access the machinery there, nothing would activate.

The third place was on the other side of the globe, but the transit-device made the distance meaningless. Some of the superstructure of the construction seemed damaged to me, but the electronic files were still accessible from the main office. I tried scrolling through the history logs, but most of the information was so much gobbledygook to me.

"Can you decipher what it means?" I asked the wherret.

"I'm not certain, Master," Scooter said. "They were apparently trying to increase the precipitation levels on those continents—about three-fourths of the potential growing area—that had arid climates. To do this they seeded the atmosphere with chemicals of some kind, but what they did had an unexpected side-effect, and created a permanent, heavy cloud cover that so reduced the ambient lighting that it killed much of the imported vegetation. The effect also eliminated all or most of the trees, and greatly increased the number of ferns, fungi, and other such growths."

"So how do we change things back to what they were, or at least to the point where conventional crops will grow again?"

"I don't know, Sir," Scooter said. "This type of science is far beyond my knowledge."

I sighed. "We need Zalmanna. She's the only one that can provide us with the data that we require, and use it to suggest some reasonable course of action."

So we transited back to the main Station, and there I informed the rest of our party of the situation that we faced.

"We...go back to Yelloweyen?" Shah'rah said.

"No," I said. "*I* have to go back there—just me! She's still a prisoner on that world, and we need her brains *here*. But the rest of you can remain safe on this world."

"No!" she said. "How...we go from this place if you not return? None of we...can use transit-thing. No, we go...or we stay. Together."

Her diction was gradually improving, I couldn't help but noticing. I looked over at Hawk and his men for their response.

"Sir," he said, "We won't stay behind, any of us."

I already knew that Scooter would feel obligated to join me, so I said: "Very well. We'll leave here first thing in the morning."

Then I took the wherret outside to where the monkey-man and the natives were waiting. I told them what we needed to do, with Scooter translating for Yé-Yé-Za-Zou.

"No," Nonnengagué said. "We don't want any of the Overseers returning here, ever again."

"If you want me to fix your world," I said, "Then I must have help. Mistress Zalmanna is a prisoner of her own people. She'll come with us voluntarily, and give you every possible assistance. She wasn't the one who did this to you."

The spokesman reluctantly agreed, but the Mouchard wanted nothing to do with Mistress Z. or any other Tyro. However, I told him (through Scooter) that we could send him home to his people before we left. The poor ape-man was so overcome with feeling at the thought of being repatriated that he came running over and wrapped his long arms around my legs, wailing his gratitude (well, I believe that's what it was) over and over again.

I tried to pry him loose myself, but it actually took several of Hawk's men to separate the creature from my limbs. We led him back into the Station, and I opened a gateway through the void that linked with the transit-mirror buried beneath the great amphitheater on Mouch. Then, with a whoosh and a prayer, we sent the terrified official on his way. No doubt the story of his grand adventure "out there" would be passed down in his family for many generations to come.

I wondered if we could send some of the natives of Festuca there as well, if the day came when no other option was possible. Right now we seemed to have few other choices.

Ah, well, as the grain farmer was wont to say, "Sufficient unto the hay is the weevil thereof!"

CHAPTER FOURTEEN
"OH, THAT WASN'T A
VERY NICE THING TO DO"

I'd not yet tried transiting without some medium to fix the link at one of the two nodes. Yes, I'd managed to use the Hand of Morlock to open a gate to the æther on my side of the equation, but always there was some device at the other end to which I could anchor my psychic probe. But if I was going to move our group from Festuca to Yelloweyen without setting off alarms on the latter world, I would need to have to find a way of creating a window on the far side as well. To do that would take considerably more power than I could generate from my own efforts, combined with those of Scooter.

However, I still had the two matched copies of *The Necropompeion*, and I decided that I would employ their combined energy to generate a clear passageway for a period sufficient to transport me and my comrades from one world to the other.

The wherret and I worked for several days to rig a connection that would augment the power levels that were necessary to provide the edge needed to maintain a safe ætherlink. As Scooter had once said, given enough energy, we could access the universe itself.

Once we were ready, I tried opening several short links to places on Festuca, and actually sent my familiar back and forth several times without difficulty. Then we were ready to proceed.

We made our temporary farewells to the natives of this

planet, locked the Station down again, and then I opened a door through the æther. I had a clear image in my mind of the room where we'd been confined during our last days on Yelloweyen, and as soon as I recreated the picture, I was able to poke a small hole in the fabric of space and time, just enough so that I could "Yellow-eyeball" the place before we transited there.

But no one seemed to be present—indeed, the room was completely dark—so I pried the aperture just a bit wider, and stepped through onto the other world. One by one, my fellows followed me as I held the link open with Scooter's help. Then I quietly shut things down.

I'd already briefed Hawk and his men about what we needed to do. They carefully and slowly checked every cubicle for occupants, and when they found none, I lit five small flames at the tips of the fingers of my left hand, and held it on high.

The main room was clear as well.

I enabled one of the glowlights, just so we could see well enough to maneuver without hitting any of the furniture. We had to find a facility that included a link to the Station database.

Hawk checked the corridor, and then motioned us to follow him. We located a door across the hall; he was able to jimmy the lock without difficulty. Inside was an office, including a desk that had a localized sky-orb of some kind. Although access to any sensitive information was restricted to those who possessed the magic passwords, I was able to pose several general queries that received responses.

"Where is Mistress Zalmanna?" I asked.

"Mistress Zalmanna is in Room PL-5005-P," came the response.

"Display that place on the Station map," I ordered.

We were shown a location several corridors over, with a dotted red line indicating how we could get from here to there most efficaciously.

I couldn't transit us there, because I'd never seen the inside of the room, but with any luck, we'd be able to walk there without being detected.

As we were approaching the doorway of PL-5005-P, we could hear loud voices emanating from the cracked opening.

"…tried everything we could possibly think of, Administrator, but we found nothing," said Tyro Brentinna.

"Then look even further," came the unmistakable voice of Mistress Zalmanna. "There must be some trace, however obscure, of where that damnable mage took them. He never even hinted to me that he had this ability."

What was this?

"But there's nothing…," Brentinna said.

"Find something!" Zalmanna interjected. "And if you cannot, I will find someone else who will. Do you understand?"

"Yes, Mistress," came the faint reply.

I motioned to Hawk to follow me through the aperture, and pushed the door fully open.

"Greetings, ladies," I said. "How good to see you both again. My, how our fortunes have turned, Mistress Z."

"You!" she said, her despite clearly evident in her voice.

"Yes," I said, "Here I am, back once more. We need your help, my dear, and since you want to know more about transiting without mirrors, I'm happy to assist you in return. You'll get to experience the experience first-hand, so to speak."

She jabbed a finger down onto the console, immediately setting off an alarm.

"Oh, that wasn't a very nice thing to do," I said. "Hawk…."

The Sergeant jumped forward, and he and several of his men corralled both of the Tyros, while I reopened the link back to the transit-mirror on Festuca.

"Take them through!" I ordered, "And don't let either one of them out of your sight."

"Yes, Sir," he said, and pushed Zalmanna through the connection.

"Wait, you can't do…," Tyro Brentinna said, but the rest of her speech was cut off when she entered ætherspace.

I quickly shooed everyone else back to Festuca, and Scooter and I jumped through the opening ourselves, closing the aperture behind us. I have no idea what the Station guards thought when they investigated the sudden disappearance of their two chief administrators—but I wish I could have been there to see!

CHAPTER FIFTEEN
"BEFORE THEY TEAR
YOU LIMB FROM LIMB"

"Let us go!" Mistress Zalmanna said.

"Certainly," I said. "Hawk, take the two ladies outside and release them. I'm certain that the Festucans, if they're present, would very much enjoy having a conversation. They've been *so* anxious to meet you."

"What are you talking about?" she asked.

"Well, it seems that your 'people' didn't make a thorough enough survey of the damage that they caused to this world sixteen years ago. There were survivors."

"What?" Brentinna said. "But why would Homeworld abandon them?"

"If I had to guess," I said, "I'd say that this experiment was a bit of an embarrassment for them, and that they didn't want anyone telling tales. So they shut everything down, withdrew their personnel, and forgot about this planet."

"That cannot be true," she said.

"I think it is. In any case, I don't intend to confine you—there's no place for it here anyway. Hawk, take them into one of the back rooms and keep them under close guard for a few minutes."

"Yes, Sir," he said, and he and his men almost literally dragged them out of the main part of the Station.

The next thing that I did was to put an ætherlock on the sole transit-device at Festuca, so that neither of the two Tyros could access any part of it without my permission. I tucked my sky-orb away into the pocket of ætherspace where I kept my other goodies, so that the ladies couldn't call for help; and I made certain there was no back-up device anywhere on the facility. Then I had Hawk search the women for weapons or other gadgets, and these were locked away into the armory closet. Finally, I let them go.

"What do you want, Morpheús?" Mistress Zalmanna asked when she confronted me.

"Your help, ladies," I said. "We have a problem here"—and I explained our conundrum.

"Why do you care?" Tyro Brentinna asked.

"How could I *not* care?" I tossed back at her.

"I don't understand."

"No, ladies, you wouldn't," I said. "Nevertheless, I intend to try to save the remnants of these people, if I can. And if I can't, you'll help me transit as many of them as I can find through the mirror to another world where they can rebuild."

"What if we don't agree?" Zalmanna asked.

"Then I'll leave you here to discuss the matter with the Festucans. I'm sure you'll come to some kind of arrangement before they tear you limb from limb."

"You wouldn't."

"I will! Count on it, Tyro," I said. "I'm fed up with your arrogance and condescension. It's about time you folks took responsibility for your mistakes—and this was a particularly horrendous one. Millions died here because of something that the High Council authorized.

"In the meantime, I need your expertise to determine exactly what happened here, and why—and what we can do to fix the situation, if that's possible. Neither I nor anyone from the rest of our group has the knowledge to interpret the data. But you do."

"Very well, if we agree to assist, what will you do for us in return?" Zalmanna asked.

"I'll let you leave this world in one piece. That's it! No other promises!"

The two Tyrosians put their orange-topped heads together for a few moments, and then turned back to me.

"Very well. We agree to help, in return for the restoration of our freedom."

"So mote it be," I said.

"So mote it be," they echoed.

But I still didn't trust either one of them.

CHAPTER SIXTEEN
"THEY COULD ALL DIE"

Nonetheless, even though I had no more faith in the two Tyrosian ladies than I did in His Nibs, I had no choice but to work with them, if I wanted to solve the problem of the atmospheric pollution of the world called Festuca. Only they had some basic knowledge of the scientific and technological framework that might have been used in the experiment conducted by the Overseers sixteen years earlier.

I took them to the three sites where the great machines had been erected. One of the structures had fallen on its side, and was clearly useless. One had lost whatever energy source had powered it. The third emplacement seemed, at least on the surface, still functional in some respect.

"You say they were trying to increase precipitation over the three-fourths of the planetary land mass that is mostly arid?" Mistress Zalmanna said, trying to sort through the paperwork that had been left scattered on the floor of the one-room office building.

"So it appeared from the notes that Scooter found in the Station logs," I said.

"The transcriptions indicated that they were trying to inject different aerosols at varying levels into the atmosphere," the wherret added. "Then something went drastically wrong."

"According to the facility database, the last chemical that they employed here was rhumadyne," said Tyro Brentinna, manipulating the controls of the main console. "They started running the application on xix Piegrech 11612, and then abruptly shut down the site completely nine days later. There is no indication of precisely what happened. They might not have known themselves."

"This is a very odd kind of substance to employ for this purpose," Mistress Zalmanna said. "There must have been something peculiar in the air that gave them the idea that this chemical might work. This is just not something that I have seen used anywhere else. Among other things, it has a tendency to bond with other gases, and is very difficult to control."

"Then what do we do about it?" I asked.

"I have no idea," Zalmanna said. "This is beyond all my experience."

"Mine also," Brentinna added.

"If we tried seeding the arable parts of this world with vegetation that would help pull the offending particles out of the atmosphere, that might prove efficacious," Zalmanna said.

"But we can't do that if it's too dark outside," I said. "The plants just won't grow. And even if we did, it's potentially a very slow process. These people need help now. In another ten years, they'll all be dead from malnutrition and associated ailments.

"Is the machine still active?" I added.

"Yes," she said. "But this device is intended to disperse chemicals, not retrieve them."

"Can you change its engineering to allow it to collect particles?"

"Perhaps," she said. "But only one of these constructions is active, and obviously three were needed to disperse the original application. We lack the materials and manpower to fix the other two emplacements."

"But can you fix this one?" I asked.

"As I said, perhaps. We will not know, Morpheús, until we try."

"Then try," I ordered.

However, I took them back with me to the main Station, and arranged for Hawk and his men to shadow their every move. I didn't want either of them working unsupervised, for a variety of reasons, including the potential danger from the natives, who justifiably hated all Tyros for what they'd done to their world. Shah'rah volunteered to be an observer as well, and I gladly accepted her help. Those two ladies would *never* be able to run a scheme by her watchful eyes.

Scooter and I alternated over the next several weeks between the great machine and the Station, trying to ask appropriate questions of our two laborers, as well as discover anything else of importance in the database archives. My lack of experience in searching such files was a major hindrance, however. Nothing about locating the appropriate data seemed easy to me, even though I was now fluent in the Tyrosian language.

Finally, Mistress Zalmanna came to me while I was inspecting the facility, and said that they'd done all that they could do. "This machine can now serve as a collector of rhuma-dyne particles," she said, "But we think that much of the original chemical aerosol has bonded with other substances, making it almost irretrievable, even if we had a hundred such emplacements. Also, with only one structure available, it will take fifty or more years to cycle through the entire atmosphere—which obviously is well outside your time frame. There is nothing else that we can do here to make the system more efficient. It is what it is, since it was not designed to do this in the first place."

"In other words, it doesn't work," I said.

"Essentially," she said. "I did warn you, Morpheús."

This left us in basically the same position as before. When we got back to the main Station, I asked Scooter to bring the Festucan spokesman, Nonnengagué, to me, and when he arrived, I walked with him under the dead trees, away from the facility, and explained to him our dilemma:

"I can start this machine, and it'll begin reprocessing particles from the atmosphere immediately, but you won't see a lightening of the cloud level for many years—too many years, in my estimation, for you to survive.

"On the other hand, it's possible that I might be able to relocate some of your people to another world—there are many that are empty or nearly so—where you could start over again. What do you want to do?"

"I must consult with the others," he finally said, after a pause; his long, striped, black-and-ochre hair drooping over his shoulders. "This is not a decision that I can make on my own, you understand. The problem is, I only have contact with a small number of the survivors—those living in this region. The rest are scattered in pockets around the globe, we believe. We have no idea how many of the people actually remain. Some have come to us looking for food, so we know they exist.

"Is there no way, Master Morpheús, that you can provide us with seeds that will grow in this dim light?"

I shook my head "No."

"I've discussed this with the two Tyros," I said, "And while they agree that creating such vegetation is certainly a possibility, to do so they would need the expertise of their scientists back on the Overworld. However, in my estimation, if the High Council of Tyrotarichos became aware of your survival, they would likely cut all outside access to Festuca permanently by destroying the transit-station. They don't want their semigenocide to become known among other races, so they'll do everything possible to cover up their mistake."

"But the same thing will happen if the two Overseers are allowed to go free," the man said.

"That's why they can never be permitted to return to their people," I said.

"Oh. Do they know this?"

"No, and you won't tell them if you want my continued help. I won't harm the two ladies, but I do intend to neutralize any future evil influence they might bring to bear on the survivors of Festuca."

"I thank you for that, Sir," the spokesman said. "I'll let you know tomorrow or the next day what my people say."

"Husband," Shah'rah said, startling me with her presence, "I been with, uh, these peoples. Hungry, all hungry, all time.

Please help them. Please."

But when the Festucan spokesman returned the following afternoon, he indicated that no one wanted to leave.

"You told them that they could all die if they remain here?" I said.

"Yes, but they would prefer that to exile. We've always been tied to the land, Sir—always! It doesn't matter that the air has become blighted, the trees have all died, and much of the greenery has turned brown. It's still our home. We live here or we die here—not some strange world in another place. That's our final word."

"Very well," I said. "I'll try to find something else to help the situation."

But my imagination had been blown away by the depressing vistas stretching before me, and the eternal gloom that enshrouded this ghost world. I could feel the oppression of the millions of souls who'd perished here over the last sixteen years. All of them were looking to me for answers.

And I had none.

CHAPTER SEVENTEEN
"NOT EVERYTHING HERE IS DEAD"

I'd taken to walking in the countryside near the main Station on Festuca, and also near the great machine that the two Tyrosian ladies had altered. The natives didn't bother me, and the remaining indigenous fauna was rather small and inoffensive, other than a few poisonous pink toads that were easily avoided. I could see something of what this once-beautiful world had previously been, and desperately wanted to find a way to restore at least part of that beauty again, and to make the land viable for the local populations.

But I lacked the knowledge that I required to take the appropriate steps. I needed help, and I knew someone who could perhaps provide it. Twice before I'd called upon the great mage, my ancestor, to assist me, and I had one more turn left at the magic ring with him. I'd hoped to save that option until I reached Naprimér, Lady Niobë's world, but this was more important right now. People's lives depended upon what I did, and I couldn't afford to make a mistake. If I accomplished only this one thing in my life, I would die happy.

I sighed, and as if in counterpoint, a slight breeze began whistling through the bare tree branches of the dead forest where I was striding. I think the spirit of Festuca herself was urging me forward.

I took a deep breath, and then repeated the archaic, arcane formula out loud: "I invoke the name of he who gave me flesh, faith, and foresight. Parakôdês of the Red-Lands, awake thou from thy sleep!"

At first nothing happened, and I wondered, as I had done at the time of the second visitation, whether I was too far "out" to get a response. I should have known better.

As I walked along an old animal path, I slowly became aware out of the corner of my left eye of a short, shadowy presence that gradually solidified next to me. It had the appearance of an adolescent boy of perhaps ten or twelve.

"My dear son," Parakôdês said, "I see that trouble shadows your soul. I felt your distress even within the orange groves of the Red-Lands where I now rest."

"Grandfather," I said, "these people have been wronged by the Tyrosians, and driven almost to the point of extinction. I have to save them, if I can. No one else cares."

"You have three of the implements that you need," my ancestor said.

I found his current youthful appearance very off-putting, and told him so.

"Would you rather that I display the mien of an elderly gentleman? What difference does it make, really?"

"I've always thought of you as old and wise, Master," I said. "In your present visage, your voice hasn't even cracked yet."

We were gradually emerging from the ruin of the devastated trees, and into an open field that had once been filled with crops.

"I'm a Dream Weaver," the ancient mage said. "I alter men's sensibilities. It's what we do, Morpheús—you and I and Mathurin and the others of our race—or should I call you by your birth name, Oridión?"

"I don't like that name, Sir."

"Six of one, half a dozen of another." He sighed then, and I felt displeasure oozing from his shadowy appearance. "My child, what do you want of me that you can't find within yourself?"

"I lack The Fourth Elephant's Egg, Master," I said. "I don't even know what it is, and I don't know how to apply the powers

I've already been given in a way that'll solve the basic problem."

"You'll find the Fourth Egg in due course," he said, "But that's not the problem here. The problem is *you*, Morpheús. You say that you care about these people. Have you talked to any of them?"

"I've spoken to their local leader, Nonnengagué, several times. He's the only one who appears to know the Tyrosian tongue."

"But have you talked—*really talked*—to any of the others?"

"No, Sir," I admitted.

He stopped then, just short of a gray brook that was bouncing through the detritus of dead vegetation, and bent down to pluck something from the bank. He took my right hand, opened it, and put a small green shoot in my open palm. It was still damp from the pervasive mist and sprinkles from the stream.

"Not everything here is dead," he said. He chuckled: "Not even me."

It was the first glimpse of green that I'd seen in my two visits to Festuca.

"You have enough power to save this world." He swept one small hand over the desolate brown fields that stretched before us until they disappeared into the shrouded horizon. "These can be made green again, and the rest will take care of itself.

"But you lack any real connection to the people here, and without that, Morpheús, without real feeling, your energy will always be insufficient to the task. It's not enough to know intellectually what must or should be done. You must also find the link to the land and all of its inhabitants, at every level.

"There's enough light here to facilitate plant growth," the old mage said. "Dimness can slow the development of fruits and vegetables—and those that survive might not have the same flavor—but they'll still mature in due course. No, the problem lies elsewhere."

"But where, Sir?" I asked. "I'm no scientist, and even the two Tyros don't understand what's happening."

"What was the event that precipitated the crisis?" Parakôdês asked.

"They injected rhumadyne into the atmosphere, Master," I said.

"Then I would look there, my son," he said. "If that substance combined with something else to create an unanticipated reaction, it could have resulted in a 'Great Dying' of the non-native plant life."

"How do I counteract the poison?" I asked.

He actually chuckled. "Truly, I have no idea. But the answer's there inside you, and inside this world, if only you take the time to look. You're a Dream Weaver, Sir—begin acting like one. Grow up and find your potential, before the universe cracks in twain, spewing chaos in its wake. If you can mend this place, this backwater in the Fifth Circle, you can fix anything—*anything*! But if you continue keeping yourself apart from life, life will abandon you—and everyone else that you know. There's no place to hide when your world is collapsing."

Then the boy—for so he appeared to me—slowly ambled away (I wanted so desperately to go with him, and knew that I couldn't); and when he came to a dead tree canted over the brook, he placed his right hand upon it, and spoke in a low voice, *"Fiat vita!"*—and, wonder of wonders, it seemed to me that I could see his power flash within the heart of that old, furrowed trunk, and then spread out steadily from that one central point, down into the roots and up into the remnants of the limbs of that once-mighty behemoth of the forest; and then sprinkles of green began appearing on the branches, as new leaves sprouted for the first time in sixteen empty years, and great, yellow flowers and lush, oblong purple fruits emerged in turn, until the entire plant had joyfully, even playfully shaken itself awake after its long slumber, and flashed its brilliant colors to its gray-infested neighbors, as if to say, "See! See what I can do!"

Then Parakôdês looked back over his shoulder at me, and said: "See!"

"Master of Mages!" I said, overwhelmed with awe at what I'd just seen.

He turned back to that beautiful sea of green that flared above him, and seemed to merge right into the massive tree trunk, gradually disappearing from sight. "Remember," I seemed to hear him say, "That you may not call upon me again in this life. Recall this, Morpheús, when you come at last to the banks of the Great River which we all must pass."

And that was the last that I saw of him.

CHAPTER EIGHTEEN
"DO WE HAVE A CHOICE?"

A great philosopher once said, *"Cogito, ergo sum,"* which is to say, "I think, therefore I am." What I had to do was to make magic—*real* magic—to find the Dream Weaver that I supposedly contained within me. I had my ancestor's example before me, and what he'd accomplished, I would try to duplicate.

After marveling over the revivified tree for more than an hour, I finally wandered back to our compound, and when I didn't see Shah'rah, asked Eagle where she'd gone.

"She's visitin' the local tribe of Festucans, Sir," he said, "With that, you know, leader fella, I don't ken his name. The Tyros, they've gone off to the great machine with Hawk."

Although I'd interacted with the natives' spokesman, Nonnengagué, on several occasions, I had no idea where their main village was located. I asked Eagle if he knew.

"I can take you there, Sir," he said. "Got nothin' else better to do, that's for sure."

So he led me through the countryside in a direction not far removed from the path I'd taken myself earlier in the day, and after a half-hour's leisurely stroll, we came to Pissapapilis. I'd expected something quite primitive, but the reality was very different: a collection of fairly-well-maintained houses fashioned of brick and wood, clustered around a large, domed green building that appeared to serve as town hall of some kind. Perhaps a third of the structures looked abandoned.

Nonnengagué, who appeared to have the status of the local

Mayor or Administrator, had been tipped off by someone that we were coming, and was waiting for us at the central facility.

"Welcome, Master Morpheús and Eagle," he said. "What news do you bring us today?"

I was about to respond when we were interrupted by a ten-year-old boy running down the street, screaming something at the top of his lungs. I thought maybe he'd stepped on one of the poisonous toads, but had no idea, really, since he was speaking Festucan.

The Mayor and the lad exchanged a volley of rapid-fire speeches, before Nonnengagué turned to me again and said: "It's a miracle, Master, a true miracle! The Gods be praised! Chuchaqué says that a tree has come alive in the Molondronne Forest. It's impossible, but it has leaves and flowers and ripe fruit all at the same time."

"That's what I was coming to tell you, Sir," I said, "but I'm glad that the boy brought you the news first. It's not the complete answer, but it's a start."

The word was obviously spreading rapidly, because the remaining townspeople (who included, I suspected, some survivors from the outlying countryside as well), were pouring out of their shops and houses, and crowding around the Green Dome, as I called it—the center of government for this region.

"Husband!" I heard my wife say, "is true?"

"Is very true," I said, wrapping one arm around her waist. It felt warm and yielding and almost homey to me, and I realized very suddenly that I was becoming quite attached to the ex-dancer. I grinned in spite of myself at the thought.

"Sir, I wonder if you could translate for me," I asked the Mayor.

I walked up the steps of the Dome, and then turned and addressed the gathering citizens: "People of Festuca," I spoke through his voice, "I promise you that I won't leave until the greenery of this world has been restored, at least to the extent that you'll be able to raise some crops again. It won't be perfect, but you'll have a future once more—for yourselves, your children, and your grandchildren."

They began cheering at the first good news that they'd had in a very long time.

"But I need your help, citizens. Someone must go forth into the neighboring towns, and tell them what's happening here. Without the communication links that used to unite this world, we have to accomplish things another way—the slow way. But if each village will do the same, we'll gradually spread the word to every land and every country farm that still survives.

"A new day is dawning. You'll be free of foreign overlords, free to peddle your crops wherever you will, free to come and go through the æthernet as you yourselves determine. I'll train you myself, once we've solved the problem of the fields.

"But first things first. Now I must return to the Station, and prepare myself for the road that lies ahead."

Then I embraced the Mayor, and followed my wife and Eagle back to our headquarters.

By then Hawk had returned with Zalmanna and Brentinna.

"Ah," I said to the Tyrosian ladies, "I have a new task for you."

"We want to go home," Mistress Z. said.

"I assume you've already tried activating the transit-mirror," I said.

Zalmanna looked down at the floor.

"Of course," I continued. "Well, you won't get anywhere that way unless you continue to work with me."

"Do we have any choice?" she asked.

"'Do we have any choice?' *Master*," I repeated.

"Master," she added, most reluctantly.

"Nope, not a one."

CHAPTER NINETEEN
"WALKING INTO THE TRUNK OF A DEAD TREE"

The next day the town of Pissapapilis invited us to be guests of honor at their first general celebration since the collapse of their economy, sixteen years earlier. Some enterprising soul had gone to the lone revived tree in all the Molondronne Forest, and had picked the ripe fruit now hanging from its restored limbs. Everyone would at least get one bite of a sweet something that they hadn't tasted in almost two decades.

I ordered Hawk and his men to break into the sealed storage room at the site of the downed machine, and to bring back some of the foodstuffs there to help freshen the pot, so to speak.

After their own processed victuals had been eaten, the villagers had survived on edible fungi, fern-like plants, insects, small rodents, and a few tubers that grew solely underground. The absence of vital nutrients had clearly increased their suscep-tibility to disease and the other ills of malnutrition, and vastly reduced the population. The Mayor estimated that ninety-five percent of the inhabitants from twenty years ago had perished in the interim, with relatively few births of new children to make up for those who died.

But before I departed for the festivities, I walked outside, where I wouldn't be interrupted or overheard, and tried to contact the Lady Niobë again. This time, I was able to get through without difficulty. She looked better physically than she had during our last several communications, and I told her so.

"I feel you're getting nearer to finding a solution to our problem," she said, "And that you'll soon be coming to Naprimér."

"Well, as to that, there's been a brief delay," I said, and explained the terrible situation that we'd found on Festuca, and my third and final meeting with the ancient mage.

She sighed: "Of course you must help," she said, "Even if it means that you can't transit here immediately. But do you know what you're going to do yet?"

"To be honest, no," I said, "even though I told the Festucans otherwise. When I saw my ancestor, he said that what I needed was already in hand. But he never tells me exactly what I'm supposed to do with the implements, or how to get from here to there. The last that I saw of him, he was literally walking into the trunk of a dead tree, just after he'd made it come completely alive again."

"You actually saw Parakôdês accomplish this task?" she said.

"Yes."

"Amazing! *How* did he do it, Morpheús?"

"I'm not really sure," I said. "He was able somehow to interface with the remnants of the tree, and revitalize it with his energy. He must have also purged or cured it of whatever ailment killed it in the first place. I've never heard of such potent magic before. He said that I carry all of the elements of a Dream Weaver's talents in my blood—*his* blood—but what does that mean, exactly? How do I find and apply such gifts, whatever they are? Or, to put it more plainly, how can I make a dead plant become productive again?"

"Tell me precisely what you saw," she said.

"He put his right hand on the trunk, spoke the words 'Let there be life,' and put his energy directly into the dead wood—I could see it spreading out from that central point to infuse the rest of the tree. It was a miracle, Lady."

"No!" she said, "it was a working—a great spell, to be sure, but a construct nonetheless. What can be done once, can be accomplished again. I know this, and so do you. It's just like the technique that Mathurin showed you to open an unlinked gate into ætherspace. You followed his example there, and now you're able to copy his actions.

"This is just the same, even though it involves a different kind of magic. You'll need the power of the two books, the knowledge of the Pathfinder-*cum*-Firedog, and perhaps the assistance of the wherret and the two Tyros as well—but you can do this, Morphy! You can do this! It's analogous to what you'll have to do to cement the fractures in the structure of the universe."

Now it was my turn to sigh. Every time I contemplated the responsibility that had been dumped on me, I got the shaking shivers. It was too much for one man to bear. I mean—why me? All I'd wanted was a little adventure in my life, and now I was being asked to save the æther as we knew it. It was impossible, just impossible.

"Niobë, I need your help," I said—and I wasn't kidding either.

"Yes, I know. You require an anchor, some certainty in life that will allow you to re-create the world as we know it in some new guise. I do understand, really. I've been trapped in my own semblance of reality for a good many years, and I've posed all the same questions, and received all the same answers.

"I have no panacea for what ails you, except to say that I *will* be there when you call. I feel increasingly certain that we're in this together, that it will take both of us to find a solution.

"But right now, you have to focus on finding an answer that will fix enough of what's broken in the world of Festuca to give you the knowledge to move on. Concentrate on small solutions first—the larger ones will come from your understanding of the process, once you gain the confidence to move forward.

"I believe you can do this. I know that you have the strength and integrity to find a way. Look inside. Look to your friends. Look to the people.

"Now I must go. Do take care, Morphy."

"And you, dear Lady," I said. And then I cut the connection.

She was in many ways more accomplished in magery than I—I could see that clearly now—but it was up to me to make things work, to envision the new reality that I wanted to create. I had to weave the dream into the fabric of the land and its people.

Parakôdês had shown me the possibilities when he'd transformed that single tree into a living, productive being. I would take Niobë's suggestion, and start small, discovering and uncovering the means within and without my being to adjust this once-beautiful world to my own beauteous vision of what it might become.

And then, out of nowhere, I had the strangest thought, and wondered if my old mother was still alive somewhere in Zmyrna. I hadn't even considered my family in many years, and I didn't even remember how old she would be. I tried figuring it in my head.

I'd left Nova Europa in 1622, and according to my last contact there, at least three years had elapsed whilst I'd been traversing the æthernet, even though it seemed much less than that to me. She'd been born about 1539, I think, figuring back from the date of my own birth, so she'd be perhaps eighty-six (or older) now.

I wanted to see her again, if she was alive, and tell her—what? That I missed her? That I was sorry that I'd been such an inattentive son? That I wish I'd stayed at home?—but I'd truly never felt that way. Or just maybe that I still loved her, in spite of everything.

What was the *matter* with me? I hadn't been troubled by such questions in decades. I felt like my insides were being torn up and rearranged in spite of myself, and put back in some kind of foreign order that I didn't comprehend or even desire.

(Her name was Selíni, the moon, and I remember that she'd always shown with an inner strength and purpose that had cemented the ties in our family.)

I wondered if Markos, my next younger brother, had become an apothecary, as he desired, and if my sister Patáta had married Gordion the blacksmith, and if Aunt María had continued making those marvelous pieces of pottery.

I'd neglected them for far too long. But would any of them remember me?—or would I just become another hoary family story about the wild, wayward son who'd left to make his fortune, and then never returned. I had to find out someday.

Scooter suddenly interrupted my reverie. "Master," it said, "It's time for us to go."

CHAPTER TWENTY
"OH, YOU WHERRETS!"

Nonnengagué, the Mayor of the town of Pissapapilis, was waiting to greet Shah'rah, Scooter, and me at the edge of the village—I'd been told that the Tyros wouldn't be acceptable, and so I'd left Hawk and his men at the Station to keep an eye on the two ladies, whom I'd never trust again with anything.

"Welcome, Master Morpheús, Mistress Shah'rah, and Wherret Scooter," the little man said. Then he proceeded to introduce us to the leading men and women of his small community, one by one. They passed in a kind of blur. There may have been as many as two thousand souls left in the area, and most of them were present to meet us. Many grasped my hands and tried to kiss them, obviously in gratitude for the effort that I hadn't yet made to save their civilization. I tried to beg off, but relented when Shah'rah trod on my foot, and whispered in my left ear, "Be good."

Afterwards, Nonnengagué led us to the Great Hall of the central administrative building that we'd previously seen—the Green Dome, I called it—and invited us to join him at the head of the long-table. Some kind of sweet-and-sour fermented drink was served—I have to say that it was utterly vile, and I could barely choke it down without vomiting—and this was followed by the first course of what they obviously intended to be the greatest feast served here in sixteen years. I noticed that some of the dishes included the contents of the canned rations that had been stored in the secure bins near the fallen machine.

"I apologize, good Sir, for the blandness of the food," the Mayor said, "but we have few seasonings remaining to us other than plain salt. Most of the others were produced from cultivated plants that died with all of our other crops, and our stocks have long since been depleted."

But they did their best with what they had. I tried to eat sparingly, not wanting to take food quite literally out of their half-starved mouths; but they kept urging me to try this or that or the other, and of course, I had to sample at least a bite or two of each. Some—like the ear of a roasted purple fungus—were surprisingly tasty, with a pungent resonance that agreed with me very well indeed. Others had almost no flavor to them at all, or were bitterly unpalatable. All of the dishes were tested first by Scooter, of course, to make certain that they wouldn't harm the two visiting Nova Europans.

Finally, the very thin wedges sliced from the ripe fruit of the opolento tree that my ancestor had revived were distributed throughout the crowd, and I heard "oohs" and "ahs" as this delicacy was sampled for the first time in almost two decades.

Then the boy Chuchaqué came forward, and was presented to me by his great-uncle, the Mayor, who said: "He requests a boon from you, Master Mage."

I looked at the lad closely for the first time, and suddenly realized that Parakôdês had copied the boy's visage in creating the shadow-image of himself that he'd employed during our recent conversation. There was a message inherent in everything he did, if only I had the sense enough to comprehend it!

"What do you wish, Chuchaqué?" I asked, smiling at him to diminish his obvious terror of this visitor from another dimension. His uncle repeated the question in Festucan.

"I...I...," he stammered, and then flushed red, one hand tucked behind his back. He pulled a pot filled with soil from its hiding place, and thrust it abruptly into my arms.

"What's this for?" I said.

"I...I...," but he was no more coherent than before. I could feel his fear, and I tried to send him waves of calm through the æther, not knowing whether the technique would work on this species.

"I think he wants you to grow more of the opolento trees," Nonnengagué said. "We've saved the seeds harvested from the fruit." He dropped a dozen oblong, dark brown pits onto the palm of my other hand.

"If you don't mind…," I said, and popped one of the seeds into my mouth, trying to probe its essence by sucking on it. But I just couldn't reach through the hard covering that shielded its life force. So I crushed it with my teeth, and savored the energy that flowed from its essence.

Suddenly I was overwhelmed with images, and almost dropped the clay container being held in my left hand. Shah'rah threw her arms around me to steady my abruptly weak legs. She couldn't know, of course, that I was being besieged, almost inundated, with pictures from the life of my ancestral mage, and being overwhelmed by the great knowledge that he'd possessed during his existence on this sphere.

"I must sit," I managed to gasp out. A chair was brought to me.

"Are you all right, Master?" Scooter hissed in my right ear.

But I was still trying to cope with the onslaught of information that had unexpectedly been thrust upon me. I shoved the data back into a corner of my mind for later examination.

"I'm, uh, I'm fine," I finally managed to say. "Really."

"The food didn't disagree with you?" the Mayor asked.

"No, it was nothing like that. There was something in the seed itself that affected me. I wasn't expecting it, and so was unprepared for its potency."

Chuchaqué had run away during my "fit," scared half to death, no doubt, that *he'd* been the instrument of this terrible tantrum, and would be blamed for the inevitable disaster to follow. I asked that he be brought back again, if he was willing— for I would never force myself upon a child.

Slowly, tentatively, he approached the "Great Mage," looking down all the while at the tiled floor. I still had the pot that he'd given me.

"Is this what you want?" I said. His uncle translated for me.

He very delicately raised his eyes to focus on the container of native soil in front of him. I popped another seed in my mouth, and when he would have bolted again, said, "Wait!" I spit the moist pit onto my hand, and then very carefully pushed it into the center of the dirt. Gathering my energy into a small cone, I thrust just a pip of it into the seed, and said, *"Fiat vita!"* Within seconds a small green shoot erupted from the dark earth, and curled its way upward, stopping when it was about three inches tall.

"Water this regularly for a week," I said, "and then replant it in fertile soil. It will eventually grow into an opolento."

He looked at the new plant so intently that I thought his soul had been captured by one of the faeries. Then, for the very first time, he gazed at me and smiled, and said in broken Tyrosian, "Tha-ank yo-uh, poh-leese."

"You're welcome," I said, and grinned back at him in turn. "You're very welcome."

Everyone in the room began talking at once, and hooting in the sound that I later learned signified their especial approval of something well done and greatly accomplished.

The Mayor kissed my hands—both of them—and said: "You have restored our faith, man from the stars. You will make us whole again." Then he began sniffing, unable to hold his emotions in check. "You have no...."

They fêted us well into the night, and in fact didn't want us to leave—ever, I think!—but I told them that we had much to do the next day, which was only the truth, and that we had to get our rest.

Fifty of them followed us all the way to the Station, to make certain that the ghosts wouldn't capture our spirits along the way; and for the first time, I felt an optimism that I could actually make a difference—with these people, and with all of the others yet to come.

"You did good," Shah'rah whispered in my left ear.

"Well, you did maybe OK," Scooter immediately added in the other.

"Oh, you wherrets!" was all I could mumble in response.

CHAPTER TWENTY-ONE
"BAD DREAM"

I'd been able to germinate the opolento shoot because the seeds had originated from the fruit of the tree that Parakôdês had restored. Whatever poison had been present in the dead wood had been purged by him, and I'd sensed glimpses of his life and knowledge stored within the pit itself, almost a psychic echo of what he'd accomplished in bringing the plant back to life. But I still wasn't quite sure what he'd done to restore the flora in the first place.

I'd brought back with me a dozen seeds from the hundreds collected by the Festucans at the feast, and the next day I transited to the one working atmospheric machine together with the two Tyros, Scooter, and Hawk.

I knew that the Overseer scientists who'd worked there had established a number of secure, sealed storage bins filled with foodstuffs, sample seeds, and other supplies. We used a Dissolve-All solvent to remove the Avert-All spell that prevented random tampering with the contents, and quickly took an inventory. I found a selection of grain seeds, and took a small number, together with the opolento pits, to the bank of a nearby brook. I planted one of the trees next to something that was supposed to become a kind of wheat, added a sprinkle of water, and then gave each a small piece of my energy.

The tree immediately sprouted, just as the one at the Festucan festival had the previous day; but nothing happened with the other plant. I felt beneath the soil until I reached the small, ungerminated seed, and found it still alive; when germination had begun, something in the dirt had blocked its continued development.

I sighed: this was way beyond my knowledge. I straightened up and rubbed my hands together.

"Ladies," I said to the Tyros, "I want you to take samples of the soil around these plantings, and analyze them for rhumadyne and its derivatives. See if you can find anything that shouldn't be there."

I knew that the office at the machine site had a room attached with analytical laboratory equipment, none of which I understood. I realized enough, however, to fathom that some of it might be able to penetrate the chemical reaction that had occurred to poison much of Festuca's plant life.

After they'd gone, I touched the one good sprout—that of the tree—and then fished around in the dirt again for the wheat seed with my other hand. I tried to compare the two, but their genetics were so different that I couldn't in my own mind isolate the problem.

"Perhaps if you try copying what Master Parakôdês did, Sir," the wherret said, "You might have better luck."

But I didn't know how to do that, not really, despite having seen the old mage accomplish what I regarded as a miracle, and having received a loose assortment of his memories and lore—none of which I'd had time to access yet. I obviously needed a break, and so I walked with Scooter on my shoulder back to the machine, and from there we transited to the Station using the local *viridaurum* mirror the Tyros had left.

My wife was waiting for me.

"You, uh, become tired, *caro*," Shah'rah said, trying to enunciate each word carefully, when the wherret and I emerged from the transit-device. Scooter promptly scooted away to perform the nasty things that those little creatures do by themselves.

"Yes," I said. "It's not going very well. I can make one of the opolento trees grow from a seed, because it's already been cleansed, but I haven't been able to figure out yet how to accomplish the same trick with any of the other vegetation. I need some time to think."

"You need rest," she said, reaching up to brush a wayward lock of hair out of my eyes. "Come, husband, I fix you…food."

Shah'rah dragged me back into the kitchen and dining area, where she unpacked several pouches of Tyrosian grub, added some spices to mitigate against the strange flavors, and dished them onto a plate for me. The victuals had heated themselves in their containers as soon as their seals were broken.

"Not bad," I said, as I spooned down something that looked like a meat stew. Somewhere she'd found salt, a substitute for pepper, and several powders with a taste similar to garlic and onion. I really had been hungry, and hadn't even realized it.

The Tyros traditionally stocked their outposts with plenty of alcohol-free ales—at least, they tasted like something potent, but had no sting to them at all. They could be quaffed hot or cold.

I yawned once, and then again, quite noisily. I was still trying to get past the celebration we'd had at the Festucan village the previous night.

"You lie down now," Shah'rah said. "Sleep."

She led me to the cot that we'd appropriated for our own bed, and tucked me in. I remember thinking that I could certainly get used to this kind of attention! But I drifted off very quickly, and almost immediately was immersed in a strange dream.

I was looking for something or someone, and I was lost, wandering this way and that in the dead Molondronne Forest, unable to find my way. Every so often a voice would call to me— of Niobë, Shah'rah, Scooter, Zalmanna, even Scarabbaios— but when I followed the sound, it led me deeper and deeper in amidst the crowded skeletons of the decaying trees. Finally, I saw a light shining in the distance, and followed it until I came to the one living plant—the opolento that my ancestor had revivified—even though I remembered somehow that it was not actually part of the old decaying forest.

Master Parakôdês was there waiting for me, in the guise of

the old man he'd been when first I'd seen him, embodied within the sculpture in my home in Barstölný. He shook his head when I tried to speak, putting an upright finger to his lips. Then he pointed at the trunk next to him, just at the spot, three feet above the ground, where he'd touched the tree, making it come alive. He motioned to me to approach, and then stepped aside as I stooped to examine more closely the white mark that he'd left there. I touched it with my own hand, and felt the energy still emanating from the spot. I looked up at the semi-transparent image of the man, and he smiled at me. Then a gust of wind literally swept him away.

But when I tried to find my way out of the maze again, I was blocked at every turn by the debris left over from the Great Dying. The dead branches pulled at my cloak, trying to retard my advance. I could not escape! Finally, I yelled out, "Shah'rah!"—and felt someone put her arms around me and hold me close. After that I slept soundly for several hours.

When I awoke, she was sitting next to the bed in a chair, watching me intently. "You have bad dream, *no*?" she asked.

"Yes, but it's better now," I said, "thanks to you."

"I have bad dream on some day," she said, "but no one there to help, ever."

"I'll help," I said. "All you have to do is ask."

CHAPTER TWENTY-TWO
"SHHH"

The two Tyrosian Overseers were still working at the great machine, according to Eagle, so I transited there while it was still light.

"What have you found?" I asked Zalmanna.

"There are several compounds mixed in with the surface layer of the soil that apparently derive from the rhumadyne that was injected into the atmosphere," she said. "These include a dioxide, a trioxide, and a carbonate of some kind."

"What does that mean?"

"Only that there are three possibilities for the agent that has poisoned or retarded the growth of these plants—and we are unable to tell you how to treat them to mitigate their influence. Because rhumadyne bonds so easily with other substances, these could actually represent different stages of the evolution of the chemical."

"So you have no solution?" I asked.

"You must understand, Master Morpheús, that neither of us are trained scientists," Brentinna said. "We know how to operate some of the analytical equipment—although not all—but we lack the specific knowledge to recommend a course of action. We would have to return to the Homeworld in order to find someone sufficiently proficient in the chemical arts to tell us what to do—if, in fact, there is a solution.

"You will recall that the technicians assigned here abandoned this planet, which provided valuable food resources to our race; they would not have done this, in our estimation, had they known of any method to counteract the damage that had occurred."

Since it would be dark soon, I had them shut their equipment down and reseal the facility, and then returned with them and Hawk to the Station.

After grabbing a meal with Shah'rah and my comrades-in-arms, I went outside and contacted the Lady Niobë again, but her time was short, and she basically gave me the same advice as before. "The key is Parakôdês's tree," she said, after I told her about my dream. "What exactly did he do there, first, to revive the plant, and secondly, to purge it of its poisons? If you can fathom that, you can solve this problem."

Scooter agreed with her assessment. "It seems to me, Master, that you must go back. He was telling you that there's something in the trunk that you missed."

Even Shah'rah chipped in: "*Mi esposo*," she said, "I worry *muy mucho*. So tired you are. *El árbol del opolento* will speak to you, if you ask it."

That night, I was drifting in the Land of the Lost again, struggling to find my way through the Dead Forest—and evidently tossing and turning in the process—when I felt her arms go 'round me once more, pillowing my head on one of her soft, warm breasts. "Shhh," I heard her whisper in my ear. Then she kissed me on the forehead, and again on the nose, and finally full on my lips.

After months of wanting to respond in kind, I finally let myself go—I couldn't help myself—and kissed her back again. Of course, there was almost no privacy in our sleeping quarters, which included four cots (Hawk's men slept on blanket rolls in the main room), housed in cubicles separated by very light partitions—and no doorways. I was too reserved to carry our bedplay to its logical conclusion in such a public forum, although I don't think Shah'rah shared the same inhibition.

Still, she seemed to understand my sensibilities better than I, because she reached down and grabbed me lightly, and then proceeded to demonstrate the skills she'd acquired in her profession of dancer-*cum*-whatever. I never had a prayer of backing away or stopping the grand exaltation that soon appeared. She raised her hand to her mouth, and licked her fingers like a well-satisfied cat. Who *was* this woman?

"Shhh," she whispered again, when I tried to express my feelings for her. I don't know why she quieted me then, when I was finally willing to tell her the truth.

Strangely, I also felt something more than the physical pleasure of the act, as gratifying as that was; it almost seemed to me that some kind of psychic energy had been released—and yet she had no training of which I was aware, and no hallmarks of Psairothi power. I probed the surface levels of her being, and was startled to find a node of golden energy there, well protected and well nourished.

"Yes, husband," she suddenly spoke within my mind, surprising me in a way that I had not experienced in decades, *"I possess a certain talent, as you would call it, although in Andalusia I would have been burned as a witch had that fact become known. My governess, Doña María Aliccia de la Cítera, was the first to recognize my ability, and she taught me both how to use it and how to hide it—and many other things besides, including the Latin tongue, although my understanding of Greek remains poor."*

"But...but I speak Latin, as you well know," I said to her mentally. *"Why...?"*

"I did not wish to reveal myself until I was sure," she said.

"But...I probed you!" I said. *"I felt nothing of this, nothing at all. I looked at your past life, and...."*

"Don Mórpheo," Shah'rah said, *"dearest Mórpheo, you never, ever understood what I felt for you. You had to reach that place on your own, before I could unveil my true nature to you. You have many reserves encircling your soul, dear one, walling it off from your humanity; what you failed so often to see is that I'm cursed with similar restrictions—just in different ways."*

I realized then that I'd been systematically blinding myself all these years to the wonderful possibilities of life, that I'd automatically thrust aside any commitments or connections or underpinnings to other people—because they might interfere with my profession, my career, my devotion to my art, or any damned excuse I could find. They were actions of a moral coward.

That was why I could never truly understand other people—or even myself. My absence of sympathy was symptomatic of a deeper problem—my total lack of *agápê*, to use the old Greek term. He who cannot love another cannot even love himself, not really. All these wasted years devoted to…what? What had I ever accomplished that amounted to anything at all?

Even here, even on Festuca, where an entire planet was dying, I'd made no difference whatsoever. It was Master Parakôdês who'd cured the tree. He'd tried to tell me—they had *all* tried to tell me—but I'd never listened, never understood. I was a fool.

And this woman, this good and beautiful woman, loved me—*me!*—and I didn't know why. I was shopworn goods, even by comparison to her ex-lover, Sevastiano the spy—old, tired, and not much fun to be around.

"I love you, Shah'rah," I finally said out loud.

"Well, it's about time," she whispered back at me in Latin. "It's about bloody time, husband." Then she kissed me once again.

CHAPTER TWENTY-THREE
"THE WHERRET WHO
ATE THE BEETLE BALM"

The next morning, I felt like singing, but managed to control myself long enough to realize how strange that might appear to my fellow-travelers. Still, I fielded several curious looks from Hawk, Scooter, and the two Tyros, all of whom seemed to be eminently aware of the change in relationship between myself and Shah'rah. How they fathomed this mystery, when it took *me* ever so long, was totally beyond my comprehension.

"Gee, someone's very happy. You do rather look like the wherret who ate the beetle balm," my familiar whispered in my right ear.

"Never you mind," I said, but I couldn't help but grin. The new day seemed like the start of a new life to me.

I wanted to go back to the tree that Master Parakôdês had restored. He'd left something there for me that I'd missed—once again! I took with me Shah'rah and Scooter, but left the two Overseers with a make-work task (overseen by Sergeant Hawk) at the great atmospheric machine. I didn't want them to learn anything more than necessary about what I was trying to do.

It took us almost an hour to wander through the Festuca landscape on the way to Brushy Creek, where the opolento stood. I wanted to savor the terrain with my wife before getting down to business.

"Well, I guess she is a tasty treat by human standards," Scooter whispered, watching Shah'rah's slim body saunter around some bushes—at which point I shoved it down my arm and onto the ground.

"If you don't have anything good to say," I told the creature, "then you can make your own way."

"Well, I never…!"—but I missed the rest of its complaint when I hurried after my lady.

The site of the tree had apparently became a kind of shrine to the inhabitants of Pissapapilis, because we found a dozen Festucans there, the boy Chuchaqué among them, marveling at the bright green foliage, the colorful flowers, and the ripe fruit—all produced out of season and out of sync with the normal progress of nature.

"*Quaqué* Morpheús!" several of them said, gabbling with each other in their native tongue. They all wanted to touch my cloak, my hands, or anything else they could reach of mine.

The boy ran off, and soon brought back his great-uncle, Nonnengagué, the local leader, who was fluent in Tyrosian.

"They just want to pay their respects, Master," he said.

"I do appreciate that, but please tell them that I must have some time alone to hug the tree," I said.

He and his fellows exchanged several sentences, and finally agreed to depart for the nonce.

"What happens if I really do save these people?" I asked my wife. "Do we have to stay here forever?"

"I certainly hope not," she said in Latin. "I would find the unceasingly adulation…tiring."

"As would I. Where's Scooter gone to?"

I looked around, but the little creature was nowhere to be seen. "Scoot!" I yelled.

"Coming, Master!" the wherret squeaked, and finally appeared with the remains of some kind of centipede-like creature dangling from its lips. "Whatever else they have on this world, the insect life is still flourishing—or rather, it was!"

"I'm going to need help from both of you." I slowly approached the revived opolento, and located the spot where I remembered the "boy" Parakôdês having rested his hand. I had to squat down to examine the site more closely, and finally just sat on the damp soil and debris. "I remember seeing some kind of energy flowing from the mage into the dead wood, and then spreading up and down to encompass the entire tree. Link with me, please, while I probe this area."

"How do I do that?" Shah'rah asked. "Your magic is so different from what I secretly learned in Andalusia that I feel at sea."

"She speaks!" the wherret hissed, chuckling.

"Curb your disrespect," I ordered. "Scooter, provide the bridge, please."

"I hear and obey, o wise one," the creature said, and nipped me slightly on the ear, swishing the tip of its tongue into the drop of blood that appeared. Then it then hopped from me to Shah'rah's left shoulder—she jumped at the unexpected motion—and did the same to her before she could react or object.

For the first time, we three were tied to each other psychically, and I felt instinctively that *this* Lady provided a much stronger complement to my powers than Niobë ever had.

"I officially stand up as straight and amazed, kind Sir," the wherret said. "The woman, she has much to contribute."

"Indeed she does," I agreed. "All right, folks, let's see what there is to see here."

While Scooter watched my psychic back, so to speak, I put myself into a light trance, and opened the third eye on my forehead to examine the surface of the bark from close range. It glowed in several æthereal colors—a bright emerald, a suave ochre, and a demure violet.

So, the master mage of yore had accomplished several different workings simultaneously! I shook my head slightly in sheer wonderment. This was a conjoined spell like none I'd ever seen before, and it had taken a truly talented and knowledgeable magus to bring it off.

But what had he done, exactly?

"Scooter," I said, "Can you find me a piece of loose bark on the surrounding ground that originally derived from this tree, but was *not* affected by the re-engagement of vital force?"

The wherret jumped to the surface, and quickly moved from piece to piece of the nearby mixed detritus of failed vegetation, until it held up a small section and yelled, "Aha!"

When my familiar brought it to me, I clutched the dead wood in my dexter hand while placing the right against the spot touched by the great master of mysteries. This time I—and Scooter and Shah'rah—probed both pieces of bark simultaneously.

"Look here!" I said, mentally pointing to the differences betwixt the two. "The green aura is the residue remaining from Parakôdês's reanimation of the life force of the wood. I know of no mage currently living who can duplicate this immense working, including me.

"The yellow-brown aura is the spell that cleansed the opolento of its poisons, changing the rhumadyne into inert compounds that don't affect the viability of the plant.

"The purple haze, however, is the most important part of this working, because without it the tree couldn't draw enough nutrients from the topsoil to survive. It takes the rhumadyne that's become layered over this planet and converts it into thalassine, which can then be readily absorbed by the tree.

"We don't have to regenerate *all* of the existing vegetation on the world, just provide enough of the third element to allow the Festucans to germinate the seeds that they—and the Tyros—still have stored. If we can do this much, they'll be able to raise food crops again within short order."

"But can we do this, husband?" Shah'rah asked.

"Yes, we can," I said.

CHAPTER TWENTY-FOUR
"AIN'T WORTH A POT TO PISS IN"

I put the two Tyrosian Overseers to work on a series of magical experiments that would allow plant life on Festuca to convert the Rhumadyne that permeated the atmosphere and soil into thalassine. I had a pretty good idea of the nature of the spell that would be needed, and gave them the basics of what I wanted them to accomplish. It would require a number of trial-and-error workings to narrow the possibilities to a level that could actually achieve the desired result.

After several weeks, they'd progressed far enough that I took over the process, working with Scooter and Shah'rah—for even though my wife was essentially untrained in the art, she had an instinct for the right path that was unerringly correct. She would review my work for the day, and say, "That process looks promising," and I found that she was almost always right.

Finally, I reached a point where I felt I'd duplicated the effect that Master Parakôdês had achieved with the purple haze. It was probably not exactly the same procedure, because each mage of power tends to find his or her own path to a particular result; but it was close enough to work.

So I implanted a seed of the wheat-type grain into a pot of soil, infused the pip with a small amount of the energy produced from the spell, watered the dirt, and used my essence to germinate the plant and grow it to a size of perhaps three inches— enough, in this case, to determine whether or not it was capable of surviving and thriving on its own.

Once I had a seedling that was viable, I showed the pair of Tyros how to achieve the same result. After another couple of weeks of successes and failures, we walked out one day to a desolate field south of Pissapapilis, cleared away the dead brush with a sweep of char-fire and a breath of quick-wind, implanted a row of seeds with a shallow-digging spell, created a mini-rain cloud over the land and doused the area with a splash of water, and then germinated the entire line of plants, bringing them to the point where they could be seen by everyone, with Scooter and Shah'rah supplementing my directing energy whenever it became depleted.

By the end of the afternoon, we were all exhausted, physically and psychically—but we'd done it! For the first time in sixteen years, a crop of cultivated plants had been sown on Festuca, and showed every sign of eventually maturing into an edible grain. My repeated psychic probes of the vegetation showed that all were sound—and more to the point, purged of the noxious rhumadyne.

The boy Chuchaqué was the first villager to venture on the scene—he tended to shadow my steps much of the time—and when he saw what we'd done, he yelled out loud for anyone to hear: "You, uh, done it, Master!" (He was trying to learn Tyrosian as quickly as possible.)

Then he ran off to get his great-uncle, the Mayor, and soon the place was overflowing with exulting Pissapapilitans.

"We're saved! We're saved!" Nonnengagué shouted. "Oh, thank you, Master Morpheús, for bringing us such life." Then he threw his arms around me and kissed me on the chin—which he could only reach with some assistance.

Over the next few months I and my crew gradually restored fields of the vegetables, fruits, and grains for which we were able to find seeds—plus a few spice plants, and some odds and ends, including decorative species. In addition, some of the native vegetation had survived the poisoning from the sky (or so we eventually discovered), albeit just barely, and we were able to revive some of that flora as well. Of course, this represented just a fraction of the diversity that had been present prior to the experiment conducted by the Overseer scientists—but it was the best we could do under the circumstances.

The restoration of the ecosphere would take generations, I knew, but once Festuca was able to feed its own population again, it could start exporting grains within, perhaps, ten or twenty years—and purchase additional seeds from outside trading partners. The great Tyrosian machine would slowly continue to clean the atmosphere of the rhumadyne compounds that had so adversely affected the planet.

I spent several additional months training a half dozen of the local population in the use of the transit-machine at the main Station, and found three potential adepts (including my boy shadow) who could learn, with time, to accomplish much more with themselves and with the equipment at the Station and the three machine sites. I implanted in their minds the knowledge that they would eventually need, and the keys to access it when they'd progressed to the point where they could assimilate it. I also completely locked down the main trans-æthereal transit-mirror so that no one could arrive on Festuca from an outside world without the permission of the Mayor of Pissapapilis. I wanted the Festucans to control all access to their world, without interference from outside powers.

Which brought us to the little problem of the two Overseers.

I simply couldn't allow them to return to Tyrosian space. At the least, they'd report the existence of this place—a fact that had obviously and very carefully been eradicated from the Overseers' records.

Under normal circumstances, if the Tyrosian scientists or officials ever tried to return to Festuca, they'd find the receptor off-line, and assume that it had permanently broken down. Such things happen, and no one would think to investigate—and there was no way for them to do so without physically sending a team to the closest neighboring stations on all sides, triangulating a fix on Festuca, and transiting into an uncertain reception, with no sure means of returning home. They simply wouldn't take the chance.

But if the two Tyros went back to Yelloweyen or their Homeworld, they might prompt the High Council to return with another occupying force, or simply order the destruction of the Festucan Station—or even of the entire world.

No, I couldn't take the chance. Both ladies had demonstrated more than once their complete untrustworthiness. Neither was reliable, and I didn't have confidence in any of their kind.

But for similar reasons, I didn't want to leave them behind either. Who knew if they could cobble together enough equipment and/or spells to free the Station transit-device—or to convert one of the short-transit-mirrors at the three machine sites for long-transit? Or they might be able to use their powers to subvert several of the acolytes that I'd created, and pick up enough information from their psyches to circumvent my locks.

So I took a walk in the countryside with Shah'rah, Scooter, and Hawk, and explained the problem to them. I particularly wanted the Sergeant's advice, since he was our expert on security matters.

"Well, Sir," he said, rubbing the stubble on his chin a couple of times, "I think you're dead right 'bout those ladies. I seen a lot of 'em this last six-month, and they ain't worth a pot to piss in. Far as I'm concerned, wouldn't trust 'em to do anything, no how! You need to send 'em someplace very far away."

"I agree with Hawk," Shah'rah said. "Perhaps the planet of the Pachyderms."

"But there *is* a transit-device on that world, Master," Scooter said. "We built it ourselves."

"There's no power source there," I said. "We used the linked books to activate our makeshift mirror, and took them with us."

"We don't know for certain *what's* there, Master," the wherret said. "We saw very little of the place, and the elephantoids were always coming up with new surprises. No, we can't take that chance."

"I agree, Sir," Hawk said. "Wherever you send 'em, we have to be certain that they'll never return. Perhaps the grave would be the best solution. Dead women tell no tales."

"No!" Shah'rah said. "Whatever they've done, they don't deserve to die."

In the distance, even through the ever-present haze I could see a tinge of emerald lining the bottom of the visible horizon. The crops of Festuca were beginning to mature, and showed every sign of producing an abundance of food for the semi-starved natives.

"I know what to do," I finally said.

When I told them, Scooter began to laugh in that huff-huff-huff way that it had. "Oh, Master," the wherret said, "You've done it again!"

CHAPTER TWENTY-FIVE
"WATCH OUT FOR THOSE VEILED LADIES"

"What I want," I told the two Overseers, "is to find some small Tyrosian outpost not far from the border of your space with the Volúcri Predation. Can you do this?"

"Not without accessing the sector database at Brannyboy, Master," Zalmanna said. "There is very little shown on these local machines."

"I can't let you do that, for obvious reasons. Very well, ladies: please get your belongings together. You're going on a little trip."

"What do you mean?" they both said.

"I can't let you remain here, and I also can't let you return to your own people," I said. "You're simply not trustworthy. So we both have a choice: you either go where I send you, without complaint, or you stay behind."

"But you just said, Master, that you could not let us remain here."

"I can't let you remain here *alive!*"

"Oh," Tyro Brentinna said. After a long pause, she continued: "I speak now only for myself, Sir, but I would rather have any possibility of life than death."

"Then you shall. What about you, Zalmanna?"

"I…I would be disgraced in any case for allowing myself to be taken in this way. I too choose life."

"So mote it be," I intoned, sealing the bargain magically. "Return here in one hour, if you please."

Then I went outside and used the sky-orb to focus on the coordinates that I remembered from my visit with Mathurin.

"Morpheús! How good to hear from you again," the old mage said. "You've progressed, I see."

"Thanks to you, Sir, and to Master Parakôdês. I have a request to make"—and then I explained my situation to him. "Sir, can you help?"

"Of course. They'll be just as comfortable here, I suspect, as our old friend, Doctor S., has been. He's become a, uh, celebrity on what they call the 'tee-vee'."

"What's that, Sir?" I asked.

"It's very hard to explain," Mathurin said. "But yes, do send them along.

"Where are you going next?" he asked.

"Back to your old haunts on Naprimér," I said.

"I remember the place quite fondly," he said, "But watch out for those veiled ladies, Morpheús. They hide more than their faces from us."

"Their world is occupied by the Volúcris now."

"Really? How did the Bird-Men advance so far? They had no transit technology when I knew them—and no technicians."

"I think Scarabbaios gave it to them, Sir," I said.

"Ah, that sounds like something he'd do," the old mage said. "Then you have a double problem. You need to move them back to their own space again, if you can do that."

"Are you aware of any weaknesses that they possess?" I asked.

"They tend to believe their own propaganda rather over-much," Mathurin said. "That makes them quite vulnerable to certain realities. You should be able to find a weakness in their society that will allow you to turn them back on themselves."

"I'll watch for it, Sir."

"Assuming you're successful in restoring this Niobë to her previous position of power, what then, Morpheús?"

"Then I have a universe to fix, remember?"

"Ha! Good luck with that!" he said. "But remember that the

Napriméroi have their own agenda, and it may not be the same as yours, irrespective of what she tells you. Do not underestimate her, my son.

"I remember dealing with her ancestress a very long time ago, and while it was generally a pleasant association, I had several very narrow escapes—and you'll note that I left the place abruptly, and never returned. The reason why was to avoid becoming entangled permanently within their social structure—as they envisioned it. It wasn't *my* vision of paradise, despite the obvious short-term benefits. I had better things to do with my time than playing house for eternity.

"At least on this world I get to watch grown men and women trying to re-create what we'd already accomplished millennia ago with physical constructs. I find that amusing—and I even help them every so often. Of course, they're nowhere near as proficient as we were.

"However, send me the twin Tyros, and I'll instruct them about life in a world without magic. That should keep me going for a few more decades! Take care, my son."

"And you, grandfather," I said. Then I closed the link.

A little later, I returned to the common room of the Station, and cut open a hole through the æther to Mathurin's World (whose name I'd never been told).

"Wh-where are we going?" Brentinna asked, obviously afraid of the unknown.

"You're about to embark on a grand new adventure, ladies, and to meet a legend in magical history."

I stepped aside, and motioned them to enter the opening in space and time. Gingerly, they walked forward, and then were quickly swept away into oblivion.

"An elegant solution indeed, husband," Shah'rah said from behind my back.

"Well played, Master," Scooter said from my shoulder.

"Glad they're gone, Sir," Hawk added from across the room. His handful of soldiers grunted their assent.

"Very happy to have the Tyros leave our world," Mayor

Nonnengagué said. I'd brought him there to witness the Overseers' departure.

"They will never trouble you again," I said. "That's my pledge to you."

CHAPTER TWENTY-SIX
"SOMETHIN'S NOT QUITE RIGHT THERE"

"It's time!" I told the Lady Niobë when I contacted her that evening. I made sure that Shah'rah, Scooter, and Hawk were present to observe our conversation.

"You mean you've finished the cleansing of Festuca?" she asked.

"That won't be completed for decades," I said, "But it's far enough along that the villagers are already harvesting the first of the crops whose growth we accelerated. Runners have been dispatched from Pissapapilis to the neighboring regions, inviting the surviving communities there to acquire their free, rhuma-dyne-purged seedlings whenever they choose. I've arranged for the few transit-travelers that I trained to erect similar centers at the sites of the three great machine-works of the Overseers, which were located equidistant from the other emplacements around the globe. The word should get out fairly quickly, and some semblance of normal life re-established within a few years.

"How many people will actually be saved still remains to be seen. I'll probably return here at some later date to check on their progress. But I think they'll be just fine for now.

"So we'll be ready within a few days to transit to Naprimér. The question is: where? I need to have either specific coordinates or a visible destination in order to travel there—and I suspect your system of measuring leys is very different from ours.

"The other problem is this: we're talking about the longest single transit-jump any of us has ever made. I'm quite sure that we have the power to facilitate the leap, but when we emerge on the other end, we'll be suffering from extreme long-transit-shock, and will probably need days—perhaps many days—to recuperate."

"That's a major problem," she said. "I can obviously let you link to my rooms here through the sky-orb, but this location isn't secure—and neither is any other site to which I have access now. I can give you pictures of 'safe' places where you could land on this world, but no one there would know who you are—and I have no way of communicating easily with my friends on the outside. You would be sufficiently out-of-place and -culture that you'd be apprehended very quickly as strangers—the Volúcris restrict all travel to and on Naprimér. So I'm not sure how to proceed."

"What about Zezament as an intermediate stop?" I asked. "Isn't that relatively close to your planet?"

"Yes!—and that world has somehow managed thus far to stave off occupation by the Bird-Men. Indeed, that might well do," she said. "You could recuperate there for a week or so before coming here. I think you have it, Morpheús!

"I visited there just once, when I was a girl, but I remember the ruins of an ancient aqueduct a few miles outside of the capital, Zazzou. It's quite distinctive. Let me give you the image."

She reached a hand down to the bowl of water that served as the receptor for her makeshift sky-orb, and touched the rim with her left index finger. The moisture resident on the inside slope of the cup was sufficient to establish a direct mental connection between her and me, and I jolted as the link was suddenly forged.

Niobë, I noted, had very carefully parceled her thoughts into secure compartments within her being, just as I had as a matter of course (to protect myself from unexpected Psairothi attacks and intrusions). She placed in the front of her mind the memory she had of her visit to Zazzou, and the trip that she and her guardian (an aunt) had made to the famous Pits just outside of town. These had been caused by some curious geological phenomena that remained unexplained, but they looked from above like nothing more than a series of cavities filled with very sharp, very pointy teeth. Running parallel to the Pits on one side was the remnant of the arched aqueduct that had once carried water from the distant mountains to the old city. The crosshatching of stone supports was quite distinctive.

"Yes," I finally said to her out loud, "That'll be sufficient to provide a transit-anchor on Zezament. I'll let you know when we've arrived there. Is there anything you can tell me about the natives?"

She lifted her hand from the bowl. "Physically, they're much like us," she said. "In fact, some of our philosophers believe that the place was settled in the distant past by voyagers from Naprimér."

"Do any of them speak Tyrosian?" I asked.

"I doubt that many do—but there may be a few. I only know of a handful of specialists and leaders on my world who can understand the language. It's one of more than a hundred tongues that I learned as part of my early training, using mental techniques that force-fed the information deep within my unconscious mind. Still, without the embedded translating effect of the sky-orb on your end, I would have had great difficulty in understanding you at the beginning of our relationship, not having heard or practiced the language in a very long time."

"What about social customs—anything we should be aware of in advance?"

"They're an accommodating people, but they don't appreciate being laughed at—so be careful what you say, if indeed you can communicate with them at all. Their language is very different from ours, but we maintained relations with them until the Volúcris arrived, and so we have a number of individuals here who can speak their tongue—and vice versa."

"Say something in their lingo—and yours," I said.

She rattled off a couple of sentences, and then repeated whatever she said in her own language.

"I think I know some words of both, Master," Scooter said. "We do a lot of trading in this area of the Fifth Circle, and have gathered bits and pieces of most of the languages spoken by the civilized worlds. I can probably make do once I hear how the people there actually speak to each other."

"Good," I said. "We'll be there soon, Lady," I told Niobë. Then I bade her farewell, and shut down the link.

"There's somethin' very odd about that person, Sir," Hawk said. It was the first time that he'd actually seen Niobë's image. "Somethin's not quite right there."

"Shah'rah?" I said, wanting her opinion.

"She seems to me perfectly normal, given her social status and former role as a political leader. I wouldn't trust her very far without understanding her motives better, but I sense that she sincerely wants and needs our help, and intends to aid us in turn."

"That was my feeling, too. What exactly do you mean, Sergeant?"

"I can't put my finger on it, Sir, but mark my words, I dinna like somethin' about the Lady."

"Well, until we find out what it is, I'm not going to worry about it," I said.

Truth be told, however, I had the same vague sense of uneasiness as Hawk. I just didn't want to admit it to anyone.

CHAPTER TWENTY-SEVEN
"A NEW DEITY TO OUR PANTHEON"

The night before we left the world of Festuca, Nonnengagué the Mayor again wanted to fête our little party of adventurers, and so the eight of us who remained—myself, Shah'rah, Scooter, Hawk, Warbler, Eagle, Bird, Roc, and Raven—walked the crooked path from the Station to the village of Pissapapilis late that afternoon.

The mist was still an ever-present caress on our bodies, and the shadowy light was hardly cheering, but the townsfolk had ignited a corridor of torches to welcome us, just outside of the main entrance, together with their wives and children and extended families, all smiling at us.

With the help of the recently-departed Tyros and Scooter and Shah'rah, I'd accelerated the maturation of some of the food-stuffs we'd planted, so the villagers would have access to a constant source of supply even before we departed—and they'd taken this precious resource, and prepared for us a series of breads and cakes and salads and even a dessert based around the fruit and leaves of the one large opolento that had been restored by Master Parakôdês (I'd been unable to duplicate his act, unfortunately).

That huge tree continued to bear and bear and bear—new flowers, new stalks, and new fruit—on a constant basis, as if to make up for the decades in which it had lain dormant. Already some enterprising planters among the natives had taken shoots from the revived growth and repotted them in clay jugs and at other sites around the area—and all had prospered with the same vigorous growth as the parent.

The Festucans had very little protein to serve us, but what they had, they shared—certain kinds of large, snail-like creatures boiled in the shell, a crustacean that still flourished in the local streams, grubs sizzling on an open griddle, something that looked like a cross between a frog and a small snake, and some other delicacies—just a bite of each, enough to sample the flavors.

But the baked goods—what can I say about them but, "Oh, my!" The men and women who were regarded as the leading cooks of the region had outdone themselves on our behalf. They served us sweet tarts filled with a compote of opolento pears and other ingredients whose source I really didn't want to know; small loaves of dark, light bread twisted into loops and fried in grease, and then covered with a layer of something that tasted like garlic; a cake fashioned (I was told) from the flour ground from the leaves of a giant fungus that flourished in the dead forest, and then baked with the sugary detritus of the boiled stalks of the quelmandre fern and pieces of a cricket-like insect that gave the mix a nutty flavor; the "tricorn hat," a long bread fashioned from three kinds of dough twisted around each other, baked for several hours in enclosed ovens, and then lathered with gentle squeezings of the barreme-bug to give its crust a flavor similar to butter. Despite the somewhat limited menu, what the Festucans served us was one of the best meals that I'd ever eaten—anywhere.

We stuffed ourselves until we couldn't even contemplate another bite, and then had to carry back with us all of the leftovers that we could handle—and more!

But before we departed, the leader of the community prompted his great-nephew, Chuchaqué, to step forward and present each of us with a medallion that the local smith had fashioned. "For we thought," Nonnengagué said, "that you ought to carry with you something to remember us by."

I held out my hand to allow the lad to slip the bright gold-red disk onto my open palm. It was fashioned from an alloy of cuprite and something else that I couldn't identify, and fitted itself between my fingers and my thumb. There was an image of a man etched there, crouched over a large open pot, stirring something with a great ladle.

At my raised eyebrow, the Mayor said: "This is Cochingué, the god of cooking and making. For your lovely wife, Chingdaqué, the goddess of love. For your familiar, Criwadué, the god of serving. For your sergeant, Churrigué, the god of bravery. For his brave men, Granizadué, the goddess of storm. They will watch over you and keep you all. They were our forebears once.

"And now we add a new deity to our pantheon: Morfegué, the god of transforming. For that is how we shall remember you, great mage of mages."

"But...," I tried to say. Alas, however, there is really no appropriate response to having been elevated to godhood. You can't honorably refuse, and yet no one knew better than I that I was no supernatural being—not even close!

"Ah, exalted Master, you seem to be undergoing a metamorphosis right in front of my eyes," Scooter whispered in my ear, chortling under its breath.

I shrugged my right shoulder in warning, threatening to dump the little creature on the ground.

"Thank you so very kindly, people of Festuca, for this great dignity," I said. "You"—nodding to the Mayor—"and your good people and this fair world will always have a place in our souls. I regret that we must leave so soon, but I shall return one day. That's my promise to you: I shall return."

Then the villagers brought still more presents for us to tote back to the Station, accompanying us on our walk through the greening fields and dead woods. We had to store most of the supplies and gifts in compartments, other than the surplus of perishable items, which I ordered Hawk and his men to distribute to the natives living near the three great atmospheric machines. They received these most gratefully.

The next morning, we finished packing our few belongings, together with the modern weapons that the Sergeant had scavenged from the four Overseer emplacements, and gathered our party during the brightest part of the day to pick at a small lunch that Scooter and Shah'rah had thrown together.

I'd placed a "word" lock on the only door to the Station, and given the Mayor the combination of tones that would open it, so that the Festucans could access whatever information and supplies they could readily scavenge.

Once we'd tidied up the small mess, we were ready to leave. I had no idea of the time differential between Festuca and Zezament, or what we would find on the other side, so we would just have to throw the dice, and see what happened.

I fixed in my mind the image of the decaying ruin outside Zazzou on Zezament, opened a gate into the æther, and felt for the right place. Then I twisted the leys, and one by one, we leaped across the empty void once more.

CHAPTER TWENTY-EIGHT
"WE CAN PAY!"

"Where are we?" I said.

I tried to stay upright—my weight seemed almost to have doubled, instantly. From where I stood, I could see the discarded relics of an ancient civilization tumbled about us on a series of low, overgrown hills cuddled against the bank of a small river— but *not* the ruins that we wanted! I'd reached out through æther-space to access an old, weathered aqueduct on the planet called Zezament, not far from Naprimér—but what *this* place was, or where it was located, I hadn't a clue.

My fellow travelers very slowly picked themselves up from the rough ground where they'd been rolled with the impact of the leap through the void. With great effort, several managed to leverage themselves to a standing position, groaning over the aches and bruises they'd incurred in their toss-and-tumble landing. The effect of long-transit shock had already seriously debilitated all of us, even my familiar.

"I think perhaps you miscued, Master," Scooter said, coughing several times to clear its lungs. "This is not where we were supposed to land. The gravity here is about twice what we're used to."

"Gravity?" I was unfamiliar with the term.

"The force that governs how much we weigh, Sir. If the world is quite large in size, it attracts us more strongly, and we feel the additional pull as 'gravity'."

Great! We'd just made the longest jump that any of us had

ever experienced—and the first transit where I'd had no spatial coordinates or direct visualization of the terminus save what the Lady Niobë had been able to lend me—and that being just the distant memory of a visit that she'd made to Zezament as a young woman. And now I'd brought us to a place where we could hardly walk or even move around normally, and were nowhere within site of any civilized beings.

"What do we do now, husband?" Shah'rah asked, gasping as she tried to remain standing. She plopped a hand on my left shoulder to steady herself, nearly knocking me down.

I had no energy left to think, so I very slowly led my hobbled, wounded warriors down a broken cobblestone avenue towards the stream. Not far from the bank, I pointed to two low walls that met at right angles, and we sat there on the broken stubs of the bricks, staring at each other. Finally I pulled off my pack, and started scrounging for something to eat, and the rest of my weary travelers followed suit.

We munched on pieces of Festucan bread slathered with a buttery substitute made from pressed beetles—it was actually quite good once you ignored the sickly green color and faint odor of decaying flesh of the "spread"—plus some opolento pears.

This was as sound a place as any to pitch camp for the night, which appeared to be approaching fairly rapidly. Hawk set up a rotating watch, using him and his five soldiers, but nothing disturbed our rest.

The next morning, we were all still fatigued by the constant pull on our bodies of this world and its ever-pervasive high "gravity," so I conducted an informal council sitting on the ground, while picking over the dregs of a light breakfast.

"We need to discover where we've landed," I said. "I have no idea what went wrong, or where we've materialized—and not knowing that, I'm reluctant to try transiting anywhere else. The one inflexible rule of æther travel is that you must be aware of precisely where you are at the start, and precisely where you're going at the end—otherwise you just won't get there."

"Well," my wife said, "it's obvious we're not going to find any help around here."

"Sir, we can't walk very far in our present condition," Hawk said, "and we don't have enough food to last more than a few days at best."

"What about hunting?" I said.

"We're all worn out, Sir," he said, "and in any case, even if we could snare somethin', we gotta be careful—we don't know what we can safely eat."

We were still contemplating what might be possible—I considered building a raft, but we didn't have the tools for such things—when the Sergeant abruptly said, "Shhh!"—and motioned us to hide ourselves behind a broken wall.

Sure enough, someone was coming—actually, some *ones*—but they were speaking in a language that I didn't understand. "Can you make anything out?" I hissed at Scooter.

"I think so, Master," the creature said. "If only they would approach a little closer."

As if obeying his command, the party of natives moved slowly but inevitably in our direction. I peeked through a hole between the cracked bricks where the mortar had fallen out, and saw them come around a nearby corner, following the ancient cobblestones. Something about them struck me as very odd—and then I realized that they were all quite short, indeed, no taller than children on Nova Europa, with thick, muscular arms and legs. Their leader was pointing at something nearby—a structure that remained partially intact—and gabbling about it to the others. Was this a tour of some kind?

Scooter nipped my ear, and spoke directly to my mind: *"Yes, Master, this human is showing the other members of his group the sights of this elden city of theirs, relating the history of this place, and lamenting its destruction by some foreign invader more than a thousand years ago."*

Armed with this information, I stepped tentatively into the middle of the old avenue, and said in Tyrosian: "Greetings, o wise one. Could this humble being beg some assistance from a fellow-traveler?"

"Wh-which?" came the tentative response from the guide, who stepped right back onto the foot of the person trailing him, and almost fell over. "Not know much word, this."

From my shoulder, the wherret said in the same chirrupy voice as the native's native tongue (and then translated his words to me): "We're lost, we're hungry, we're tired, and my Master and his seven companions would appreciate your assistance, if you don't mind. We can pay."

Always the magic words—"We can pay!" That one little sentence can open so many doors in life.

"Ah," the leader said (with Scooter translating in my ear). "We would be honored to assist such, uh, larger-than-life adventurers. Where do you wish to go, kind sir?"

"What world is this?" I asked; the wherret spoke in my name.

"You don't know? How strange. This is Zezament the Beautiful, the Lush, the Bountiful, with vast spacious skies and amber waves...."

"Yes, I've heard that one before," I said. "How do we reach Zazzou?"

"I can arrange for transportation," the guide said, "For the appropriate level of compensation, of course."

"Of course," I said. "Is there no place in the universe where greed isn't the prime factor?"

"Do you want me to translate that, Master?" the wherret said.

"No," I muttered. "Tell him that we appreciate his generosity."

The native spoke a few more sentences. "Of course," Scooter translated, "I must complete this tour first."

"What?"

"I have a contract to complete. We Zezamentors always fulfill our agreements. Barring issues of death or serious injury or public safety, I'm required by law to honor all previous commitments first, before proceeding to a second. Not to worry—we should be finished with this visit to the notable ruins of the Rakkou District within a couple of days."

"Days?" I asked.

"Yes. Perhaps the day after tomorrow, or maybe the day after that," the guide said.

"I'll pay you more!"

"Alas, if I accepted money to break a signed contract, I could be sued by all of these good folk"—he motioned to the crowd of natives behind him—"and if the cases went against me, as I would expect (for the law is very precise on these matters), I would be stripped of my clothes, my family, my honor, and my livelihood. No, this would not be a very good thing at all. So, very sad to say, I must take care of Number One before addressing Number Two."

But it was actually three days before the stocky little man—whose name was Klouter Revou—returned with a stream of mechanical vehicles large enough to accommodate "The Giants from Beyond," stashed two of us in each truck-bed, and hauled us off in short order to the capital city, Zazzou. By then the constant drag of this planet's great mass had worn us down to almost nothing.

I noticed that we passed right under the ruins of the old aqueduct on the outskirts of town.

CHAPTER TWENTY-NINE
"THE ROTTY-GUTS AND THE WIGGLY-WORMS"

It was obvious to even the casual observer that Zezament had benefited substantially from the incursion of the Volúcris into this sector of the Fifth Circle. Everywhere one looked in Zazzou City, merchants were busily gathering goods from other worlds, and redistributing them for great profits to those of their fellows who were now interdicted for political or other reasons. The Bird-Men had been very good for business, since they tended to restrict visitations to their own sphere of influence.

I also noticed a heavy security presence throughout the town—something that I presumed was repeated on all parts of the globe. The Zezamentors may have been small in stature, but they intended to secure their hard-garnered wealth with blatant force, if necessary.

Lodgings were difficult to find, but the guide Revou "knew some people," and for "a few ounces more," secured us pleasant if unspectacular accommodations at a boarding house in the Etou-phou Ward. "Madame Lou-Tou runs a clean place," Revou told me through Scooter, "and so long as you pay on time, you should have no trouble. She's not like Prou-Krous-Tou, who makes his customers fit his beds, whether they wish to or no. She actually caters to you 'Big Ones.' Ha—say's you're less trouble, if you believe that."

"What about someplace to eat?" I asked.

"You might try The Old Goat," he said through my translator.

"It features some exotic excrement they call food, but I'm told you foreigners masticate such things."

Well, Madame L.T.'s establishment at least featured full-length beds and clean sheets, and the proprietress was a jolly lady of perhaps three-and-one-half feet in stature (if she stretched), always laughing and having a good time—and she knew passable Tyrosian.

I asked her about the Goat.

"Ha!" she said. "That boob Revou! His cousin owns that place, and if anyone there could actually cook, why, they'd draft him at the Royal Palace. Old King Bou-Bou xxxi is always looking for someone with a cuisinal talent.

"No, no, no, you don't want to eat there—you'll just get sick with the rotty-guts and the wiggly-worms. No, try The Beastly Burp or Touny Macarouny. They feature native dishes that can safely be eaten by you lot, and also have the Tyrosian fare with which you might be more familiar."

I thanked her for her kind assistance, and suggested to the rest of my party that we bathe, change clothes, and then venture forth to one of the local eateries, using several of the taxi-bikes. We voted for the "Touny," whose name was just a trifle less offensive than the "Burp," and which was located closer to our establishment than the other—a major factor for us, given the heavy gravity—but also discovered, to our great delight, that the seating had been constructed in such a way that the eatery could accommodate both large- and small-sized patrons, and that the menu was equally flexible.

The restaurant offered deep-dished meat pies whose savory flavors reminded me very strongly of Old-Town Paltyrrha, strong, lusty ales, huge loaves of dark, sweet bread to sop up the rich gravies, vegetable-and-shellfish stews seasoned with a variety of sharp spices reminiscent of pepper and paprika, several kinds of fish grilled in a light sauce that tasted a bit like garlic and butter touched with lemon, and a dozen different varieties of cakes and tarts and what they called "sugar-sticks," which came in several different flavors, including something that was fiery hot as well as sweet.

Of course, there were offerings that I didn't particularly enjoy, but none of us went away hungry, and at least some of us were stuffed so full to the gills that the devilettes danced decidedly undelicately through my gulliver all the night long.

Being unable to sleep during the first part of the dark, I took out my sky-orb and attempted to contact the Lady Niobë on Naprimér. She responded almost immediately, but asked me to try again a little later, which I did.

"Sorry about that," she said, when she answered again. "I was, uh, indisposed. Where are you? When you didn't call me right away, I became worried that something had gone awry with your transit."

I told her of our little adventure in the countryside of Zezament.

"Yes, they're a mercenary people, although fair and honest within certain limitations. We had a trade mission there once, along with an embassy, but the Volúcris maintain tight control over any communications with worlds outside of their sphere of influence."

"Is there anyone here that I can contact for assistance?" I asked.

"Everyone that I knew is dead or retired now," she said. "Well, except for the King, but you could never gain access to him. The security surrounding him is very tight."

"I can't get over how hard it is for us to move around physically on this world. The least effort seems to wipe us out. And the people here—they're all just half-sized compared to us."

"Yes, Zezament can be difficult on outsiders who come from lower gravity places. I was young when I visited there, but even then, I could only last about a ten-day before I had to return home. Our legations rotated their personnel every few weeks."

"Well, we're going to be stuck here for a few more days at least, recovering from long-transit shock," I said. "But we can't stay much longer than that, or the 'rest' will be harder on us than just simply moving on. I'll contact you again tomorrow. We need to make plans concerning our final transit to Naprimér."

But events forced our hand sooner than I'd planned, it so happened!

CHAPTER THIRTY

"LOU-TOU'S NUMBER ONE SLEEPING EMPORIUM FOR THE BETTER-CLASS FOREIGN GENTLEFOLK AND THEIR PASSIVE PETS"

A loud banging on the outside door of our establishment, "Lou-Tou's Number One Sleeping Emporium for the Better-Class Foreign Gentlefolk and Their Passive Pets" (as the stocky little proprietress had so proudly informed us yesterday), woke me from a dream in which I was being pursued by King Bou-Bou and Queen Evetéria 'round and 'round a table piled high with sweetmeats and sprouts, overseen by a green-skinned bogy who kept throwing rock-hard missiles of the latter at my face. I hated the rotten little vegetables.

I staggered out of bed, Scooter hopping to my shoulder from where the wee creature had lain on the floor, and flung a cloak across my back, with the wherret pulling it up and tucking it under its body. At the least, now that I was awake, I wanted to employ the garde-robe to empty my bladder.

"Master Morpheou!" I heard Madame's shrill voice yell from down below, "someone official to see you!"

Shah'rah poked her drowsy face up from a nearby bedroll. "What's happening?" she asked.

"I don't know yet. Remain here, please. You too, Hawk," I said, when I saw the Sergeant roll out of his cot. He quickly roused his fellow guards, and they armed themselves as a precaution.

I managed to get down the stairs without taking a tumble, only to confront a pint-sized man who displayed a royal blazon on his gilt-edged shirt; he was accompanied by two of the local gendarmerie. He handed me a piece of flat, shiny material, on which were written some letters.

I turned it up and down, and finally said: "I don't know what this means."

"We've, uh, received a demand from the Bird-Folk to escort all recent arrivals from other worlds to their embassy for vetting by their representatives," the official said. "Naturally, our gracious King refused, since our laws specifically protect the comings and goings of all merchants, travelers, and good-people. This is our usual practice in such matters.

"However, you and your party appear to serve no function here—indeed, you large folk can scarcely move about—so this is our notice that you must vacate Zezament by this time tomorrow, or be seized and deported by the State. You'll be given free passage on the ætheroprobe to Delirant. I'll leave two of my men here, at the front and back doors, to assist you in your swift exit of this planet.

"Thank you for your attention."

Then he gave me a low bow, and sauntered off down the street. The reddish-orange suns had barely skipped over the horizon, and I glared at them with two equally bloodshot eyes. This day was not beginning well!

I trudged slowly back up the staircase, and gave my fellow travelers the sad news: "We have to leave!"

"Thank God!" Shah'rah said. "Another day here, and I wouldn't be fit for anything. I can hardly walk as it is."

"I certainly don't want to go to Delirant, though," I said. "I think it's finally time that we paid a visit to Naprimér."

So we gathered together our meager collection of belongings once again, and then they crowded around me while I cut a hole in space and time. I set the image in my mind of the high and low geography of the Lady Niobë's suite, and reached out, twisting the leys to make the link. Then I opened a door through the æther at the other end, and pulled us through.

CHAPTER THIRTY-ONE
"OH, CAMEL DUNG AND BIRD'S TURDS!"

The first thing that I saw was the shimmering nude body of Lady Niobë stepping out of a large tub of steaming water.

The second thing that I envisioned was a black-furred, six-legged creature flying through the air, all claws outstretched, aiming right at my face. Fortunately, Sergeant Hawk had reflexes like a cat, and forehanded the animal right out of the air, knocking it against one wall, where it moaned a couple of times before slinking back to its naked mistress.

The third thing that I realized was that Niobë, like her distant cousins on Zezament, was also short, perhaps four feet in height, although much better proportioned than the natives of the massive planet from which we'd just transited. She displayed twice the mammary appendages of any human that I'd ever seen on Nova Europa, and evinced absolutely no shame at being viewed without clothing by eight strangers who'd appeared literally from nowhere.

The gravity of this place was higher than would have been normal on my own world, but not by much.

"Well, I guess you've arrived," she said in passable (if oddly accented Tyrosian), reaching over to pull a long red-and-black-striped hand-woven shawl about her shoulders. It barely covered anything of note, being just enough to call attention to her nether regions. "You must have had an emergency to come so quickly. Welcome to Naprimér, Master Morpheús." She bowed her head in a slight nod.

"And you must be Shah'rah," she said to the former dancer, "and Scooter, the wherret," she added to my familiar. Of course, no one understood her except the little creature and me, so I translated for my wife.

Then I introduced her to Hawk and his five men, relaying their words back and forth.

"You are all graciously well come to my world. I apologize for Sable. Sometimes she becomes overzealous in her efforts to protect me."

The six-legged feline was crouching behind the protection of her mistress's bare legs.

"I realize that this place isn't secure, Lady," I said, "but as you indicated, we needed to decamp from Zezament rather quickly, and your rooms were the only structure that I'd viewed sufficiently well on Naprimér to provide the placement needed for a secure transit."

"You're right about the absence of security," she said. "I can be interrupted at any hour of any day, without warning, by my son, by high-level officials, by attendees, even occasionally by the Volúcris.

"But I know of several places on this continent where you'll be safe for the nonce. If you don't mind the intrusion...."

She quickly stepped across the tiled floor separating us, reached up and placed her hands on either side of my forehead, the two strings comprising the shawl dancing across her quartet of breasts, and gave me the first image that I needed.

But before she could transmit the next, Sable suddenly squawked, almost like a bird. I heard a distant rattling, and Niobë hissed at me, "Quickly! You must leave! They can't know that you're here!"

I drew a circle in the air, opening a door into ætherspace, fixed my mind upon the vision of the refuge the Lady had given me, and established the link. My people knew what they had to do. One by one they quickly jumped through the gate.

Another rattle, this time closer. "The second door!" Niobë

whispered in my ear. *"Move!"*

Without thinking, I wrapped my arm around the woman's slim waist, lifted her off the floor, and stepped straight into the void. The cat-creature was right behind me, following her mistress into the emptiness that I'd created. As soon as I walked on terra firma again, I shut the two openings behind me, just after I heard a plaintive query, "Madame Nio…?"

"What have you done, Morpheús?" the Lady said.

"I've just arranged your escape from an oppressive prison," I said.

"But they'll…," she said.

"They'll do *what*?" I responded. "They've just found themselves an empty room—a mystery, if you will. There isn't a mage anywhere in this sector who can trace where you've gone. You're known to have great mental powers. Your vanishing will simply become part of the legend surrounding you. The Volúcris are not magically oriented, and neither are most of your people. They will *not* understand what's happened here."

"But they're not stupid, Morpheús," she said. "The Bird-Men may be, as you say, insensitive to magical influences, but they're very, very thorough about their security. They'll search my known haunts, widening the circle layer by layer, looking everywhere I might have gone. This place could be one of them, if they venture far enough back into my past."

I looked at our surroundings for the first time. We were standing inside a large, stone room, flanked by two giant bronze statues that could barely be seen in the dim light cast by widely spaced torches. The breath of a warm breeze was gently twisting the ends of the Lady's shawl over the tips of her breasts.

"Perhaps, uh, you'd better find some clothes, Lady," I said.

"*Where*, Master Morpheús? If you'll recall, I didn't exactly have time to pack. And I don't think your wife's outfits will come close to fitting *me*."

But Shah'rah had already come over to assist, and was mentally measuring the smaller woman's dimensions.

In height, I was just shy of an *orguia* in size, or six feet based on the old Attic Greek model. Shah'rah measured *diploun bêma-kai-imipodion*, or about a half-foot shorter than I. But Niobë was at least a foot less in size than my wife, and perhaps a bit more. She looked almost like a teenaged girl until you saw her eyes; one had the sense that they'd witnessed far too much ever to recapture innocence.

"I can make a wrap for her," Shah'rah finally said. "It won't be perfect, but it'll hold against anything except rapid exertion. I don't know what your native dress is like, since I haven't seen any of your women clothed."

"Thank you for your help," the Lady said.

"What *is* this place?" I asked.

Hawk and his men had already spread out to take an inventory of our surroundings, which consisted (apparently) of a number of interconnected rooms—how many, I had no idea.

"The Tomb of Matrin," Niobë said, then laughed at my expression. "Yes, we were a bit premature, but the people demanded it."

"Who's the other figure with him?"

"His consort, S'rënë, my ancestress. This memorial was created about fifteen hundred years ago, according to the date on the dedication stone. Every morning a procession of devotees comes at sunrise to leave presents and food on the steps at the entrance, secured in tubs and baskets so that the animals can't interfere, with two guards posted; and every evening at sunset they return to remove the uneaten remains, and then distribute the orts to the poor. No one is allowed inside this building except on special anniversary dates. That's why I knew it would be safe as a temporary refuge.

"But we can't remain here long. There are no private quarters in which to hide, particularly when they discover that someone's eating the food."

"How will they know that?" I asked.

"Because I have to go outside and fetch it. The two burly witnesses standing to either side will be utterly astonished at the sudden appearance of a woman from the past," she said. An exasperated tone filled her voice. "No, they won't interfere, but they will report the miraculous re-emergence of the unclothed S'rënë—you'll note that that's the way she's depicted on the monument—to the authorities back in the capital. The Volúcris will have a fairly good idea of what's actually occurred, and will immediately investigate."

"Then where will we go?"

"I must think about this overnight," she said. "So long as we remain within the confines of the memorial, and keep our voices low, we should go undiscovered." I passed her words along to the rest.

"What about The Fourth Elephant's Egg?" Shah'rah asked. "Isn't it supposed to be here somewhere?"

I translated her Latin for Lady Niobë, who responded: "That's entirely possible. Do you have any idea, Morpheús, what it is we're supposed to be looking for?"

"No," I said, "but I know someone who might."

I pulled The Second Elephant's Egg out of the pocket of ætherspace where I'd secreted it. This was the Pathfinder, which included a half-alive personality in the shape of a canine animal.

"Firedog!" I said.

"Yes, Master," the chocolate creature responded, its ears pricking up. Everyone within range of its voice seemed to hear its reply in their native tongue.

"Do you know where The Fourth Elephant's Egg is?" I asked.

"Yes, Master," it replied.

"It's very literal," I said to Niobë, "Almost a child in some ways." I translated separately for Shah'rah and Hawk.

"Where is it located?" I asked.

"In this room, Master," came the response.

"Show me!" I commanded.

But the firedog remained stationary.

"Show me!" I said again.

And again, it failed to move.

"What's wrong with it?" my wife asked. "It was fine just a moment ago."

"Firedog, take me to The Fourth Elephant's Egg," I said a third time.

But once more, nothing happened.

I shook my head in frustration, and then looked at the others: "I don't know why it's not responding."

"Ask it," the Lady Niobë said.

"Why have you not obeyed my command?" I said to the canine creature.

"We *have* obeyed your command, Master," it said.

"Then *where* is The Fourth Elephant's Egg?" I demanded.

"It is here, Master."

"*Where*, firedog? Where specifically is it located?"

"The spot where you are now standing, Master."

"What exactly do you mean?" I asked. For some reason, I just wasn't "getting it."

"*You* are The Fourth Elephant's Egg," it said, "you and Mistress Niobë."

"Oh, camel dung and bird's turds!" I said. "Oh, shitters critters!"

Things were much, much worse than I'd thought.

CHAPTER THIRTY-TWO
"WE ARE NOT THE FOURTH ELEPHANT'S EGG"

I was stunned at what the firedog had said. The Lady Niobë and I together constituted The Fourth Elephant's Egg? But we weren't magical artifacts, not by anyone's consideration. So how could that be possible?

But then I remembered the little things that'd been said to me along my journey, the imprecise implications and insinuations.

I recalled also that Niobë and I were descended, apparently in the direct line, from Master Mathurin or Matrin and S'rënë, his temporary consort, and that according to Naprimér legend, the two mages, instructor and pupil, had together remade the rifts on this world—and by implication, had healed the divisions throughout the Five Circles.

I then revisited in my mind's eye the unforgettable image of The Maker-and-Fixer-of-Things on Pachydermia, the he-and-she-in-one-body.

I must have said something out loud without realizing it, because Niobë suddenly said: "Yes, that makes a certain kind of odd sense. But I still don't understand what it is we're supposed to be doing here."

I turned to the firedog again and said: "What is the role of The Fourth Elephant's Egg?"

The "dog" canted its head to one side and raised its left ear, as if listening for the moan of the ætherwinds. "The Fourth Elephant's Egg shall employ the other three Eggs to restore balance and harmony to the Spheres, Master."

I had the distinct impression that it was reading from the tattered pages of an old, old book.

"How does it do that?" I asked.

"Since we constitute one of the lesser Eggs, Master, that understanding has been placed beyond our ken."

"By whom?" Niobë asked. "*Who* is your Master?"

"You are, Master," it said.

"No," she said. "Who has placed 'that understanding beyond your ken'?"

"We do not know, Master," it said. "This is the reality of our existence, and we cannot say what we do not understand."

"What about the statues, Sir?" Scooter said, interrupting the exchange. "Is there any other source of power here?"

I queried the "dog."

"Yes, Master, the great images of Master Mathurin and Master S'rënë are themselves reservoirs of energy that can be used by The Maker-and-Fixer-of-Things. Indeed, this entire building is a locus that brings together the BaseLines of the leys that underlie the structure of the universe, and a focus that will allow the transmission of healing waves to every corner of the Seven Spheres. It was erected on this site for that reason, and rebuilt several times."

"How do we access these forces?"

"We do not know, Master," the firedog said. "We are not The Fourth Elephant's Egg."

"So what do we do now, husband?" Shah'rah said.

And indeed, that was the pertinent question. Apparently, I had the potential, with the assistance of the Lady, to manipulate grand energies to reshape the social and political structure of the known universe—but to what end? I remembered as a child building a castle of sand on the shore of the Gulf of Zmyrna—and even then, although I knew it was an impermanent thing, I was devastated when it was crushed by a bully who pooh-poohed my architectural fancies. How could I access these enormously potent tools, and what could—or should—I do with them once I knew how to manipulate them?

I told Niobë that we could feed ourselves from the stores in our packs for this day, and to find us the best quarters for the night that she could; and she led us through a complicated maze of rooms to a back area where we spread our blanket rolls out on the floor, and made ourselves a cozy *crèche* where no one would disturb us.

That night I dreamt that Master Mathurin stepped down from his great statue, and came to me.

"How fare you, grandson?" he asked, when he stood in front of my recumbent form.

"We've made it to Naprimér, Sir," I said, "and the shrine that they built for you and Lady S'rënë."

"Ah, yes, the lovely S'rënë," he said. "I remember her well. She had a fiery disposition, as I recall. Once our business was finished here, I wasn't unhappy to leave. She would have been impossible to live with for very long."

"They declared you 'dead,' Sir," I said.

"Of course they did—and she killed me too," he said, smiling, "or, at least, she thought she did. She wanted all of the power for herself. She never understood that it always takes two to heal the rifts in ætherspace."

"Why, Master?"

"I don't know why, Morpheús. Ah, you look shocked, grandson. No, I don't know everything. Some things just 'are' the way they are, and you have to adapt to them. Whatever being established this pocket of the universe—it may have been the spirit we call God or some other intelligent creature—they left it imperfect, and every so often it has to be 'retuned,' if you will, and the fractures in society and space mended. There were others, perhaps many others, who came before me, and still others who will appear after you're gone. How many of these Dream Weavers have lived before or will live in the future, I also don't know."

"Why here, Sir?" I asked.

"Why not?" he responded. "For whatever reason, Naprimér

is a place where many different lines of control happen to merge or coexist or impact upon one another. There are others of this ilk scattered throughout the Circles, but standing on one central node means that you stand on all. Because of this, if you have enough power, if you have enough will, if you have enough courage, you can sway the very universe itself.

"Look upon the Spheres as a kind of giant clockwork. They swirl in and around each other, going about their business, paying little attention to the creatures who inhabit them. But gradually, over a long period of time, they wind down, they move out of synchronization, and grow old and tired and rather cranky. Eventually, if left to their own devices, they would become inert, and all life on these worlds would die.

"So they have to be recharged. And that's what I've done in my existence, and what you have to do now. There's no one else to take your place. But you need Mistress Niobë as a counterbalance. You cannot accomplish this on your own. There's something in the female principle that ameliorates the male element, and makes it function or focus better. You'll see."

"How do I do this?" I asked.

"It's different for each of us. You can call upon my spirit in the sculptures, just as Niobë can appeal to her ancestress there. Ultimately, however, you two must find a way. You'll know it when you see it."

"What about Shah'rah, Master?" I asked.

"What about her?"

"Does she have a role to play here, Sir?"

"Yes," he said, "but I don't know what it is, any more than I know why the wherret is present. They were not elements that featured in my own epiphany, although I did have access to the Eggs, in the forms that they took at that time. As I say, each instance is different.

"However, I did have with me a friend whom we called 'Lamb,' who knew my every whim, and helped me immensely during this period, when I felt very uncertain of my role in this great working. Alas, 'Lamb' did not long survive the turning of the wheel, and I wonder sometimes if that was the sacrifice that I had to make in order to restore order to the universe. I don't honestly know.

"And now I must return to the place whence I came. Good fortune to you, my boy."

I awoke just as his image was beginning to fade away—enough to see that my experience wasn't *just* a dream after all.

CHAPTER THIRTY-THREE
"A ZIP-PORT AT TONTONTO"

The next morning, I asked the Lady Niobë to fetch some of the offerings that had been left on the great stone foresteps of the memorial. As she'd expected, the sudden appearance of her nude body while the penitents were still depositing their gifts caused a certain stir among the populace.

I heard the people shouting. Niobë later translated for me: "S'rënë has returned! The prophecy is fulfilled! The wonder of the ages has come back to us again!"

Of course, they didn't dare touch or approach her, and she said not a word to anyone—well, it wouldn't have been appropriate, if she was whom they thought.

"How long have we got?" I asked her when she reappeared holding a basket of bread, fruit, and a few vegetables. The fresh food provided a very pleasant change.

"A day, or at most, maybe two," she said, throwing the wrap that Shah'rah had made around her. "The Volúcris will know I'm here by this afternoon, so it's only a question of how quickly they'll respond. There's a zip-port at Tontonto, which is about fifteen leagues from here. If I were still running things, I'd have a force ætheroprobed there by this evening, and thence march to Caribbë tomorrow morning. But the Bird-Men are hard to predict. They always must first decide which of their leaders has sufficient rank to deal with major issues of this kind."

"We need to be ready for them," I said.

I called to Hawk, who reported immediately. "Have you

taken a survey of this building complex?" I asked.

"Yes, Sir," he said. "I know where everything is."

"How big is one of their squads?" I asked Niobë.

"They usually number between ten and twenty-five individuals. It's not fixed—they don't think that way. They're always heavily armed, and they usually wear some kind of body armor over their chests."

"Very well," I said. "Sergeant, I want to engineer a situation where you and your men, at little risk to yourselves, can lure the Bird-Men back into the maze of passages behind the display room. I'll create an opening into ætherspace at a place where it can't easily be seen in advance, and then shunt them to another world."

"But where?" Shah'rah said. "I wouldn't want them to kill or injure any innocent on the other side."

"Niobë, how do the Volúcris handle the cold?" I asked.

She smiled slightly, and it wasn't a pleasant sight to see. "Not well, Morpheús. Do you have something specific in mind?"

"On our way here we encountered a world of ice and snow called Quidni. We had to flee for our lives when the natives attacked the lone transit-station there. The Overseers were all killed. I suspect that none of them would shed any tears at seeing the Quidnis and Volúcris exterminating each other—and the Bird-Men have nowhere to go there, no possible refuge, and no way of contacting their own people."

"Sounds like a good option to me," she said.

Thus, together with Hawk and his men, I rehearsed a number of scenarios that might play out the next day—or whenever the aliens finally arrived.

"Do you know where the main portal to their home world Volucripimpant is located?" I asked the Lady.

"Of course," she said. "It's near the administrative complex in Carrou Town."

"Then I suggest that that might be our next stop. If we can find a way to destroy the link that Doctor Scarabbaios built for them, they probably won't have the technological knowledge to regenerate it, at least very quickly.

"Can your people handle the remaining Bird-Men on their own, if the Volúcris can't reinforce their soldiers here?"

"Yes, but that's dependent on not having to fight two battles at once. The men must stand by our side in the struggle."

"Well, that's your problem," I said. "You'll need to talk with your son before we attack the Volúcris. Otherwise, all of this may be for nothing."

I got no response from her, which didn't bode well to me, but perhaps I was misreading things. The culture clash between male and female in this society threatened to tear apart everything that had been so carefully maintained over a period of millennia.

We made it an early evening, although Hawk posted his usual round of guards throughout the night, just in case the enemy unexpectedly appeared.

We rose before sunrise, made our ablutions, played at breakfast with the remnants of yesterday's offerings, and prepared ourselves for whatever might come.

Of course, nothing whatever happened that day, except that the crowd of natives had grown by a factor of ten when the Lady Niobë made her second awe-inspiring appearance (well, at least they *seemed* to be inspired) as S'rënë the Unclothed.

"Where are they?" I asked her, when the sun began to ooze into the horizon.

"Well, as I indicated, the ways of the Volúcris are something unfathomable by humans. They'll probably be here tomorrow."

But they weren't, and again we were left wondering what had happened, and what we ought to do. I decided to give the process one more day. Alas, however, that I waited too long!

CHAPTER THIRTY-FOUR
"I DON'T ASSOCIATE WITH LESSER BEINGS"

They came in the middle of the night, overwhelming poor Raven, who was on duty at the time, and taking us prisoner before we could even fully come awake. Their raucous squawks—their voices reminded me of that of oversized crows—echoed through the back halls where most of our party was situated.

There must have been a hundred of them. We were dragged to our feet, trussed with ropes, gagged with rags, and loaded into several carts that were powered by some silent, invisible force. Somehow they missed Scooter and Sable, however.

The road back to Tontonto was quite rough, and I was aching all over by the time they hauled us out, force-marching us a block to some large, cylindrical building (I could only see its silhouette highlighted against the slightly lighter sky). This was obviously where the zip-port was located.

The ætheroprobe was an immense complex of machinery teaming with Naprimerans and a lone Volúcri overseer, including a trio of actual operators. A great metal circle circumscribed where the opening into ætherspace would be forced. There was a sudden whoosh, and I felt the back-blast of air that was moved by the operation of this strange and complicated gadgetry. Once again I marveled at the differences between transit-travel on Nova Europa and this far-distant world.

But the result was the same in the end. We were shunted to the capital city, Mirabör, and from there taken to several old-fashioned prison cells in the dungeon of Lady Niobë's former residence in Castle Réstiff. We were stripped of our clothes and tightly bound to the walls, so we couldn't use our arms or legs. Our captors did remove our gags, a small kindness, and put small tubes accessing a supply of water near each of our mouths. When we had to do the dirty, we did it right underneath.

"Is anyone there?" I yelled out, when our jailers abandoned us.

Each of our group sounded off, one by one, except for the wherret.

"Has anyone seen Scooter?" I yelled, my voice echoing back several times.

"The wherret escaped, Sir," Bird said. "I saw it bite one of the birdies on its wing-hand, and then it ducked under it and ran away."

"Good," I said. "Maybe it can help us."

"But how, Sir?" someone shouted back.

"Oh, you'd be surprised," I said, but the truth was, I didn't have an answer to that particular question. I knew the wherret was a devoted servant, but it would have to find some way to travel halfway across the planet to reach us, and that would have been difficult for any of us. I didn't want to tell the others that, though.

"Scooter'll be here!" I added, more to build everyone's spirits than anything else.

They didn't bring us any food that night, nor did they replenish the candles. Once the wicks gradually sputtered out, the area was drenched in a fathomless dark. I could hear "things" scuttering around the cell and corridor, but I couldn't see what they were. That made their presence, of course, that much more intimidating.

Finally, after an interminable period of waiting, some human guards appeared, and mumbled a few sentences at us. Of course, I didn't understand the native tongue, so I had no idea of what they were saying. They did bring us candles, some old bread, and a few pieces of overripe fruit. Then they splashed us with a bucket of water to rinse off the unmentionables, unchained us, thrust our old clothes in bundles into our arms, and after we'd dressed, prodded us with spears into the corridor. We were off to see the wizard—or some such personage!

We trudged up and down the stone corridors of that fortress, gradually ascending through the structure, until we were assembled as a group again in a small anteroom. I was tempted to try opening a hole into ætherspace, but was never given the chance. We were kept under *very* close guard, with sharp steel points jammed at all times into our backs.

Finally we were urged forward through a doorway, and emerged in front of a small set of thrones, one occupied by Lord Sadokéy, the other by one of the Volúcri leaders. The latter had a fancy headdress with long feathers of red, blue, green, and white pointing out every which way, and a harness encrusted with gold strapped about its chest.

It said something to us in a tongue filled with sibilants. A human standing off to the left of the twin thrones translated for us, but since I had never learned the local language, I didn't understand.

"You'll have to speak in Tyrosian," I said.

The translator cleared his voice, hissed something at the Bird-Man, and then tried again, using the Overseers' tongue: "Lord Ssissever wants to know why you have come to Naprimér."

"This is just one of many worlds in the Fifth Circle that I've visited," I said.

"But why?"

"I've heard much about the beauty of this world. I wanted to see it for myself."

"How did you get here?"

"I transited," I said.

"Are you a spy for the Tyros?"

"No."

"Then why do you speak their language?"

"Tyrosian is used by many races to facilitate trade and travel."

"Are you a spy for the Tyros?" the Volúcri asked again.

"I've already responded to that question."

"This Naprimeran woman with you is a traitor to her race. How did she join you?"

"Of her own free will," I said.

"You mean that she is able to travel through the spheres on her own?"

"You would have to ask her that."

Lord Ssissever turned to his human counterpart, and said (through the translator): "Sadokéy?"

The collaborator looked down at his mother and said: "How did you reach Caribbë, Lady Niobë?"

"I transited there," she said.

"But how?"

"I don't know. I just did."

"But such things never happen accidentally. They require machinery and operators. How did you accomplish it?"

"I don't know," she repeated. "The last thing I remember, I was standing in my rooms here in Réstiff, and then I was at the Tomb of Matrin. The transit was instantaneous."

"That's impossible," the human nobleman said.

"Nonetheless, that's what happened."

"Did you encounter these foreigners there?"

"Yes."

"What did they want?"

"They seemed happy to see me," she said. "They wanted to know all about the monument and its history."

"Why?"

"You'd have to ask them that."

"You—what's your name?" Sadokéy said to me.

"Morpheús."

"Where are you from?"

"Nova Europa."

"What…where is that?"

"You do not have the understanding that would allow me to convey any sense of the actual distances involved," I said. "My world is a very long way from here."

"How did you know about Naprimér?"

"We know about many things."

"Are you Tyrosian?"

"I've already answered that question."

"You are spies!" the Volúcri lord said through his translator.

"No," I said.

"Why did you want to know about the Tomb?" Sadokéy asked.

"The man you called Matrin is my ancestor—and yours. I wished to honor his memory."

"Why did Lady Niobë meet you there?"

"She knew a great deal about the history of Matrin and the building of the great monument. She was very helpful to me."

Ssissever interjected himself again: "What was the little furry creature who accompanied you?"

"What creature?" I asked.

"I was told that some hairy animal bit one of our soldiers—and then escaped."

"That may be," I said, "but I don't associate with lesser beings. It must have been a wild thing that was seeking warmth and safety in the building."

"Ssss," was all that the Volúcri was able to say.

"What about your familiar, Lady?" Sadokéy asked.

"I don't know what became of her," she said. "She wasn't captured with the rest of us."

"She wasn't found at the site."

"Then she must have escaped," Niobë said. "I haven't seen her since we were captured."

"Take them back to their cells," Ssissever ordered. "We must consult with our superiors on Volucripimpant."

And so once more we were forcibly marched in single file down long, dank corridors of cold, dripping stone. We'd almost reached bottom, when I noticed a movement in the near-darkness, just out of the corner of one eye. It rather looked to me like the long, furry body of some wild thing that had sought warmth and safety in the building!

CHAPTER THIRTY-FIVE
"MUST'VE BEEN THE NOSE TAX"

"Well, you took your sweet time finding us," I said to the wherret, when it finally appeared in the dim candlelight.

"It hasn't been *that* long, Master," Scooter said. "And then I had to make sure that the guards were out of the way before I actually came down here. I brought Sable as well—she's with the Lady."

The creature began picking the locks that fastened my chains to the wall. "Tough little things, aren't they?" it commented, as its small hands went to work.

"Yes, and protected against magical interference as well," I said. Then I felt one pop loose, and a few minutes later, another. The third and fourth fasteners soon followed—and I was free!

We crept silently from cell to cell, opening the doors and loosening the restraints, until our little force was complete again.

"What do you suggest, Sir?" Hawk asked.

"Niobë?" I said to the Lady. She was stroking her familiar, who was curled over and around her shoulder, upper left breast, and neck, and purring her contentment at being reunited with her mistress.

"What about my quarters?" she asked the cat-like creature.

"No one there now," Sable said.

"Morpheús, can you open a small window there so that we can check for intruders? I need some clothes and implements, if I'm going to be able to help you."

I crouched down, huddling close to a nearby candle that Scooter held for me, and opened a small circle into ætherspace, and then made a similar oval cut in Niobë's quarters. I nodded to her, and she eased a piece of her consciousness through the opening.

"It's clear!" she said, and so I widened the gateway sufficiently to allow us to pass to the other side. Then I closed the flaps of real space behind us.

"I love the way you do that," she said. "You must teach me the technique sometime." I saw my wife give the Lady a very odd look.

Niobë dashed into her bedroom, packed some clothing and other essential aids into a tote-bag, then pulled a mage-pouch from behind the wall, and widened it sufficiently to add a number of strange-looking artifacts that she located in odd corners of her residence.

"I'm ready," she finally said. "We must depart before they discover our absence from the dungeon. I know a place where we can go"—and she stood on her tiptoes and gave me the image with a quick double-touch to my temples, Sable scowling at me through her whiskers all the while.

Even though the Lady was certain that the other site was safe, we followed the same routine of checking the place out carefully through a view-cut before making the actual transit there. However, the structure—whatever it was—seemed free of interference, and so we made the journey safely.

"What is this place?" I asked, looking around in wonder. We were standing in the middle of a large, open, round room topped by a translucent dome, surrounded by a series of concentric circles of what looked like small, upright podia or lecterns.

"The Church of Churches of Lady Mariah of Nazareth, who was stoned to death to save womankind. She was one of the seven aspects of the Goddess: baby-child, girl-child, young woman, warrior, mother, matron, and grandmother," Niobë said.

"But...but, in our world, it was Jesus of Nazareth who was the Son of God," I said.

"Holy Mariah had a son named Yeshua," she said, "who helped spread the word about his Mother, but it was Her daughter, Lady Magdalena, who founded the institution that continues her teachings to this day, and who provided the continuity that was needed to strengthen and maintain the Church."

I shook my head. There was no point in arguing the subject. Obviously, religion had also developed differently in the Fifth Circle, although perhaps ultimately to the same end. I wasn't a theologian, and I knew from practical experience that it wouldn't have mattered to Niobë if I had been.

She believed what she believed, just as I did. And I'd seen too much over the past months and years to regard any "-ism" as the last Word on the subject.

The domed structure was quite simply a triumph of architecture, pierced at regular intervals on its sides with what appeared to be small, eight-sided stained glass windows, and covered with something that wasn't glass, but allowed the light of the sun to stream through in beams that illuminated various parts of the interior. Even as I watched, one of these rays was suddenly cut off and replaced by another, and then another, and so on in slow progression as the day progressed. Whoever had designed this place had a genius beyond compare for matching form with function and artistry.

"Why isn't there anyone here?" I asked Niobë.

"As with our other ceremonial buildings, this one is only used on certain occasions," she said. "One's devotion to the Goddess proceeds first from the heart, and not from any place dedicated to Her Memory. So I knew there would be no one present here today."

"But we can't find refuge in this Church," I said.

"No, but there's a nearby village that has an establishment devoted to travelers, and the area is so isolated that it'll take weeks for word of our appearance to trickle back to the capital. No, we'll be safe here for a few days."

Then she led our way up an aisle and out the main door at the back of the structure, and from there down a well-trodden path to the Seven-in-One Inn.

"Yer a bit out-o'-season, Lady," the proprietress said, when we banged on the door. All I could see was her bulbous nose poking out into the light. Scooter translated for me, since the wherret had picked up enough of the local lingo by this point to do the honors.

"But we still need lodging for the night, Lady Karnikä," Niobë said.

"I 'members ye," the old woman said. "Yer were 'ere for the Night of the Transforming, nigh unto, oh, eleventy years ago."

"Yes, I was," the Lady said. "I'm surprised you recall me."

"I always knows the classy lassies," she said. "All yer lot need rooms? Yer write 'em down in this book, like. Got the pick o' the place, yer do."

"You still provide meals?" Niobë asked, pulling out a couple of coins from a money belt strapped 'round her waist.

"Oh, aye. Take me a bit, though, mind. What's about that one?" she said, pointing at Scooter.

"It'll eat almost anything," I said.

"That's good, cuz I eats most anything too! Might even eats 'im, ha, ha, ha! Puts 'im on a stick, I would! Roasts 'im real good!"

"Everyone has to be a clown," the wherret said.

"Oh my Goddess!" Karnikä said, "'E talks! Nasty thing!"

Scooter stuck out its long tongue at the old lady and went "bleh" with it.

"I wouldn't taunt the wherret," I said. "They have a vicious bite, and don't like being touched. Do you, Sweetums?" I said, stroking its back

"Oh, no, Master," Scooter said. "Ohhh, it feels like dying!"

"Nasty, nasty!" Karnikä repeated. She backed away from the door. "Yer keep 'im outside there, yer 'ear?"

"Sorry, but where Master goes, I go," the little creature said, and jumped to the floor, scooted past the proprietress, and raced inside.

"Oh, nasty, nasty, nasty!" the old woman said, grabbing

a broom and chasing after the wherret. But she wasn't quick enough, even with that huge proboscis of hers leading the charge, and Scooter just toyed with her a few moments before tiring of the game. The rest of us had already found places at a table in what passed for the adjoining dining room.

The innkeeper finally brought us some beautiful crystalline cups and several pitchers full of an ice cold, dark drink that had a slightly bitter taste to it.

"What is this?" I asked Niobë, after gentling sipping at the brew.

"We call it *trinkmacher*," she said. "It's derived from an herb that's grown in the north, and it's known for its restorative properties, as well as just being a refreshing drink without the usual alcohol content."

It took Mistress Karnikä about an hour to prepare our meal, but we patiently sipped the cool tonic and nibbled on hard twists of rolls covered with some kind of pungent seeds, and some raw purple vegetable stalks that tasted a bit like sweet turnips.

Finally, the proprietress led in a procession of pint-sized servants laden with large trays, and plopped them down in front of us. Then she held out a pewter cup: "No free lunch!" she proclaimed. Lady Niobë dutifully deposited a coin. Karnikä shook the cup again, and another copper joined its cousin.

"Must've been the nose tax," Scooter whispered in my right ear.

I snickered, and Karnikä gave me a dirty look. "Nasty!" she exclaimed. "Yer all nasty! All save the purty Ladies. Nasty!" Then she snorted—I swear she snorted—and waddled away, with her, uh, nose clearly out of joint.

CHAPTER THIRTY-SIX
"HOW DO WE JIMMY THIS ONE TO MAKE IT GO 'BOOM'?"

"Tell me again how the Volúcris first came here," I said to Niobë, who was sitting across from me at the dining table in Mistress Karnikä's Seven-in-One Inn.

"I initially received a report of an earthquake in Carrou Province, to the east of here, and sent one of my ministers to investigate, since I couldn't seem to get any direct accounts from the area. She reported back to me, before I lost contact with her, that an army of bird-creatures had emerged from a great rift in the sky, and were now marching on Mirabör.

"I called out the local police, which is all that I had, but they were no match for the heavily-armed creatures, and had to fall back. When I saw that all was lost, I fled with my government to Sisquiyou Provence.

"The Volúcris—for such they proved to be—quickly assumed control of the central apparatus of government, and set about subverting the male population, beginning with my husband. He was named the new leader of the Council. The bulk of our security forces went over to him in short order, since most of our warriors are male. The female officers were arrested, executed, or sent fleeing. One by one our populations were overwhelmed, and I was seized and sequestered after returning to the capital and attempting a counter-coup.

"Our technicians then erected a large, new transit facility to service the ætherrift that the Bird-Men had created with the equipment that Doctor Scarabbaios had built. It was incorporated somehow into the gate that they'd erected at Carrou Town. This facility is very tightly guarded by the creatures, who allow very few humans inside. It's linked directly and solely with their homeworld.

"That transit-node and the equipment linked on both ends must be destroyed if our people are going to have any chance of throwing off the Bird-Men's yoke. The rift must be sealed forever. I suspect that this crack in space and time may be prone to widening, even without prompting, and could one day threaten the very existence of this world—or our sphere."

"Your son Sadokéy has been there," I said.

"What? How do you know?"

"When I sifted through his mind, I saw an image of an emplacement that could only, on reflection, have been that station. Scooter, link us together and show Lady Niobë the building interior."

"Yes, Master," the wherret said, and after drawing a little blood from my arm, scooted under the table and climbed onto the Naprimeran woman's lap. The transfer was quickly made.

"Yes, that's it, I'm quite sure," she said. "Do you have enough data to transit there?"

"I think so," I said. "The question is, what do we do when we arrive?"

"How many armed guards will be present, Sir?" Hawk asked.

"Probably not a lot—they'd interfere with day-to-day operations, and after years of never experiencing problems, they'll be complacent, even with the Lady being at large."

"If we can generate a power overload in their main console," Niobë said, "It would not only destroy the enemy equipment in Carrou, but also create an energy pulse that would surge through the established ætherpath right back to Volucripimpant, and blow out the main machine on their homeworld. I don't believe that they have the ability, without the presence of Doctor Scarabbaios, to replace it. The few hundred Bird-Men left on Naprimér would be relatively easy to subdue."

"If you can unite your population…," I said.

"Well, yes, of course," she acknowledged, "But I have no doubt…."

"Lady, a little freedom is a dangerous thing," I said. "You may find that the men on this world may not want to return to female rule."

"I find that rather un…."

"Just consider the notion, please," I said. And then, changing the subject: "I'm not at all familiar with your zip-ports and ætheroprobes. How do we jimmy this one to make it go 'boom'?"

"If you can get me there, I can take of the rest," she said, smiling slightly. "It would be a pleasure."

"Very well, then. We'll get a good night's rest, and make the transit tomorrow. Shah'rah, you'd best remain here."

"No, husband," she said. "Where you go, I go."

"There's no need," I said. "This particular jump is liable to be exceptionally risky, and I don't want to see you put in harm's way."

"Nonetheless, I'm coming."

I couldn't convince her otherwise, so I left it at that. I chomped down one more of Mistress K.'s sausages, belched a couple of times to show my appreciation (I was told by Niobë that this was appropriate behavior), and was just beginning to rise from my seat when the little crew of servers appeared again with dessert.

"Oh, you remembered!" Niobë exclaimed, clapping her hands together. "How marvelous!"

The concoction was at least a foot high and four feet wide. It looked like a white-ashed volcano covered with some sweet, gooey preserve that dribbled down the sides in splotches and streaks of red, purple, and pink. Suddenly a flame erupted at the very top of its peak, and little sparkles of blue fire flew into the air above our heads.

The platter was placed right in front of the Lady, for whom it was obviously intended, but she insisted that plates be handed out to all of us, and we each received a portion.

The sweetness of the dish was tempered with some hot spices, giving it a very distinctive and unusual flavor, rather like mint easing into pepper. The body of the creation had a consistency and taste not unlike lumpy pudding. It was quite yummy, actually.

That night Shah'rah and I shared truly private quarters for the first time since that evening on Festuca. I suddenly realized as I undressed that the wherret was missing. The little creature always slept under, next to, or on my bed. We hadn't been apart for more than a few days in many years.

"Scoot!" I said, looking around the small room. "Scooter!"

"I locked him out," my wife said in a decidedly odd tone from across the room.

"Why?" I asked. Wherrets were very different from us, but they had a pack mentality, and utterly craved company; indeed, they almost had a physical need to be close to…someone.

"Because," she said.

I looked up. She'd fashioned a costume for herself from odds and ends of cloth, feathers, and fur—and they didn't cover much!

"Husband," she said, "I once danced the 'Snake-Arms' for you, but have you ever experienced the 'Constrictor'?"

Strangely, I'd completely lost my voice by then, so all I could do was shake my head "No."

"Then this'll be the first time," she said, and set in motion that marvelous body of hers, all curves and swerves and jangled nerves, and I found myself wishing before that short night ended that dawn would never come again.

CHAPTER THIRTY-SEVEN
"COPPER TONE!"

Getting inside the Bird-Men's Carrouvian zip-port-station wasn't the difficult part; and we had surprisingly few problems subduing the operators and their handful of guards. We'd caught them, after all, completely by surprise.

No, the real issue emerged almost immediately, when Lady Niobë said, "Uh, oh," from the main control panel.

"That doesn't sound good," I said, as Hawk and his men mopped up the remaining resistance. We were fortunate that none of our men were injured.

She raised her head from the console, and looked back at me. "I can't get access," she said. "They've put on a fail-safe of some kind."

"Cripes," I said. "Scooter, lend us a paw!" I yelled, as I headed towards the great machine. "You too, Shah'rah!"

I used the wherret quickly to link all five of us together (including Sable), and then I saw what she meant. Although the Volúcri technology was primitive by Tyrosian standards, it possessed certain mechanical elements that greatly increased the complexity of the interconnections within, making it difficult for us to understand what each component was actually accomplishing as part of the whole, or how they worked together.

"This could take hours!" I said.

"We don't have hours!" Niobë said.

"Sir, they're sending reinforcements," Hawk yelled from the main entrance to the complex, before he and his soldiers began laying down a covering fire from the Tyrosian zappers.

"How long can you hold them?" I asked, over the gradually increasing noise level behind me.

"Five or ten minutes, no more," he shouted.

"Very well, then, we'll do this the hard way," I muttered to myself, and then told Scooter to maintain our link while I released my hands, and pulled the copies of *The Necropompeion* from the pocket of ætherspace where I kept them secure, along with the governing medallion of Master Melanchthon. I accessed the combined power of the twin books, holding it in check with the energy provided by the others in the chain, barked the command, "Back away," and then suddenly poured a huge surge of ætherforce into the console.

The effect was immediate. Small webs of lightning started to enshroud the controls, and then rapidly began to spread, both in number and intensity.

"Let's get out of here!" I yelled over the now constant din. I forced the two ladies back towards the still-open flap into the æther, pushing them through head-first. Hawk and his men dropped a small explosive just outside the entrance into the chamber, and then joined me at the gate, diving through one by one. I looked back just before leaping through the gap myself, only to see the control panel completely covered by roving sparks of electricity.

"She's gonna blow!" I said, and then backed through the opening to safety, quickly closing behind me the flaps through time and space. Even with the "net" cut off, I could feel in my bones the explosion that followed. It must have obliterated much of the town of Carrou—and a reciprocal area on the Bird-Men's home planet.

Back in Mistress Karnikä's establishment in the village of Ramöllie, we checked each other over for injuries—I had a slight burn on my left elbow—and then exhaled our general relief at apparently having cut off the Volúcris from their homeworld without losing one of our group. I told Lady Niobë, however, that she should expect significant casualties among the civilization population of Carrou Town. I also needed to seal the great rift in ætherspace, but that actually proved relatively easy to accomplish, since it proved to be merely an extension of what I'd already learned in creating and closing personal transit-holes in the fabric of space and time.

"I should get back to Mirabör," Niobë said afterwards. "The government will be in chaos."

"Contact your allies first," I suggested. "Find out what the situation is. If the Bird-Men are still in control, you could be arrested and/or executed immediately upon your arrival."

It took several tries over many hours, but she was finally able to use my sky-orb to establish a link with one of her friends, a former member of the ruling Council, and talked for almost an hour with her before shutting down the connection.

"The Volúcri regime has fallen," she said, "but Lord Sadokéy is still in control. The aliens are being tracked down and exterminated, one by one. Their firepower may be greater than ours individually, but without the possibility of reinforcements, they're ultimately doomed. Just in a few hours they've already been pushed back to three surviving bases, and those are being heavily bombarded, and are certain to fall within the next few days.

"But my son says that his regime was forced into collaboration, and that he will lead the effort to continue the reforms of society and government that he and his father began."

"Can you safely challenge him?" I asked.

"Yesterday I would have said yes, but he controls the security apparatus of the state, and those elements have apparently rallied around him. Thus, he can use brute force, if necessary, to maintain his hegemony. Still, I must return immediately, or lose any possibility of prevailing."

"Very well," I said, "we'll come with you."

"No, you should probably remain here, where you'll be safe," she said.

"I need you for the next phase of what we have to do," I said. "I can't afford to have you taken or killed. The stability of the

Circles is more important than either of us."

"Very well," she murmured reluctantly. "We should leave at once."

So we again gathered our wits and belongings together, having barely had a chance to rest and recoup our energy, and I was just about to cut another circle in the æther when I was confronted by Karnikä.

"Yer can't jes' leave me," she said, almost whining; Niobë translated for me. "Ain't gots no other sleepers right now." She held out her cup again.

"What do we owe you?" I asked through the Lady.

"Gold," she said. "Needs gold."

"Nope," I said, "No pays gold."

"Silver," she said. "Takes silver."

"Nope," I said, "No pays silver."

"Uh, copper?" she said. "Please?"

"Copper," I agreed, and tossed a small, octagonal coin with a square hole cut through the center into the open mouth of the container.

She rattled it around a couple of times, until it created almost a musical note, then smiled slightly and said: "Copper tone!"

CHAPTER THIRTY-EIGHT
"A MELODIOUS MELODRAMA"

We transited back to Lady Niobë's quarters; the lone guard that was posted there immediately rushed off to report her return. We followed behind him at a more leisurely pace, heading down the long stone passageways towards the throne room where we'd been interviewed previously by Lords Ssissever and Sadokéy. Both beings were actually present there, but Sadokéy was doing the questioning this time, with the Volúcri leader being confined with heavy chains.

"My Lady Mother," her son said in passable Tyrosian, bowing his head. (I realized afterwards that he *wanted* us to understand him.) And then something very strange happened. Sadokéy rose from his chair and moved down to the secondary emplacement. Niobë put Sable on her shoulder, and slowly ambled up the stairs, her back and neck straight, her demeanor regal, and seated herself on the primary throne.

"Seize them!" she ordered, as soon as she'd presented her face, and we suddenly felt our arms grasped by the surrounding guards. Hawk and his men were disarmed, and the rest of us were stripped of our packs and gear.

"I'm sorry, Master Morpheús," she said, "But you understand that I must act first for the benefit of my people. Now, if you will kindly hand me the first three Elephant's Eggs...."

"I did warn you about this woman," Scooter whispered in my ear.

"This was just an act, then?" I asked.

"More of a melodious melodrama," she said. "I had to find a way of freeing my poor countrymen from the alien yoke, which I couldn't accomplish on my own, and simultaneously gain the ability to defend our world in the future. With the Eggs, I'll have the power to manipulate time and space in such a way that I can lead us into the future—a very bright future, I might add."

"And if I don't give them to you?" I said.

"Then I'll have to have your wife tortured in front of you. I can see the affection you've developed, and I strongly suspect that hurting her is the only pressure to which you'd respond. Don't doubt, by the way, that I'll do exactly what I say."

I sighed. I didn't doubt her in the slightest, and I knew that I couldn't abide seeing someone I loved being hurt on my behalf. I'd finally realized, fool that I was, that Shah'rah meant enough to me that I'd gladly sacrifice my life, my fortune, even my soul for her.

"Don't do it, husband," my wife said.

I didn't respond to her, but just reached into ætherspace, and pulled the implements—the Hand of Morlock, the Pathfinder, and the two copies of *The Necropompeion*—from their hiding place. One of the guards took them to the Lady. But I left the medallion created by Master Melanchthon to govern and direct the power of the books safe in its hidey-hole.

"Ah," she said, as she turned the precious objects over and over again, almost caressing them in her lust for control. It didn't even occur to her that something was missing.

"Can you feel them, Mother?" her son asked.

"The power is there, my son, and I know what to do with it. I won't need Morpheús's people any longer. You may dispose of them as you will. Just don't let the mage see where he's confined, or he'll escape again."

"Very well," Lord Sadokéy ordered. "Take them all to the dungeon, but make certain to blind Master Morpheús before he's chained. We can put the rest of them on trial whenever the Council's reconstituted, maybe in a week or two."

What happened next occurred so quickly that, although I've

reviewed the events over and over again in my memory, I'm still not certain of the why or how of it.

All I know is that my dear wife suddenly stomped her heel hard on the foot of the short man holding her loosely in his grip, prompting him abruptly to let go. She pulled a short sword from the scabbard of the diminutive guard next to her, thrust it immediately into his right side, and then twirled and killed the man to her right—the one who was holding me—and slashed the one behind her right across the belly, mortally wounding him.

The room descended into chaos in so brief a period of time that I'm not even sure of what took place next. Hawk and his men used the distraction to break loose from their captors, killing or injuring most of them in a quick set of thrusts and parries and rethrusts.

Ssissever yanked his chains out of the grasp of the three guards that had him pinned, and whirled them in the air until they crushed the heads of the trio—in one case severing it completely from the man's neck. Then he dashed up the marble steps towards the lesser of the two seats. Sadokéy struggled to bring his own sword to bear, but was barely able to get it pointing in the right direction before Ssissever impaled himself on the weapon, while simultaneously smashing the man's head between his claws. Both of them died instantly.

But there was no time to act and no place for us to go. The remaining guards reacted very quickly, closing in on the ring of defenders crouched around me, and overwhelming us in short order with their numbers. I was trying to focus myself sufficiently to create an opening into the æthernet, and had managed to work open part of one flap when I saw my wife out of the corner of my eye, falling to the floor; but before I could come to her aid, something struck me hard on the right side of my head, and I felt and saw and thought…no more.

CHAPTER THIRTY-NINE
"YOU'LL HAVE TO STAY HERE FOREVER"

When I finally fought my way back to consciousness, I could see nothing. I was lying nude on a soft, flat surface, covered with a sheet of some kind. I tried to raise my head, but was immediately and severely nauseated, and was forced to lie back and remain quite still for several moments to make the aching, whirling feeling diminish to bearable levels. I very carefully and slowly felt around me with my right arm, and encountered what appeared to be cold, metal railings on either side of the bed. My left arm was attached to some kind of tubing—and so was my penis, I suddenly realized, much to my mortification—and something else was wrapped around my face, poking slightly into both my nostrils. I almost pulled the nose device loose, and then decided I'd best be careful about detaching anything whose function I didn't fully understand. All of this technology was utterly alien to me—and, I suspected, to Niobë's world.

So where was I?

And then I remembered   and I found myself filled with such anguish that I involuntarily let loose a long groan of despair, almost a scream. Someone in the distance immediately came running over, leaned against my body, and said something unintelligible to me. I could only distinguish the word "Morphy," and the accent and diction was different from anything that I'd encountered on Naprimér. It sounded almost like some crazy cross between Anglo-Saxon and the Frankish tongue.

"What is this place?" I asked.

The woman—I could tell she was female by her voice— spoke again, but I understood her no better than before. I felt for my eyes, and realized that the entire upper part of my head was completely bandaged. Was I blind—or not?

The thought sent my mind whirling again, and I must have cried out the name "Shah'rah!" a second time, because my nurse—or whoever she was—said something low and soothing, and then moved slightly to one side. Within seconds, the mental pain eased markedly, and then I drifted off into sleep once more.

The next time that I was conscious, I found myself going over those last few moments in the throne room at Réstiff, again and again and again, trying to glean whatever I could from what I recalled. I remembered my wife falling, but I could never retrieve a clear image of what had actually happened to her. Was she injured? Was she dead (oh, not that, please)? And if she'd survived, where was she? Why wasn't she here? What'd happened to Scooter and Hawk and the other men? But most of all, most of all, what'd become of my dearest Shah'rah? The gorge was rising quickly again— and again I was doused with whatever tonic it was that drew a slow curtain down over my grieving soul.

I may have experienced these brief resurrections a half dozen times or more before I finally emerged from my anguished state to some reasonable facsimile of a saner world. I remember that I was drifting in and out of the depths when an old man's voice spoke to me: "Morpheús! Morpheús!"

I recognized Master Mathurin, and I groped through the darkness of my soul until latching onto his shining light, and pulled myself up from despair again.

"Where am I?" I finally was able to ask. I felt a warm hand grasp my unfettered wrist, and squeeze it slightly.

"My world," he said in Tyrosian. "Use this language to communicate, if you please, since no one here can possibly understand it."

"How…?" I mumbled.

"I heard a voice from the æther calling to me, and when I investigated, I found you there, curled up in a pocket of protected space, filled with enough warmth and air to survive for a few days, perhaps a week. I don't know how long you'd been there, but you were shivering and blue, and wouldn't have survived much longer. I brought you here, and took you to one of our hospitals.

"The back of your head was fractured, there was swelling in your brain, and you had a number of small cuts on your arms."

"Wh-what about the others?" I asked.

"There were no others, just you," Mathurin said.

"How long have I been here?"

"Three weeks," he said. "You nearly died several times, but somehow you pulled through. The technology here is marvelous, if you can afford it."

"My implements?"

"There were none—just the clothes on your back—and the medallion."

"Then the Eggs are truly gone," I said, "and my wife and familiar—I don't know what happened to them. I think they must be dead."

Then the sorrow overwhelmed me again. I wanted to die, wanted to be anywhere but here, pretending to get better while the others were...wherever they were.

"Morpheús!" I heard my name called several times before I was able to disengage myself from the dark. "Morpheús! We don't know what happened. Don't assume the worst. Maybe they survived."

"But Niobë—she's taken the Eggs, she's...."

"Yes, I know. You've told me that many times before. No matter."

"But the Spheres...?"

"Your work will wait for you. There are other possibilities," the old mage said. "There are always possibilities. Now you need to get well enough so you can think clearly again. Then you and I will find a way."

"Shah'rah!" I wailed. "Shah'rah!"—and this time, I would not be solaced. I heard Mathurin somewhere in the distance calling for the nurse in that strange language of theirs, and I drifted off again into the void.

I had a vision then. I beheld the recumbent body of my beloved tucked into a bed of her own, her chest slowly rising and falling beneath her bandages. She lived! Someone partially blocked my sight of her, leaning over her form, and raising her head to give her some kind of tonic. Then the nurse put down the cup on a nearby stand, carefully put Shah'rah's body back on its pillow, and turned to face me.

"You see!" Niobë said, "I've kept her alive. I had to keep her alive, because you and I comprise the Fourth Egg. You must return to me, Morpheús, to complete the spell. I need you. I give you my word: come back to me as soon as you're well, and I'll let the woman go. I forgive you the death of my son."

"What about me?" I asked.

"Oh, well, I'm afraid you'll have to stay here forever," she said, smiling sweetly. "We'll have a great time together, the two of us, won't we? I do think so. You'll become my new consort."

CHAPTER FORTY

"YOU CAN BE GREAT
SOME OTHER TIME"

When I awoke, I was overwhelmed with rage at the sheer insolence of this Lady, who dared to blackmail me with the health of my beloved. I chewed on this new feeling, and let it drive away the depression of mind and spirit that had so infested me. If Shah'rah still lived, so would I! If there was any road to rescue her, I would find the path.

This is what I told Master Mathurin on his next visit. He sighed and said: "My son, hate can sometimes be a useful temporary tool to focus your energies, but don't let it eat away your insides. You have to retain a positive outlook if you're going to have any chance of smoothing the cracks that now demarcate our existence. If I thought that you'd be nothing more than an agent of vengeance, I'd strike you down here and now. This Lady has poisoned herself with a false sense of duty. Don't follow in her footsteps. Use the love you've discovered with Shah'rah to heal the canker in your soul."

"But what about Niobë, Sir?" I asked. "She and I together represent The Fourth Elephant's Egg."

"She's useless to you unless she's a willing agent of change," he said. "And if she's unable or unwilling to help, then you must find some other individual that you can employ as your partner in the shaping of this spell. You're the Prime, and the other is always Secunda—a necessary complement, but less specifically oriented."

"Then how…?"

"Let yourself discover what's intended by the Universe," Mathurin said. "There's no formula set down by some significant universal Other to determine your actions in advance. *You* determine your actions—and that resolution is always unique for that time and that place."

"I think I see what you mean, Master," I said. "I wonder…."

"Ah," he said. "Perhaps you now understand, my dear son. I've told you this before, but I'll say it again: you'll do just fine, Morpheús, if you let yourself act. But first we must get you well and strong again. Follow the instructions of your physicians."

"But I don't understand the local language, Sir," I said.

"Oh, that's nothing," he said, and I felt the air whoosh as he leaned close to me, an odor of garlic gently washing my face. He placed his two hands just underneath the bandage that covered the top of my head, and slowly insinuated contact with my mind. When he knew that I would receive him without flinching, he gave me something—I didn't know what—and then released me.

"I must go now. I'll be back again soon." Then I heard him say as he walked out, "Nurse, would you check his vitals, please?"

It took me a moment to realize that I understood the foreign phrase that he uttered, and also was able to translate the soft female murmur that replied, "And how are we doing today, Doctor Morphy?"

"B-better," I said.

"You can talk!" she exclaimed, "You can talk!" I heard her yell out the door, "Doctor Karlov, please come quickly!"

I heard a set of footsteps enter my room and approach my bed. He gave an order to the nurse, who promptly left, and then a familiar voice whispered in my ear in the Greekish tongue, "Well, Master Morpheús, we meet again."

It was Doctor Scarabbaios, that two-faced old reprobate! I was stunned that he even lived, much less prospered, and said so.

"Actually, this world suits me very well indeed, much to my

own surprise," he said. "You see, the people here don't really believe in magic, except as fantastical stories. And the usual magical techniques often don't work especially well in this *milieu*—but they do function in some smaller ways, and that gives an adroit practitioner such as myself a decided advantage in certain types of dealings. Of course, I can't transit anywhere else, but my traveling days are past, and I don't miss them. And no one else can ever find me here."

"What about the two Tyrosian ladies?" I asked.

"They've done well too," the old mage said. "We don't associate much, but I see them once in a while. They've become, uh, 'executives in the entertainment industry'."

"What's that?" I asked.

"You'd have to live here to understand the context."

"So why are *you* here, Doctor Scarabbaios?"

"Call me Doctor Karlov, if you please; that's my *nom de guerre* here—'Big Karl,' if you wish—although I really prefer 'Doctor.' It has such a basic dignity about it, doesn't it? 'Doctor' this and 'Doctor' that—I just love being praised by the masses.

"Well, your friend Master M. asked me to help, and since I still have some basic healing spells available, as minor as they are," he said, "I've used them to knit your poor head back together again. Oh, don't worry—old Marty keeps me on a very short leash indeed. We trade favors, of a sort, and keep each other informed about developments.

"In any event, your main problem is regaining your strength. Your mind is sound, and your head will gradually heal, although you now have a small metal plate inserted there. However, you will discover, much to your dismay, that your energy will take a very long time to return to its original level, if it ever does. These kinds of injuries can be very debilitating, and you're going to have to be quite careful in the future. Your physicians will remove your bandage in about a week. Your eyesight will be blurry at first, but it will recover, I'm told."

"I thought I was blind," I said.

"You *have* been blind, Morpheús," the mage said. "You've

trusted way too many people in your life. Remember the old adage?—'Trust no one.' Especially not women!—they'll ruin you every time. Zalmanna, Fathria, Morganna, Johanna, Katherina, Lorrah—they all betrayed me. This Niobë is just another prime example, from what Marty tells me."

"What about Shah'rah?" I asked.

"Another comely witch? Fie! They'll ruin you, my boy. *Ruin you!* I've spent my life being ruined by bad women and dysfunctional lackeys."

"I think I'll make my own judgment about that," I said.

"You do that, boy, you do that. But…find out first what she really wants. Yes, that'll be a real eye-opener, won't it? I bet you haven't a clue. We men never do, not till it's too late. They all have their secret agendas, you know."

"And what are *your* secret plans, Doctor?" I asked. I was getting very tired of this egomaniacal rant.

"I want to be remembered for having done something," he said.

"What?" I asked.

"Doesn't matter! It's not the deed itself, Morpheús, it's how people perceive it—and *you*! If they *think* you've accomplished great things, well, that's the way the story's written, isn't it? You don't actually have to *be* great in order to *look* great. You just proclaim the fact, and let the people come to understand how great you are. Most of them do eventually, you know."

At this point I was utterly disgusted by the old fart. "I need to rest," I said. "You can be great some other time."

"Ah, the nonbelievers…," he said. "But you'll come around, Morpheús. They all do, in the end. My greatness is only exceeded by my ambition."

I closed my eyes and pretended to be asleep. At last Scarabbaios got the message—"No one is listening"—and left me in peace. A greater fool I'd never before encountered, and the sad thing was, he believed every word of this fantasy of himself.

When a man comes to regard his own propaganda as real,

he topples into the pit of solipsistic madness, which closes ever more tightly upon him, until the only possible exit is death.

CHAPTER FORTY-ONE
"SLOW, NOISY, SMELLY, AND OFTEN DANGEROUS"

The first step on the long path to my recovery was removal of the bandage covering my skull, which was cut and peeled away very carefully. I hadn't realized the weight of the thing until it was gone. As predicted, my vision was initially somewhat unfocused, but it improved very rapidly, and I was soon able to see my surroundings with much more clarity.

On his next visit I questioned Master Mathurin about my familiar, Scooter, but he knew nothing about the fate of any of my companions. "I do have a sky-orb," he said in Tyrosian, "But I employ it seldom, since I wish to keep my presence here secret. You had nothing on your person save your clothes, and no one else was in your refuge. How you got yourself there I have no idea—the magic is beyond my knowledge or ability."

This mystery puzzled me a great deal, but I had no memory of what had happened to me after I received that conk on my head in Niobë's throne room, and told him so: "I remember opening a gate into the æther, but before I could save any of my comrades, we were overwhelmed. Maybe the wherret somehow created my refuge."

"They're not really known as active practitioners of the art," the old mage said. "They're mostly a trading people, and while they possess some innate abilities that we simply don't have, and can greatly enhance another's working, they're not usually credited with much initiative. Of course, I haven't associated with them as frequently as you."

"Did Shah'rah really live, Sir, or has the Lady sent me the 'portrait' of a lie?"

"Again, I have no way of knowing this," he said. "You should be careful, however, about trusting that woman ever again—and not because all females are inherently untrustworthy, as our friend Karlov (as he now calls himself) would have you believe. She's demonstrated quite clearly that she regards her own local responsibilities as paramount over those in the greater community of beings. You and I did not and do not have that luxury."

"But how can I heal the Spheres without Niobë's assistance, Sir?"

"We've discussed this before, Morpheús. I don't know the specific means that you might employ in the Great Working. I do know that there's a way, and that you must find it through your own efforts. That's as much as I can say—and, really, as much as I know."

The days dribbled by, one after another, punctuated by discussions with Master Mathurin, Doctor Scarabbaios, and the physicians and nurses that assisted me. I spent three weeks getting to the point where I could use the facilities again, and also gain sufficient mobility that I could walk without assistance. By such small steps is progress measured when you've experienced illness nigh unto death.

Finally they discharged me into the Master's care. I was placed in a chair on wheels, rolled through the long corridors of the hospice until I reached a main exit, and there carefully installed in a large metal vehicle with four wheels that seemed to move of its own accord.

"What is this thing, Sir?" I asked the old mage, when the driver engaged the motivating force.

"As I mentioned to you," Mathurin said, "On this world magic is not considered real. Therefore, the natives must build elaborate machines to simulate transits that we would find second-nature. This is one of those devices, powered by the small, controlled explosion of gasses in the engine housed up front."

"That seems to me a very inefficient way to go from one place to another, Master," I said.

"Indeed it is—slow, noisy, smelly, and often dangerous. But that's what we have available to us."

And indeed, the automotive mechanism took almost an hour to ferry me back to the magician's abode, struggling with heavy traffic, red-and-green flashing lights that apparently indicated "Stop!" and "Go!" (although I never quite understood what the yellow one meant), and signs posted along the streets that also told us when to move and not move. It all seemed extraordinarily and unnecessarily complicated to me, and I said so.

"All of this is true," Mathurin said, "but on the other hand, they have made tremendous strides in areas such as medicine—which is one of the reasons why I settled here—that and the desire for privacy. And for those with an entrepreneurial bent, such as Scarabbaios and Zalmanna, this place is a paradise of opportunity."

I lived with the old man at his home for almost six months, until the nightmares finally abated, and I could walk and fight and exist again without wheezing, faintness, headaches, or nausea. Mistress Essora had seemingly vanished from the scene, and when I asked about her, I was told that she had her own adventures to pursue.

Finally, I was ready to depart this strange new world, and rescue my wife and friends.

"Do you know where you're going?" Mathurin asked on my final day, as I was putting the last of my small cache of weapons and implements into a new pack.

"Niobë will have guards and traps posted at all of the places that I visited on Naprimér, Sir—and I can't transit to any of them without a strong possibility of being taken. But she probably won't recall that I got a glimpse through her mind of the garden at Réstiff, an image reinforced by something that I saw in her son's memories. I have enough, I think, to find the place—and then I'll just have to improvise!"

"Be careful," he said. Then he reached into a pocket, pulled out an oblong object, and dropped it onto my hand. "This may help you."

It was his sky-orb.

"But Master, you have no other way of contacting anyone without this…."

"I can always leave this world if I choose," he said, "although I can't think of any circumstance that would prompt me to do so. No, Morpheüs, take it. I've only used it a handful of times, and it's become a temptation more than anything else. You have better need right now. If you survive, if you prosper, come back to me someday—if I'm still here—and return it.

"And now, I give you my blessing, son of my son's sons. May you find your way, and may it be one with the universe." Then he put his two hands on my forehead, and gave me—something. "What I know, you now know," he intoned. "What I've done, you now can do. What I've been, you now are. Use your powers wisely, my boy. And do take care."

I embraced him then for the substitute father that he'd become to me. "I shall miss you," I said.

Then I cut the opening into the æther (which I now found I could do without the First Egg), reached through the leys to find Niobë's hidden garden, and strode the byways of space and time.

CHAPTER FORTY-TWO
"MAKING UP THE BOGEYMAN"

I was again lucky: I emerged under the comforting blanket of night, which saved me from detection from the pair of guards that the Lady had posted in Princess Tema's Garden in Mirabör. She *had* remembered after all! I would not underestimate her again.

I very patiently crouched down behind a large plant located next to a gravel walk, trying to catch my breath. I still didn't have my complete strength back. I made a slight hissing sound.

"Do you hear that?" a man said. I was surprised and pleased to find that one of the Master's gifts had been a facility with the Naprimeran language.

"Just the wind," the other man said.

I waited for a few moments, and then tossed a small pebble across the pathway.

"What's that!" the first guard said.

"Oh, just some critter scurrying 'round," his companion said.

I flipped another stone into the brush.

"I'm going to check it out," the first man said.

"It's a complete waste of time," the other said, "but I can't stop you. Next you're going to be making up the bogeyman!"

I heard the guard coming before I could see him, and so I encouraged him with a third fling across the way.

"That's it again!" the man said, and stopped right in front of me, poking at the shrubbery with his long-knife.

"Find anything?"

"Nah, nothing." I reached out my hand and grabbed him by the calf, immediately surging up his body and into his mind. I subsumed his consciousness before he could even gasp.

"What's this?" I forced him to say. "Come here, Blocus!"

"Oh, crimey!" the second guard said. "If you're playing a joke, Goujö...."

But when Blocus appeared, and leaned over the brush to see what was happening on the other side of the path, I used Goujö's hand on his friend's shoulder to bridge my way into *his* mind—and then I was safe, at least for a little while. I sifted quickly through their thoughts and memories for whatever I could use, and harvested a series of images of rooms around the Palace and through the city, plus much practical information that I would have to examine at a later date—if I needed it.

I also discovered the fate of my companions. Hawk was a prisoner in the dungeon, but his men had all died, either at the scene or later from their lingering injuries. Scooter had escaped, as he always had a tendency to do—a wherret is never trapped for long!—and no one knew his current whereabouts. And Shah'rah—oh Blessèd Lord Above!—had survived and healed, but was being kept closely confined in one of the rooms in Castle Réstiff. The two guards had never visited there, and so I couldn't harvest an image of the place from their minds to help provide me a link for transiting. In any case, I was certain that the place was a trap—as was Hawk's jail cell.

Still—my heart expanded with the music of the Spheres. I could finally feel hope again!

I marched the men back to their posts, propped them up against the wall, put them into a heavy doze, and wiped any memory of my intervention from their minds.

Then I opened another exit into the æther, and walked through otherspace into a little-used storage compartment in the Palace. I had to find help—and soon—and there was no one to whom I could turn on this world. Except....

But the problem was, I couldn't make myself visible, or even issue a psychic call, without Niobë being aware of my presence, and the only real advantage that I had right now was my ability to operate without her notice. I was so much larger physically than the natives of this place that I would immediately stand out in a public forum. Whatever I accomplished, it had to be completely secret—from them and from her.

I decided to try something different. I very cautiously allowed my consciousness to ooze into the walls of the room in which I hid, and then began to spread it piece by piece throughout the interconnected stones of the old structure, until I and Réstiff had become one, in a manner of speaking. I still existed as a separate entity, but I was also the Castle. How much time elapsed during this process, I have no idea.

Then I began to open passive, psychic eyes throughout the entire complex, section by section, until I could "feel" everything and everyone that passed through my hallways, my vestibules, my rooms. When I felt the presence of the Lady, I walled off that area from my mind, so that her senses wouldn't detect me.

I was looking for a particular presence, and when finally I located it, deep within the bowels of the building, I gently shut my "eyes" elsewhere, and focused just on that one portion, an abandoned torture room several levels beneath the main wine cellar.

I forced a pair of lips from the mold growing on the surface of the brick, and flapped them together with a breath of rancid wind.

"Scooootteeeer!" I hissed in a barely audible tone.

The little creature, I could sense, immediately sat up on its hind legs, and peered through the gloom with its intense eyes. Wherrets could see quite well in the near-dark.

"Yes, Master?" Scooter finally said.

CHAPTER FORTY-THREE
"WHAT FORTY *BLEEMS*?"

Once I had Scooter's attention, I made a gate from the store-room to the "hole," and immediately transited there.

"Master!" the wherret exclaimed again, jumping into my arms and licking my right ear. "I was beginning to wonder how long I'd have to wait." From the tone, I almost expected tears—but, of course, Scooter's kind didn't have the proper physical equipment for that type of display.

"I was, uh, injured," I said. "Master Mathurin saved my life and then nursed me back to health. What of our companions?"

"They're mostly dead, Master," it said. "Hawk still lives, but he's not well. Shah'rah also survives, but she has no will to live—she believes that you were killed in the throne room. I told them both that you'd return as soon as you could, and that if you'd been severely impaired, you could never have made your escape."

"I don't honestly know how I got away, my friend, and my recovery was long and tiresome. So you've seen both of our friends yourself?"

"Of course, Sir. You know that a wherret can't be retarded from finding out anything that it wants."

"Yes, you're renowned throughout the Spheres as great thieves and plunderers," I said.

"Why thank you, Master. That's the nicest thing you've ever said to me."

"We need to find some way of retrieving the others," I said.

"That's going to be difficult, Sir," the creature said. "They're both very closely guarded at all hours of the day and night. Lady Niobë obviously *wants* you to make such an attempt, and seems confident that she can catch you in the process."

"Well, then, we have to make certain that she doesn't. What are their specific circumstances?"

"Well, Sir, both are kept chained to a brick wall most of the time, with heavy, magic-proofed locks. Your wife is usually guarded by several strong women in her compartment, and three or four heavily-armed men in the corridor just outside. Hawk is shadowed by two or three armed soldiers assigned to his block who check his cell every few minutes."

"So there's no quick way we could free them for transit?" I said.

"No, Master."

"Rats! Is either of them ever moved or exercised or otherwise shifted to another location?"

"Once a week, Sir," the wherret said, "Lady Shah'rah is taken in chains by a half-dozen guards to Princess Tema's Garden, where she's allowed to spend an hour sitting or strolling through the shrubbery (to the extent that she's physically able with all those restraints). On rare occasions, none of which are predictable, the Sergeant has been brought before a magistrate or inquisitor for questioning about you."

"All right. We'll retrieve my wife first," I said. "She's the more accessible of the two."

Over the course of the next week, I visited Blocus and Goujö several times during their shifts in the garden, and gradually suggested to them that they had a running feud with one of Shah'rah's sentinels. I also made certain that they'd be on duty when my wife next appeared.

Thus, several days later, as the little expedition of guards and prisoner came to the entrance to Princess Tema's hideaway, Blocus stepped forward when he saw Verol escorting her, and said, *"You have the nerve!"*

"What?" Verol said.

"You think you can escape your debt just by ignoring it? Who do you think you are?"

"What are you talking about?" the other guard asked. "I don't owe you anything."

"You hear that, Goujö?" Blocus said to his companion. "He's forgotten all about it!"

"Well, I was there, Blocus," the second man replied. "I saw him lose the money to you, fair and square. You should pay up, Verol!"

"I've never lost any money to either of you," the escort said.

"Oh, really?" Goujö said. "Then what about last year, eh? It took me eights months to collect those forty *bleems* from you."

"What forty *bleems*?"

"Give me back my money!" Blocus shouted at the other guard, pushing him away from the gate with his hand.

"It's not *your* money!" Verol yelled back. "I don't owe you anything, you bastard!"

"Bastard, am I?" Blocus wrapped his arms around his enemy and tossed him into the mud of an adjoining flowerbed.

"That's it!" Verol said, and charged his accuser. Then Goujö joined in the fray, and called for help from two other guards on the other side of the garden. Soon there were ten men rolling around on the ground, hitting and biting and blaspheming each other with great enthusiasm. My bemused wife had backed away from the fight when it had started, and ducked through the open gate into the refuge of the garden proper.

I'd been watching our little "disagreement" develop through a small hole in the æther, and as soon as Shah'rah was standing by herself, away from the others, I widened the aperture and snatched her backwards into my arms—and safety!

"Oh, Morpheús!" she moaned, when she saw who it was, and then fainted with exhaustion and the strain. I took her to our friends on Festuca, and left her temporarily in their care.

Then Scooter and I transited back to Naprimér to the dungeon below Castle Réstiff, and one by one I subsumed the minds of the soldiers patrolling the corridors of the prison block where

Hawk was being held. I needed to move quickly, before the situation changed again and security was beefed up. One of the guards then kindly opened the Sergeant's cage and unlocked his chains. Hawk staggered into my arms as I pulled him through the æther. I also deposited him at the village of Pissapapilis on Festuca.

Then Scooter and I spent some weeks there ourselves, recuperating from transit-shock and fatigue, and allowing Niobë's anger to build in the interim. I wanted her stewing like a volcano before I confronted her again. I still needed to retrieve the Three Elephant's Eggs—and then I'd be finished, once and for all, with the Lady and with Naprimér—and with all of the mostly bad memories that I now associated with them.

CHAPTER FORTY-FOUR
"WHAT DID SHE DO?"

"You're alive! She said you were, but I...I finally didn't believe her. You were gone so very long." I was standing over the recumbent form of my wife, who was looking at me with wonder—and yes, love—illuminating her gaunt face. I just leaned down and enfolded her in my arms, holding her tight, feeling her flutter like a trapped bird beneath me for a moment, before finally releasing her. For once in my life, my speech utterly failed me. We were both overcome with the joy of reunion, and my tears were sufficient, I think, to express everything that I needed to say.

Then I slowly and haltingly told her how Master Mathurin had rescued me from the abyss, of my slow recovery these past months, and that I had to go back yet one more time to retrieve the Eggs.

"I can't leave them with Niobë," I said, "any more than I could have with Scarabbaios or the Tyros or even Master Melanchthon, all of whom would have used the implements for their own ends. These are not artifacts that can be turned to some selfish purpose—they were created for higher work. They're meant to unify the worlds, not generate further divisions."

Shah'rah parted the covers to show me the jagged scar that now marred the perfect flesh of her right side. "I nearly died," she said, "but I kept thinking of you, dear one, and this inevitable day when we'd be together again, and I focused on that to pull myself back into the light, despite what that woman tried to do to me."

"What did she do?" I said, and those four words were the coldest that I've ever uttered. *"What did she do?"* I repeated, when I got no response.

I must have scared her, because she laid her hands on each side of my face, and said: "She said things to make me doubt you. She threatened me and tempted me and tried to use me to lure you into a trap. She said she needed you for the 'Grand Experiment,' whatever that was. She said that if I failed to gain your cooperation, she would torture you in front of me, and then kill us both. She's a vile, evil woman, Mórpheo, with a heart filled with needles. She blames you for her son's death, and she'll never forgive you for it."

"I wish I didn't have to see her again, but I'm afraid I have no choice."

"Then let me and Hawk come with you," she said.

"I'll think on it," I said, but the truth was, I had no intention of putting her in peril ever again. I'd come too close this time to losing her, and had suddenly realized that life without Shah'rah would be utterly empty for me.

But in the meantime, we remained on Festuca, resting in advance of the ordeal to come. Hawk had been severely injured in the throne room fray, but was now regaining some of his strength and mobility, although, as he said, "We're none of us gettin' any younger, Sir. I regret the death of my boys: they fought bravely, all of them."

"We'll erect a memorial to their names when we return home," I said.

"'Home' is beginnin' to sound good to me again," the soldier said. "Never thought I'd say that."

"We'll go back, never fear."

But I wondered in my soul whether any of us would survive the confrontation with Niobë. She had the Eggs, after all, even if she didn't own Melanchthon's medallion, and that gave her a tremendous source of psychic power. But I actually had worked with the artifacts, and knew perhaps a bit more about their functioning than she. Perhaps. She'd had plenty of time in the last six months to explore on her own—if the Eggs had cooperated. They had a mind of their own, in many ways, and could not easily be controlled by someone whose motives were suspect.

Still, she was ruthless and power-hungry, and those attributes gave her an immense amount of potential force: she would do almost anything to increase that power, and justify her acts as necessary for the advancement of her people. Her people, of course, would be far better off without her.

I had to gain an advantage somehow, however minor. I knew that she would never agree to meet me off-world, but I wondered if she could be lured to the one place on Naprimér that might give me an edge. I needed to consult with someone about that possibility, and so I told my friends that I had to depart Festuca for a few days, but that I'd return shortly. I took Scooter with me.

We actually visited several different places over the course of a week, seeing what was possible and what was necessary. I needed the wherret for some of this work, because of its ability to squeeze through small spaces unnoticed. I couldn't easily go anywhere on Naprimér, for example, without immediately being noticed, since I was several feet taller than the average human there. No wonder "Matrin" had been revered in olden times: he'd quite literally towered above them, and must have seemed, with his powers, like some god striding over the landscape. I wondered how the priestesses reconciled his presence in their mythology with their religious beliefs. Well, that was their affair, not mine.

Finally, when we'd finished with our prognostications, and I was satisfied that we'd uncovered all we could, we transited back to Festuca. I knew what I had to do. I gathered our little group of survivors together, and told them what I had in mind.

"That's a very risky plan, husband," Shah'rah said.

"Yes," I said. "If any of you have a better idea, I'd certainly like to hear it."

I was greeted with silence.

"Then I assume we're all agreed," I said.

My wife spoke for everyone else: "We'll be right behind you."

CHAPTER FORTY-FIVE
"WE SHALL NEVER FORGET"

We actually spent more a month as guests of Mayor Nonnengagué, fattening ourselves on the rich crops that his fields were now producing. It was gratifying to see that this one act by us had made such a positive difference to these people. The word had spread very quickly around this world that the town of Pissapapilis had a restorative that would regenerate their crops again, and was giving away the seeds gratis. Despite the limited transit resources available on the planet (only four stations, widely scattered), the replantings had already reached every arable part of the globe. I could see the restored confidence evident in the way the natives held themselves.

"I want to show you something," the Mayor said on the day after my return.

He led me out beyond the village boundaries, followed by his great-nephew and some of the townspeople, and took me up the slope of a nearby hill. The top had been cleared, and a structure erected there. When I realized what it was, I stopped short, overcome with emotion. They had fashioned a group of rough stone statues resembling the intrepid group of voyagers who'd come here the previous year to save their world—or at least, this is how they'd interpreted our presence. We were now legend on Festuca—and I was a god!

"You didn't need to do this," I said to my friend.

"Yes, Master Morpheús, we did! We shall never forget what you've done for us. You saved our people, you and your companions—even the Tyros, against their will. You forced them to restore what'd been lost. No, Sir, we shall never forget, and this monument will help future generations remember what happened here."

Then he embraced me, tears running down his furrowed cheeks, and I hugged him back, because he'd forced *me* to realize that I had an obligation even to those that I'd never met before—indeed, that we all have obligations to the strangers among us, whether we acknowledge them or not. This is what the Christ had said in the Bible, and what so few of his so-called followers ever followed.

Then we went back to the village and had a rousing good time over dinner. I remember that the Mayor's great-nephew, Chuchaqué, came to me and asked in labored Tyrosian, which he'd obviously been learning from his uncle in the interim, if he could come with us when we left, so that he could learn the skills that his world needed to prosper in the future. I told him that I would return for him if I survived, but I could not allow him to be endangered by this mission of peril. He seemed pleased that I would even consider his request.

But finally our time in Festuca once more came to an end. None of us were back to our original strength, but we were healthy enough to proceed. I'd decided that all four of us would be needed, and all had agreed to join me.

So I cut the gate through the æther once again, and took us back to Naprimér, to the Tomb of Matrin at Caribbë in the Province of Tontontoquë.

CHAPTER FORTY-SIX
"THAT ONE IS NOT FOR YOU"

As soon as we appeared in front of the two flanking statues of Master Matrin and his consort, Lady S'rёnё, Scooter and I flashed a set of psychic boundaries around the perimeter of the great-room, protecting us from any outside intrusion, physical or mental. The two guards standing within the new "fence line" immediately turned and came at us, but Hawk was waiting for them, and quickly took them down, despite being outnumbered.

We dragged the bodies out to the main entrance, and threw them through the invisible barrier and down the marble steps. The dead men's companions charged straight at us, but bounced off the shield we'd created. They were remarkably persistent— or perhaps not terribly bright—because they kept right on trying such tactics at the various exits around the main display room until a number of the soldiers were forced to withdraw because of the numerous small injuries they'd inflicted on themselves.

Finally, their commanding officer ordered their retreat, and trod up the stairs by himself, two at a time, stopping just at the highest level, where he knew his passage would be barred.

"Who are you?" he asked. "Why are you defiling this sacred monument?"

"You know who I am," I replied. "We'll wait just three days for your mistress to appear—no more! If she hasn't arrived by then, we'll destroy this building and these statues, and leave this place forever."

Then I turned my back on the man, and strode away from the

entrance, ignoring his repeated calls. Instead, I darkened the curtain that the wherret and I had imposed around the monument room, to make further communication more difficult. Finally, the officer got the general idea—I didn't have anything further to discuss with him—and went away.

The layout of the Tomb was fairly simply. The twin stone monuments to Master Matrin and Lady S'rënë lay side by side at the center of the open space. Each of the raised "graves" (that of Matrin was certainly empty, or at least filled with the body of an imposter) was decorated along the sides with scenes from that individual's life. There were alcoves where admirers could place small gifts, or stop to appreciate the great deeds of these two founders of Naprimeran civilization.

To the left and the right, facing each other over their tombs, were the giant stone statues of the mage and his consort. Matrin's right hand was extended towards the woman, his left arm posed upright, holding some kind of magical implement, while S'rënë's left arm reached out towards her mate, with her right hand crossed over her chest to clasp her bare upper left breast, which her shift just failed to cover; wrapped around her right arm was a chain from which dangled a pendant of power.

The heads of the two ancients barely touched the ceiling, which loomed over us in an arch at least twenty feet high above the central nave of the monument, declining to perhaps fifteen feet at the side walls.

I reached out with my mind towards the grand image of my ancestor, and found a sympathetic vibration there; but when I attempted the same probe towards the woman, I was rebuffed by whatever presence slept there.

"Let me try," my wife said, and before I could stop her, she strode over to the towering sculpture of S'rënë, and touched the Lady's right foot. Immediately Shah'rah stiffened at the contact, and seemed to enter a trance. I gasped out loud, and was about to rush to her aid when Scooter hissed in my right ear: "No, Master! That one is *not* for you! Let it be!"

I managed to restrain myself, although every instinct within my being wanted to help my wife—but the wherret usually knew whereof it spoke, and I had learned to follow the creature's advice on such matters, since it was, by nature, a rather cautious and careful being.

Finally, Shah'rah broke her link with the stone carving, and lurched backwards. I was waiting to grab her before she fell. "That was…different," she said.

Then she turned around and burrowed her head into my shoulder, before murmuring: "She, uh, she told me that she'll remain neutral in the struggle to come, husband."

"Is she actually buried here?" I asked.

"Oh, yes," Shah'rah said, "She's here, all right. She awaits the return of her beloved, Master Matrin. Only then can she rest in eternal peace."

"Mathurin told me that she'd tried to kill him," I said.

"A, well, misunderstanding, I think—I'm not really sure. They had a tumultuous relationship, Morphy. But she still loves him."

"Very well," I said. "Then we've done all we can do to prepare. The next step is up to Lady Niobë."

But Niobë did not appear on the second day, as I expected, although we waited and watched for her while the sun was high; and when the third day dawned, I wondered whether my gamble was about to be lost.

Oh ye of little faith! For the Lady could not resist my public challenge, which I was certain had now become general knowledge among the population of Naprimér, and about an hour after sunset of the third day, I finally heard the unhappy voice that I'd been expecting.

"Morpheús!"

CHAPTER FORTY-SEVEN
"WOULD YOU DESTROY THE TOMB IN ORDER TO SAVE IT?"

"Morpheús!" she screamed again. No, the Lady Niobë was not a happy person at this point in her life.

I walked out to the top of the stone stairway, lightened the curtain so that we could communicate, and looked down at her.

She was stunningly beautiful in the bright stare of the sun, wrapped in a gown of translucent gauze that highlighted and showed off her figure, while simultaneously sweeping it with swirls and flashes of bright and pastel colors that never seemed to repeat themselves. It was an amazing creation that combined the best of magical workings with a consummate sense of design and fashion. Clutched around her brow was a slim diadem of gold lamé tied at the back of the neck. Two crossed straps of black velvet overlaid her shoulders and underlaid her four petite breasts, emphasizing their prominence, and around her waist was fastened a thin strap of leather, belted at the front, which served as an anchor for the ebon ties. It was a costume that proclaimed: "I can do anything that I please."

Surrounding her at a distance of ten feet was a semicircular squad of Council guards in their equally impressive uniforms, and beyond that I could see courtiers, other Council members, and representatives of the public.

I was impressed. This woman had certainly mastered the art of political theater—and theater was exactly what she intended this confrontation to be.

"I'm here, Lady," I said, smiling slightly.

"Release the barrier and let me through," she ordered.

"No, Lady."

"What? You defy me and my authority on this world?"

"Your authority, as I understand it, extends to just one nation on Naprimér, and even that has been questioned in recent times, by your own account," I said. "I helped you to overthrow your conquerors and restore your rule, you might recall. But that assistance does not give you any authority over *me*, Lady—or even over this monument, which belongs to the ages."

She didn't respond, but gathered her energy, and flashed what she thought was an unexpected lightning bolt directly at me. I didn't even flinch, having anticipated her action. Of course, it had no effect on the screen, which I'd been reinforcing ever since the wherret and I had created it several days earlier.

"Care to try something else?" I said, and then turned my back on her and walked towards the pair of tombs in the center of the room.

She followed with a series of magical attacks on the psychic boundary that protected the great-room, and once she began drawing on the power of the twin copies of *The Necropompeion*, the whole structure began to rock and rattle.

"Would you destroy the Tomb in order to save it?" I shouted at her over the din, turning to face her again—and that gave her pause.

"Let me in," she said, "And we can decide this struggle ourselves, without affecting anyone else."

"Don't trust her, husband," my wife said, her right hand on my left shoulder. Hawk stood just behind, and the wherret sat at its usual place next to my right ear.

"Will you give me your word that if you win, you'll release my companions and let them go?" I said.

"Yes," she said, "I'll give you my pledge, as a descendant of Master Matrin and Lady S'rënë, that if you're defeated, your friends may leave this world unmolested. And you must give me yours that under such circumstances you'll cooperate fully with me in enabling the Eggs to function as intended."

"But how would my comrades actually get anywhere?" I asked. "No, that just won't do, I'm sorry to say. Your intentions may be honorable, but you've shown that you can't be trusted, even so."

"Then set a gold standard, Morpheús, by which my behavior can be measured. Surely there must be something that you trust."

"What is there that I might consider an absolute *bona fide*?" I said, frowning slightly. "*Ah!*—there is something, Lady, if you'll consent to it."

"If it doesn't compromise my position or person, then I'll agree," she said.

I drew a circle in the air, and opened a passage through æther-space. Then I reached out my hand and helped Master Mathurin step through the gateway that I'd created.

"Lady Niobë," I said, "may I present to you the mage whom you call Master Matrin." I turned the man to face his many-times-removed offspring.

She went stark white and gasped out loud, and finally sank to her knees in front of the barrier. "My Lord Ancestor," she finally managed to say.

He walked forward towards her, and reached a hand through the screen. She grasped it, and he pulled her through, bringing her almost against his body.

The old magician looked down and said: "My dear grand-daughter, I have need of thee. We all have need of thee and thy great abilities. Wilt thou help?"

What could she say? All of her people were listening, for Mathurin had made certain that their quiet conversation was broadcast throughout the square which fronted on the monu-ment. No one could best the wily old politician at this game.

"Yes, grandfather," she said. "I'll do whatever you want me to."

CHAPTER FORTY-EIGHT
"SHE CALLS TO ME"

We kept the barrier around the structure in place to keep the *hoi polloi* (*i.e.*, Niobë's people) from interfering with us during the preparations for the spell we intended to work. Although Master Mathurin still insisted that I must be the one responsible for shaping the great enterprise that would be needed to restore some balance to the universe, his presence helped stabilize the relationship between the Lady and me (and Shah'rah and Scooter as well), and made our interaction possible. Niobë had finally agreed that we must attempt to fix the larger problem before focusing on the smaller disagreement that we had over the long-term use of the Eggs—and she'd quietly handed the implements over to her ancestor.

We began a series of exercises designed to familiarize ourselves with the three Elephant's Eggs and their powers, and how we might interface ourselves with them to create one unit to heal the fractures in the Five Circles.

The Hand of Morlock helped us identify where each of the companion Eggs were located in our universe, and all of the transit-mirrors that could be made to function. The Firedog led us to the controlling consciousness or mechanism for each device, and one by one we subsumed them into our growing net. The two books of power gave us the sheer energy that we needed to reach the most distant parts of the interlocking Spheres, and break through any barriers that we encountered.

We worked unceasingly for weeks, and then months, as our

comprehension and authority slowly grew. Sometimes I paired with Shah'rah or Scooter as substitutes for the Lady, but most of the time it was she who backed my probes into ætherspace, making certain that I wouldn't lose my focus, and that no other entity dared to interfere. We had several close calls, but each was rebuffed with her aid.

I found, much to my surprise, that she *was* a necessary part of the process, and I finally understood why. She had a unique and widely varied experience of all magical forms and workings, and proved to be a steadying influence on all my activities, in a way that neither of the others could provide. Mathurin kept himself away from any direct involvement in the process.

I caught him one day standing over the grave of his long-dead paramour, Lady S'rënë. "What is it, Master?" I asked.

"She calls to me, Morpheús, she calls to me," the old man said. And he fully looked his age by this point. His absence from the mechanical world had taken its toll on his health and physique, as he'd predicted.

"My wife felt her presence here when we first investigated this place, Sir," I said.

"The stories about us are not completely accurate," Mathurin said. "Yes, she did attempt to take control of the implements, the so-called 'Eggs' that I was then employing to heal the structure of the Spheres. But in the process I was forced to kill her. I always regretted that action, but it was necessary. Our twin daughters were too young to understand what'd happened that day. And now she calls to me, as she has since the day that I put her there."

He sighed. "Don't get old, Morpheús. Don't ever let yourself get to the point where you feel worn and tired and utterly useless."

"You're not useless, Master," I said. "You've been a guide to me at every step of the process. I couldn't have done it without you."

"I think you underestimate yourself," the old mage said. "I just have one more question for you, my son: when the time comes, what will you dream for us?"

I didn't understand his query, and told him so. He just laughed and said: "If you don't know where you're going, Morpheús, then we're all in trouble."

I still didn't know what he meant, but I was willing to let time tell the tale, having come to the realization that some things require a basic context to elicit an understanding in oneself.

We finally came to the day when we were ready to try illuminating the entire web of connected transit-machines and – mirrors in tandem with the myriad Eggs scattered hither and yon throughout the Five Circles.

This was by far the grandest experiment that I'd ever attempted, and I needed all of my people involved, even Hawk, whose vital force would add to our energy base. Master Mathurin also agreed to become part of the link, although he declined my invitation to help shape the spell.

First I used the Hand of Morlock to re-establish the current locations of all of the Eggs and transit-devices in the Five Spheres, and then directed the Firedog and Pathfinder to quickly activate them in a series of linked chains. We'd found a way of contacting and employing the transit-machines without the users being aware of our internal interference; the only measurable effect was a slight slowing of transiting times, and there was enough variation in these in the normal course of events that no one would pay attention to such matters.

The most difficult task was leashing the enormous power of the combined *Necropompeion* volumes, which was always threatening to break loose and overwhelm us. We'd had to attempt many smaller experiments before embarking on this large run-through, and I knew that we wouldn't be able to conduct too many such exercises without wearing us down.

I entered into the *milieu* we'd thus established, and let myself "feel" the combined forces at my command. They were all waiting—particularly the Eggs, and rather impatiently, I might add—to be let out of their psychic cage. I realized then the potency of what I was trying to harness, and how difficult this task was going to be. Somehow I had to shape a new reality on top of the old one, a reconfiguration of the æther that would allow the Spheres to grow again, without destroying the underlying schema of things.

It was a daunting prospect, to say the least. Now I understood Master Mathurin's question a little better. If I didn't have some idea in advance of what I was going to do, I might lose everything in a botched attempt to reshape something that would resist all my efforts to force it into a new box of my own making. I had to imagine the "box" first!

However, the structure of the spell was now in place, and so I gradually disengaged each of the participants in such a way that none were harmed, and shut down the trial. By all reckoning, it'd been a great success.

CHAPTER FORTY-NINE
"I HAVE A SONG TO SING, O!"

That night I couldn't sleep, and so I gently disengaged myself from the bedcovers without waking my dear Shah'rah, and started walking the perimeter of the great-room. Around and around I went in slow, lazy circles, occasionally stopping to peer through the hazy barrier at the crowd lingering around the main entrance to the facility, or to gaze up at the giant statues of Master Matrin, as the locals called him, and Lady S'rënë.

On the third, back wall, the side that faced the open platform at the top of the steps, was a set of incuse designs that ran in a series of panels down the flat surface. They told the story in pictures of Matrin and his consort, and how he'd been nursed through a serious illness by his young *protégée*, which in turn had led to their partnership of work and spirit.

But that couldn't be true, not really, because mages rarely became sick from anything ordinary. They could be plonked on the head, as I'd been in the not-so-distant past, or pierced by weapons, or burned, or…whatever—and they certainly were as mortal as ordinary humans— but they didn't usually suffer from the ailments that afflicted the rest of mankind. We didn't shake, sniff, or snort from colds or agues, we didn't perish of cholera or the heebie-jeebies, and we just plain couldn't catch most of the usual bugs. So what did this story represent?

Psairothi adepts could be poisoned by what we called in the trade a "dragon's-draught," a specially prepared brew that included certain herbs, potions, and potencies, although the ingredients involved were hard to acquire and administer, and required a willingness on the part of the killer to debase him- or herself to a level that mitigated against any possibility of secreting the crime.

I recalled the infamous case of Madame Lestley, who murdered her lover, Master Porcypick, a minor colonomancer from Longwitch, and was quickly apprehended, tried, and condemned to 343 years of servitude as a bound sewer-swipe. Even if she'd survived the term, she would have been mindswept by the end of the period. As it was, they found her body flung up on the beach near the outwash pipe of the Cloaca Maxima in Novum Londinium.

I was still speculating on the case of Matrin and S'rënë when a voice just behind me said, "Yes, it was something like that. She wanted control of the then-Eggs (they change over time, you know), and finally became sufficiently obsessed to try the 'dee-dee'—but she had no experience of such things, and botched it enough so that I survived. She thought that I wouldn't realize what'd happened to me. I couldn't let her continue after that, but my enforced illness—and the horror that followed—forever changed me.

"It's the experiences that alter our psyches permanently that make a difference to us. Remember, my son, how you felt when you decided to live once again, and not perish in that alien hospital on my world. If you can harness that feeling of humility and gratefulness at having survived, when so many others haven't, then I think you'll understand what you need to do."

Then he shuffled away with his short, old-man steps, and went back to his bedroll. But I couldn't find any rest, not with the balance of the future at stake. What if I did something wrong? What if I miscued, and the entire structure deteriorated further—or collapsed? What if I failed—again?

The burden of the responsibility seemed overwhelming at that moment. Then I felt a soft arm curl itself around my waist, and a whisper in my left ear: "You're worried, aren't you, husband? You're worried about tomorrow, and tomorrow, and tomorrow."

"What if I make a mistake?" I hissed, looking up at the engraved panel hanging above me.

"You'll fix it, and I'll still love you no matter what," Shah'rah said.

I realized something then: this was enough! This was enough—*for me!* The love of a good woman, the unfolding of a leaf, the quick, sudden laugh of a child—these were things precious beyond any reckoning, along with so many other simple joys of everyday existence. It wasn't wealth or power or status or property that made the difference. It was the little things that mattered, the sweet sureties of life that gave it (and us) depth and pleasure and occasional songs to sing. And that was certainly enough!

A little ditty that I'd once heard in a tavern in Paltyrrha suddenly came to mind:

"I have a song to sing, o!
Sing me your song, o!
It is sung to the moon
By a love-lorn loon,
Who fled from the mocking throng, o!
It's the song of a merryman, moping mum,
Whose soul was sad, and whose glance was glum,
Who sipped no sup, and who craved no crumb,
As he sighed for the love of a ladye."

That described Oridión the Morpheús to the letter—as he once was. But in the end, of course, according to the song, the Ladye begs for the "merryman's" love, and by this onslaught of affection, he's finally and utterly transformed, chanting:

"Heighdy! Heighdy!
Misery me—lack-a-day-dee!
His pains were o'er, and he sighed no more,

For he lived in the love of a ladye!"

Yes, indeed, I had a song to sing, o!
And by all of Heaven's thunder, I would make it a good one.

CHAPTER FIFTY
"SING ME YOUR SONG, O!"

And when, on the next day, we again linked together the great Eggs and transit-devices of all kinds scattered throughout the known universe, I sang my song—of joy and life and love and all the good things that I'd experienced in my existence, and let that feeling of oneness permeate the worlds where intelligence writhed and congregated and spawned, and....

On the planet called Mixt in the Third Circle, a serial murderer named Altudo Prokay paused suddenly in his stalking of a victim, and remembered what his mother had told him when he was eight, and how her smile was the thing that he had craved most in this world; and thus distracted, he uttered the single word "Momma" and abandoned his hunt for just one night—and that woman lived, who was the judge who ultimately put him away;

In the city of Ruádish, on Prugcl in the Second Circle, a ruler named Incalfaxo, being the sixteenth of that ancient line, decided to spend the day toying with his thirty-seventh wife, Ymago, instead of authorizing an expedition against Toltolrostiu, a decision that saved the lives of thirty-seven thousand, three hundred, and forty-two innocent inhabitants of that region—and, unbeknownst to him, ultimately prevented a revolution that would have put him and his entire family to the sword;

At the great transit-station of Bucklynton, on Bucklyn, in the Fourth Circle, Supervisor Morreïton finally authorized, for no reason that he could ever identify, the passage of three underaged members of the Gambozha family, who'd been trying to reunite with their parents for five years—and in the process, guaranteed that the youngest of those children, M'am Luizha, would gain the education she needed to become the greatest composer of her time, an event that would positively influence millions of individuals yet to be born;

On the world of Less'n'More, First Circle, a runaway boy named Zafil was found starving by the side of a road in Amplvat, and instead of being sold into slavery, as was the custom in that place for undocumented minors, was adopted by a woman named Ferriya Kerkera, who gave him her love and affection and attention, thus nurturing and raising the man who later became one of the greatest mages of his—or any other—age;

On a place called Earth, First Circle, a businesswoman named Ms. Zee authorized the production of a film that she knew would make very little money, and might even result in her dismissal (which it did!); but it related the story of the perseverance of a blithe spirit amidst the horrors of genocide, a tale that she felt just had to be told—and thus prevented a similar event from occurring twenty-two years later;

In Pondrat in the Fifth Circle, a writer named Konfee Amastee Durabee, riddled with despair over her inability to make her published work better known, was about to drink herself into oblivion with an overdose of drugs, when she had the idea for a novel called *The Great Elephant's Egg*—and couldn't wait to see how the story would develop; by the time her book was published, she'd turned a new page in her life, and had put aside forever any thoughts of self-destruction; she later found her calling writing jingles for an advertising agency;

In Nova Europa, First Circle, the warring factions at the court of Queen Evetéria I finally agreed to halt their rush towards civil war, when that ruler gained enough strength suddenly to rise from her bed and preside over a reconciliation council;

On Tyrotarichos, at the heart of the Five Spheres, the High Council adopted a new policy of reconciliation towards the member intelligences, giving those races increased representation in the central government, and thus preventing a collapse in long-transit travel thirty-six years later;

And everywhere throughout the Five Circles, people paused in what they were doing—just to pick a flower, to kiss a spouse, to share a meal, to laugh out loud, to teach a child, or to savor the sheer joy of living—and to share it with others in their lives.

I don't know how long that day lasted—it seemed to take forever at times, and at other moments I was conscious of no time passing at all—but throughout that interminable, uncountable, unmeasurable period I knew that what I was doing, with the assistance of my friends, was actually helping. It was no more than that, I clearly understood—I couldn't alter the basic personalities of the individuals involved—but what I did made a small positive difference in people's attitudes—and thus the universe righted itself again.

And for another millennium or two, things would continue functioning normally once more, or what passed as "normal" on most days; and the clockwork mechanism that governed the Spheres would continue to move—tick, tock, tick, tock—until it needed rewinding again.

And that, I also knew, would be accomplished by someone else, because I could never repeat this Great Spell ever again. I wasn't even sure that I remembered now what exactly I'd done to enable the transformation. My responsibility was not ended, of course: I would monitor and maintain the balance of the Spheres for as long as I lived, and I would have to choose the next caregiver before I died, if I had the time and the opportunity.

I sighed. But here and now, I and my companions could do no more. As Barlévin often says, "Sufficient unto the day is the evil thereof."

CHAPTER FIFTY-ONE
"THEY'RE NOT PEOPLE"

Night now enshrouded our enormous working with a haze of ambiguity. I knew that my comrades were as exhausted as I, and that all of us would need a long period of recuperation before we could do much of anything else. I asked Scooter to release the psychic barrier protecting us from the outside world. It wasn't needed any longer.

What we *did* need was food, sleep, and to laugh a little. I yawned.

"You did well," Master Mathurin said, suddenly hugging me to his chest. "You did extraordinarily well, Master of Mages Morpheús. You've earned that title."

"I can never match your record, Sir," I said, "not if I saw a thousand years."

He just chuckled at the thought. "I once thought that a hundred years was a long, long life, and if only I could reach that mark, I'd be more than satisfied. And then a thousand years seemed necessary to complete all the things that I wanted to do—to see and explore the universe, to accomplish such great and glorious feats. Ah, the thoughts of a foolish man: you can't accomplish that in a thousand, or even ten thousand, cycles, and eventually you get tired just thinking about it.

"Well, my course is almost run, and I'm not sorry for it. This universe seems to have left me behind in so many ways. I always knew I was old, of course, but I never thought that I'd *feel* old. And now for the first time, I do."

"I hope you'll continue to be my friend and mentor for many more years, Sir," I said. "I count our first meeting as one of the highpoints of my life."

"I wonder if you'll repeat those words a millennium from now," he said. "You're young, Morpheús. You still have lessons yet to learn."

Always he was trying to instruct me, and always I was playing the ignorant fool. Perhaps it's ever so 'twixt the old and the new. I just didn't fully understand that part yet.

The people rightly wanted to celebrate. They didn't know what exactly had happened here, but the demeanor of their leader told them that the outcome had been a good one. I just wanted to go to bed and sleep for a week, but we had to make allowances—and I realized that replenishing the energy that we'd expended on this longest of days was a necessary part of our restoration.

So we trod the stone steps down into the great-square, and there we were hailed as conquering heroes, and fêted with as large and rich a feast as I've ever encountered. And there were entertainments of all kinds—playlets and dances and music and singing and much, much more—but I fail now to recall every-thing that happened in detail, for we were all tired nigh unto death that night. There was a strange light that blazed from the three eyes of the Lady Niobë—that much I remember—a kind of manic euphoria that I've only seen displayed elsewhere in places where folks are allowed to lose all control of their emotions.

But finally, I could party no more, and Shah'rah and I snuck off into the woods where we wouldn't be disturbed by anyone else, and slept the sleep of the righteous, safe in each other's arms.

The next morning, we staggered back up into the main room of the Monument to gather our things, and to break fast with the others. Hawk was still snoring in one corner, while Scooter seemed as fresh as usual, and Niobë was already meeting with her courtiers and military men to help restore order to the surrounding area. Shah'rah went off to freshen herself (I think she wanted a bath, or at least a dip). I saw Master Mathurin standing at the mural again, gazing up at the image of his late beloved, and slowly shaking his head—over what, I had no idea.

I walked over to him, and wished him a "Good morrow."

"And to you, Master Mage," he said. "Curiously, this day would have been my birthday on the world where I was born, a place called New Earth in the First Circle."

"And how many ales do we quaff in honor of your natal day, Sir?" I asked.

"Ha! Still gnawing at me, eh, Morpheús? Well, I've lived two thousand, six hundred, and eleven years. I was born on the same day that the great city in which I dwelt was conquered by its long-time enemy. My mother and I were taken as slaves to the rival capital, and there I saw the collapse of that other empire some seventy-three years later. I was an old man then, or so I thought. But I'd seriously studied the art, and I was already prolonging my existence with spells and herbs. And so it went. I transited off-world for the first time several hundred years later."

Just then my wife called us for the morning meal, a simple fare of cheese and bread and fruit and sour milk. Niobë sat down with us halfway through, and munched on a slice of dark loaf.

"Have you thought about where you're going next, Master Morpheús?" the Lady asked me.

"I think Shah'rah and Hawk and Scooter and I will return to Nova Europa," I said. "We have unfinished business there. I haven't thought about the longer term, but that's something we'll discuss between us later. However, I would like to take the bodies of our five brave comrades back home for proper burial with their families."

Niobë noticeably grimaced at the mention of the battle in the Throne Room of Réstiff Castle. "I can, uh, arrange that," she finally said, after delicately biting into a ripe red berry the size of a peach. The juice dripped down her chin, staining the veil attached there.

"Fie!" she said. "Kwala fruits are such a nuisance." She

yelled out, "Mikáy!"—and a young man trotted over. "Find me a replacement!" she ordered.

"Yes, Ma'am," he said, and quite literally ran off. He returned again two minutes later with the replacement veil.

"It's good to have things back the way they were," she said, after adjusting the new lace over the bottom of her face, and then stuffing a piece of pungent cheese between her cheeks.

"I'd assumed that they hadn't actually changed," I said. "Wasn't our long-distance exchange merely play-acting with you?"

"Not always," the Lady said, "I did enjoy our several conversations—and I *was* quite, quite lonely. You were the only person with whom I could talk on an equal basis. I'll miss that, particularly now that my dear son is gone.

"Speaking of which, I was wondering, dear Master Mage, if you've considered what you might do with the three Eggs?"

"They've achieved the purpose for which they were created," I said, "but they'd still be dangerous in the wrong hands. I've put them safely away for now. I might have need of them again someday."

"In the meantime, could I possibly borrow them? I want to make certain that the Volúcris are driven from this sector back into their own home space."

"And you anticipate employing the three Eggs for what, precisely?" I asked.

"Whatever I need to do," she said, smiling slightly.

"Your transit technology is somewhat primitive compared to what your neighbors have. The Eggs won't help that," I said. "Perhaps if you worked together with Zezament and the other nearby worlds in this sector...."

"The Zezamentors are such fuddy-duddies, aren't they?" Niobë said. "You experienced them yourself, Morpheús. They're children, really, compared to us, always thinking about how to make a profit on their various enterprises. No philosophy at all, no culture, no art. Really! They're such a minor people."

"When we first landed on Zezament," I said, "we found ourselves in the ruined city of Rakkouzzou. On the long journey back to the capital, I asked our guide what had happened there, and you know what he told me? He said that Naprimér had done this to them a thousand years ago. Your people invaded that world and destroyed several cities before they were driven out. Why should I help you do that again?"

"They're not people," she said. "They're sub-humans. You can tell just by looking at them."

"They look remarkably like you," I said. "Yes, they're shorter and more heavily muscled, and that's probably because they've adapted to the heavier gravity on their world. But I suspect you're actually the same race underneath your skin, so to speak."

"Impossible! Our philosophers tell us that the Zezzies are barely greater than brute animals. Yes, they speak, but that doesn't make them people."

"I don't feel like arguing," I said. "The answer to your question is quite simple, Administrator. No, you may not have the Eggs. Not now, not ever."

Then the Lady got up without saying another word, and strode away, her neck stiff, and her hair wound up and tied at the back of her head. From the rear, she looked like an oversized doll.

"My granddaughter has a very high opinion of herself," Master Mathurin said.

"In Andalusia we call such women *Las Brujas*," Shah'rah said. "They're not to be trusted. *El candil en la calle*." Then she spit on the tile.

"What does that mean?" I asked.

"She's a lamp that shines more brightly on the street than at home," Scooter said.

"Ah, nicely put," Mathurin said.

"She's a witch-bitch," Hawk said. "They'll steal a man's soul, and eat it for supper."

Then Master Mathurin suddenly straightened up and groaned, just once.

"What is it, Sir?" I said, putting my arm around his back.

"The device in my chest just activated, Morpheús. I'm all right, truly. That's what it's supposed to do. My heart apparently stopped beating briefly, and the machine put it back on track again."

But his face had gone a pasty gray, and it was clear that we had to get him back to his own world as soon as possible. When I broached the subject, however, he said: "If you send me through right now, the chances are very good that I'll die of transit-shock almost immediately on the other end. I need to rest here a few days to regain my strength. Then we can attempt the leap."

We took him to one of the back rooms, where we placed him on a soft cot that I ordered delivered right away. When he was comfortable, I spent some time watching him drift off to sleep. He mumbled something once or twice, but I couldn't catch the words.

What had I done? I'd brought the old mage here to act as a buffer between me and Lady Niobë, because I knew that I needed her to complete the spell. If he died as a result, I'd never be able to forgive myself.

If I saved everyone else and lost him—my mentor, my friend, my guide—what was it all worth? I had to return him to the physicians that could actually help him.

"Husband!" my wife said softly in my left ear. "Come, you can do no more here. Let him rest." She tugged on my arm and gently pulled me out of my chair. Then we went back to the room where Matrin's tomb was displayed.

CHAPTER FIFTY-TWO
"'THE MAN WHO FLEW'"

That day had a very strange quality about it, as if the light were bent at an odd angle, and was coloring everything just a bit "off" from what it ought to be. We were still very tired, all of us, all except Lady Niobë, who ran around giving orders hither and yon like a fowl whose head has been cut off, and doesn't know yet she's dead.

We should have been happy, should have been overjoyed at having completed such a tremendous work of magique, something for the sages and historians to write about in æons to come. But we felt instead a tremendous sadness, a deflation of expectation, I think; for now that our life's work was done, what else had we to look forward to? Everything paled in comparison. There is no future when all is past.

I found myself walking the perimeter of the great-room again, walking and walking and walking, until I imagined myself wearing a trail into the hard tile floor. How many circuits would it take to achieve that, I wondered. And always I stopped at the panel that depicted the strange marriage of Master Matrin and Lady S'rënë, and gazed up at those two lost souls. Once I thought I felt a presence at my elbow, and said without looking, "Well, Master, are you feeling better now?"

"Come back to me," was the whispered response, and when I whipped my head to the left to see who it was, I saw nothing there but an empty wind that lightly brushed my face and hair, and left me nigh breathless with anticipation.

That ended my journey for the day.

We supped that evening in one of the back rooms—just I, Shah'rah, Scooter, Hawk, and Mathurin—a subdued occasion in which we could hardly bear to look at each other, much less talk. I think my Master found the pinched atmosphere oppressive, because suddenly he said:

"There was a man named Lucano who wanted to fly. From the time he was a little boy, and saw the birds in the sky, he desired to follow them, and vowed that one day he would attain the heavens.

"He began by drawing them in motion from the observations that he'd made, but he was no artist or draughtsman, and so his scrawling revealed few secrets to him. By the time he was a young man, he was dissecting the birds before his mother could cook them, to see how and why they could soar so high in the wind. But he realized over time that the bones of these creatures were very light when compared to those of other animals, and that there was no way that he could duplicate this structure in himself. Still, the dream would not die.

"Meanwhile, his father died just as Lucano came of age, and he was forced to assume the role of provider in his family, and to work for a tent-maker, for his people dwelt in a town that straddled a trade route. Many of the caravans that passed through this region required parts and cloths to fix or replace their tents before heading into the wilderness.

"One day he was talking with a blacksmith's apprentice, and his friend explained to him the working of a bellows. 'Ha, ha, ha!' the man said. 'I hid it under my cloak one day and took it to market, and then billowed up the dress of a pretty young girl from behind. Oh, wasn't she surprised?!'

"And that gave Lucano an idea. What if he took the hot air from a bellows, and blew it up into a large cloth? Wouldn't it rise into the sky?

"In his spare time he stitched together many different pieces of cloth, and treated it with a special kind of beeswax that he made to seal all the joints and pores of the construct. He placed the huge piece of stained cloth over a light wooden frame, and attached a basket to it underneath with a charcoal burner, and made certain that everything was securely fastened, so that nothing would come apart. And then, for the first time in his life, he knew with certainty that he would finally fly!

"The great day arrived, and Lucano brought his family and friends out to view his 'Folly,' as the townspeople were now calling it. Because everyone knew that no man could ever fly.

"Slowly he began heating the coals, letting the fire spread its warmth throughout the fuel, and then he climbed into the basket, and used the bellows to blow the hot air up into the balloon (for such it was).

"As the overhanging bag gradually filled and puffed out, his chest puffed out along with it, full of the pride of accomplishment. As soon as the cloth was completely distended, and the construct was straining to leap into the heavens, he ordered the stays released, and shot up into the sky at a furious rate.

"Higher and higher he soared, continuing to puff the bellows without thinking about it. And the wind caught the balloon and began blowing it away from the town, and all of the little, bug-like people gathered down below waved and shouted at his triumph. He was so happy.

"Soon he was high over the desert wilderness that surrounded the outpost, and moving further away with each moment. The basket swayed back and forth in the wind, threatening to toss him out, but he held on, exhilarated by the experience. Something hot stung him on the forehead, and he reached up a finger to see what it was. A little piece of wax had melted somewhere up above, and dropped down upon him.

"Then more wax splattered the basket, and more, and suddenly he was losing altitude, and his fire was diminishing, and his magnificent balloon was dropping, dropping, dropping, until finally it smashed headlong into the earth.

"For all of the things that rise into the air, there is a day of reckoning, and the earth ultimately reclaims its own.

"But when the townsfolk found the wreck of his machine,

and the wreck of his body twisted in amongst the remains, they brought him back, their one native-born hero, and erected a great monument to his memory. They commissioned the sculptor Hamilcar to forge the bronze image of him and his balloon. Inscribed at the base of the display, for all to read, were the words: 'The Man Who Flew.' That was all that anyone ever remembered of him."

For a time we remained silent, and then Shah'rah finally said: "What a sad story."

And afterwards we went off to bed, each and every one.

CHAPTER FIFTY-THREE
"I MUST DO THIS"

The next morning, the third day, when we gathered to break our fast, Master Mathurin was absent, so I wandered back through the complex into the great-room again, and as I expected, he was standing in front of the mural, looking up at the image of Lady S'rënë again. "She calls to me," he said, not even aware of my presence.

"Come, Grandfather," I said, putting my arm gently around the old man. "Let's go get something to eat." He reluctantly followed.

We were snacking on some fresh fruit that the locals had supplied when he turned to me with a great smile on his face and said: "Life is good, isn't it, Morpheús? Life is so good. Why does it seem to pass us by so very quickly?"

"I don't know, Grandfather," I said, "but I think that we have to enjoy the moments that we have, and not worry much about the rest."

"Ha!" he said. "So the student has become the teacher. Oh, such delicious irony! Kudos to you, Master Mage! Kudos!" Then he bent over and kissed me on the right cheek. "You are very right, Sir. Never, ever forget that!"

And when we were done, and had delicately swabbed the crumbs off lips and fingers and beards, he suddenly arose and said: "It's time!"

"Time for what, Grandfather?" I asked.

"Come, follow me." Then he led the way back into the place

of Monuments, and we trailed behind this old, old man, unable to catch up.

He was waiting for us near the Tombs, facing the smaller icon of his descendant, Lady Niobë, who was flanked by a squad of troops. Her face was drawn and old—indeed, she appeared to me by far the elder of the twain.

"Seize them!" she commanded, and our hands were immediately secured behind our backs—all except my Master, who just stood there fronting the Lady—and Scooter, who hopped away as usual, and could not be caught.

"What is this?" I asked, trying to keep the anger out of my voice.

"It's time!" she said, echoing Master Mathurin.

"Time for what?"

"Time for you to give me what's rightly mine, Mage," the Lady said. "I've been very patient. I've helped you on your quest, I've given you all my wisdom, my energy, my strength, and I made this Great Spell possible."

"All of this is true," I said, "but I fail to understand how this obligates us to you."

"'You fail to understand'? What kind of fool do you account me, Sir? *Give me my Eggs!* Then you and yours can wander the universe wherever you wish. Go in peace."

"We will go in peace, Cousin," I said. "You can do to us what you wish, but you won't have the Eggs, ever. And even if you did, they'd destroy you. They have minds of their own. The Pachyderms understood the weaknesses of man."

Niobë nodded to two of the soldiers near my wife. One swiftly drew his knife, while the other grabbed her left hand, and while she screamed and yelled her protest and pain, between them they sliced off her small finger, and tossed it on the floor in front of me. A third man strode across the hall with a small, red-hot iron, and jammed it into the bleeding socket that was still gushing blood. Shah'rah fainted.

I struggled to free myself from my captors, shouting obscenities of my own—but I could not wiggle loose.

"Granddaughter, what is this violence?" Master Mathurin said in his gentle voice.

"I must do this," she said. "I must! You can't stop me! You can't!"

But my dear ancestor just stiffened once, as if someone had shoved a rod up his spine. His eyes rolled up, and he fell to the floor with a dull clunk.

"Grandfather!" Niobë shouted. "Grandfather!" She knelt down next to him and embraced the old man.

He opened his eyes again and weakly smiled up at her. "I am so sorry, my dear," he said, and then muttered one word, *"Amove!"*—"Remove!"—while waving the fingers of his right hand in a small, tight pattern.

The Lady went completely white, and collapsed right over the inert body of Master Mathurin.

The guards released us in their anxiety, and rushed to the aid of their mistress. She was still breathing, I noted, as they pulled her away and took her outside.

"Morpheús," I heard a whisper coming from somewhere in the æther—and not from the old man. "She calls to me, Morpheús, and I must go now. Niobë will trouble you no more, but you must leave. Leave *now*, my dear son! *Ave utque vale.*"

I saw the faint image of the Lady S'rënë rise up from her Tomb, and draw the spirit of her husband from his fallen frame. Together they went to a place that I could not follow. Perhaps they're happy out there, wherever it is. I do hope so. I'd like to think that there is another time, another place, for all of us to find rest.

I cut a gate through the æther to Festuca again, and led my friends to safety, one by one.

It was the saddest and happiest period of my life.

CHAPTER FIFTY-FOUR
"WHAT'S THAT SMELL?"

I had no intention of remaining very long on Festuca, but we were all so tired from our ordeal that the "few days" I'd anticipated stretched into a week, and the week into two weeks; and finally I realized one day that we'd been there a month. I'd been so enjoying having nothing to do and nowhere to go for a change that I didn't really want to leave.

However, I finally became bored with the inactivity, and gathered my remaining group together to ask them what they wanted to do.

"I'd like to return home, Sir," Hawk said.

"Me too, husband," Shah'rah added.

"I'll follow you wherever you go, Master," the wherret said.

"And I also want to see Nova Europa again," I said.

My wife and I strolled over to Pissapapilis later that afternoon, and searched out the Mayor.

"Your nephew Chuchaqué has expressed interest in becoming my pupil," I said to Nonnengagué. "We're leaving your world tomorrow, perhaps for a considerable time, so I wanted to ask you if I had your permission, as his nearest surviving relative, to invite him to join us as my ward."

"Of course, Sir," the Mayor said. "We need to learn enough to defend our world against all predators in the future, and I wish to establish a program to train our young people off-world. I know you'll treat him well. You and he both have my blessing."

Then he called for the boy to be found and brought to him

while we waited, and when he appeared, told him about our conversation, and asked him if he wished to go.

"Yes, Uncle," Chuchaqué said in passable Tyrosian. "This is what I asked the Great Mage when he last visited us here. I want to learn...everything. I want to see the universe. This is my dream."

"Then you shall get your wish, dear boy," Nonnengagué said. "Gather your things together, bid farewell to your cousins and sister, and be at the Station at first light tomorrow. Thereafter you must pledge obedience to Master Morpheús as if he were I, standing in my place. Do you agree?"

"Yes, Uncle."

Then the two embraced, and the child went running off to tell his exciting news to his friends and surviving family.

"He's a good lad, Sir," the Mayor said. "You'll find him an easy charge if you treat him well."

"That I solemnly promise to do," I said. "He shall become a part of my household, as if he were one of my own nephews. I shall educate him and show him the good that's in the world, and try to lead him down the proper path. And in the end, I shall return him to you as a man of whom you can be proud."

"That's all I ask, Sir," he said. "Good voyage to you, Master Morpheús, Lady Shah'rah, Master Hawk, and Wherret Scooter." Then he bowed and walked back inside the Green Dome.

The next morning, Chuchaqué was standing outside the front door when I opened it, carrying a small satchel filled with his few clothes, belongings, and several gifts that relatives had presented him. "I'm ready, Sir," he said.

"Then you can begin by joining us for breakfast," I said.

After we cleaned up the mess, I sealed the door, and we gathered together in the common room, all five of us. I cut an aperture into the æther, and easily linked to my own personal transit-mirror in Barstölný on Nova Europa. I used the medallion that Master Melanchthon had fashioned to access the power of the twin books from Hades, and then shooed each member of my team through the link. I was home again!

As soon as I stepped out of the opening, I shut down both access points, and quickly walked through the house, checking the exits and windows for intruders. Everything looked much the same as before, except for the dust that layered the floor, shelves, and furniture. I depolarized the windows to admit some light again, and noticed that the garden had mostly gone to weeds. But it too, so far as I could see from inside, seemed untouched.

"We'll need to bring that woman in to dust and clean," Shah'rah said just behind me.

"Until I know what the situation is, I don't want anyone to know that we're here," I said. "No one goes outside, not even for a moment, and we make no visible signs of occupancy. No smoke from the fireplace. Is that understood?"

They all agreed.

"I don't even know how much time has passed here," I said. "I need to contact a few old friends, if I can find them, to determine what's happened with the government."

We'd brought a little food with us, so we made a cold supper of it, sitting around my great-table that I used for company, after swiping the top with a damp cloth. The water pipe still worked, so I didn't have to worry about having something to drink. The imps and gnomettes in all the appliances were also functioning, so none had exhausted their terms of service yet.

After we ate, I got Chuchaqué situated in a small roomette in the rear of the structure—"This is yours," I told him—and put Hawk in a larger guest room. He promptly retired, saying he was "done in" from the long-transit.

Shah'rah helped me move a second bed right next to mine in my sleeping quarters, and I linked the two together with a simple joining spell. Then she stripped off her clothes, and crawled under the covers herself. "Coming?" she murmured, and when I said that I had things yet to do, she responded with a soft snore. I smiled to myself.

I went to my laboratory with Scooter, and used Master Mathurin's special sky-orb to call Magister Geraklíd, my former superior in magic. I got a very strange signal in response, a "beep-beep-beep" sound that signified that the address that I was contacting was invalid. So the Magister was no longer in office, eh? That was unsettling.

I decided to do some further investigation, now that darkness was upon us. I changed my appearance subtly, removing my facial hair and darkening my skin, and adding a double chin and paunch. I put on some brown commoner's rags that I kept in my closet for such purposes, adding a pair of worn sandals, and cut an opening in the æther to an alley on the outskirts of Barstöl Town. When I'd verified that no one was present, I slipped through the gate, and stood there for a moment getting my bearings. There was a tavern, I knew, just a couple of blocks away, if it was still there.

I directed my gaze at the dirty alleyway, and shuffled my feet as I meandered out onto the street, stumbling a few times as I headed towards my "favorite" watering hole, the Knave of Hearts. The other denizens gave me clear passage as I navigated towards that paradise of cheap ale and cheaper wine. Finally, I pushed open the old wood door, and staggered into the dim recesses.

"Beer!" I mumbled, putting a copper bit on the counter. The barkeep didn't pay me any mind, but just pushed an overflowing mug of the brown liquid at my hands.

I took it to an empty seat at a long-table, and tried not to choke when I actually sipped at the foul brew.

"Good stuff, huh?" the man next to me said.

"Great," I said. "I'd drink horse-piss instead, but the horse might object."

"Ha, ha, ha!" my neighbor said. "You're funny. 'The horse might object.' That reminds me of…."—and then he told me a long, very *un*funny story whose details I promptly forgot.

"You'd think the Queen—or is it King, now? (I forget)—would do somethin' about this rotgut," I said.

"You must really be out of it," the man said, shaking his head. "Nah, the Queen doesn't give a flyin' fuck 'bout folks like us.

Too busy playin' pah-lee-tix."

"Whatsat?" I asked.

"You know, that guv'ment stuff," he said.

"Don't follow that shit much," I said.

"Nah, me neither," he said. "There's great folk and small folk, and never the twain shall meet, they say."

"Who says?" I said.

"Ya know, the twain?"

"What about the Emperor?" I asked. "Ya know, July somethin'-or-other?"

"Oh, no, he's dead a whole year now. Fell off his horsy, they say, but some say he was kilt. His cousin Anti-somethin'-or-other took his place. They're all the same, ya know," he said.

"Yeah, damn pikers, every one," I said.

"Ain't that the truth. More ale?" he asked.

"Nah, gotta go take a leak," I said. Then I got up and staggered off, leaving my mug behind. I'm sure ole Mumbly-Face grabbed it the moment I was out of sight.

So the Queen still reigned in Paltyrrha, and there was another King of Kings in Julianople. Interesting! I yawned. The day was catching up with me, and I knew that if I didn't get some rest soon, I'd collapse. So I transited home, and snuggled up close to Shah'rah's warm, welcoming body.

My lovely wife just stirred and muttered, very romantically, "What's that smell?"

CHAPTER FIFTY-FIVE
"SO THE PRODIGAL
DOTH RETURN"

The next morning, I decided to try another avenue, and putting on my old rags again, transited with Scooter to a wooded area near the Bridge of Sighs in Julianople. Then I sent the wherret with a private message for my old teacher, Doctor Árbogast, asking him to meet me there in the first hour of the afternoon.

I was standing on the arch of the structure, looking down at the slowly moving waters of the St. Joseph Canal and enjoying the spring weather, when the professor ambled up the cobbled pathway that led to the bridge. Scooter kept out of sight, per my instructions.

"So the prodigal doth return," he said. "About time, too."

"How much time?" I asked.

"You don't know?"

"I just got back yesterday," I said, "and I've kept a very low profile. I don't know anything about anything yet."

"Remind me: when did you leave?"

"July, 1622."

"Then you've been gone almost five years. Today is the day before the Nones of April, in the Julian Year 1267."

"1627!"

"Yes," Árbogast said.

"I can't believe that's possible. Of course, time moves differently in the Otherworlds, and I was never sure of how many months or days elapsed between certain events. So what do I need to know?"

"The times have been getting increasingly perilous," the teacher said. "Old Emperor Stephanos died shortly after you left, and his idiot son, Autokratôr Ioulianos, quickly managed to expend most of the treasury and goodwill that his father had gathered during his long reign, and finally died a questionable death early last year. He was succeeded by Philippos, who claimed to be (and might have been) a natural son of the old Emperor, but was unable to hold his position for more than six months. Then the usurper Bakchos, head of the Imperial Guard, took control for four months—but General Prince Antiochos immediately began his long march through Asia Minor with his army. By the time he reached the Sea of Marmara, the accidental Autokratôr's head was waiting for him on a pike over the main gate. This happened in December, and our new Emperor's been trying to settle everyone's hash since then."

"What about Kórynthia?" I asked.

"The old Queen suffered a stroke some years ago," my former instructor said, "And was confined to bed. Although she retained enough of her senses to review documents (and mark them with an "x"), she could no longer attend the Council meetings or any public functions. The political situation declined very rapidly, as each faction supporting a different candidate for the position of Heir Presumptive began actively pushing and pulling the apparatus of the state.

"Then, early this year, the miracle happened: Queen Evetéria regained enough strength to organize and attend a Reconciliation Council. All of the candidates were present, and she named the least likely of them, Lady Karlyna, as her chosen candidate. This was a brilliant move, because the Princess Karlyna, as she now became known, was unmarried, and so were most of the male possibilities—all except Duke Zoltán, who had the strongest legal claim and the largest amount of territory.

"So the other claimants all supported the new heir, figuring they could marry her at some point, and either reign jointly, or control her actions. They did manage to band together long enough to purge some of Evetéria's councilors, ministers, and other officials, substituting a list of incompetents that wouldn't oppose anything they wanted to do. Except, of course, that none of them can now agree on what they want to do. And so the government is more paralyzed than ever. The poor Queen has been left slowly swinging in the political winds, powerless and friendless in this time of need. But she's still alive, and still keeping her hand in the game. It's better than an outright civil war would be—but not by much."

"I had no idea," I said, "and there was nothing I could have done in any case while I was in the Otherworlds. What's happened to Magister Geraklíd?"

"Dismissed, supposedly for mishandling funds," he said. "They allowed him to retire to his country estate. Of course, all of the so-called 'actions' against former officials have been indefinitely postponed, because none of the suitors can agree now on a course of action. It's a terrible mess.

"Meanwhile, the Liets have been encroaching along the northeast border of Kórynthia, and no one is paying attention while they seize the disputed lands that they've long claimed as theirs.

"As soon as the Heir Presumptive picks a husband from among the claimants, or as soon as one them prevails and is sanctioned by the Queen, then we may have the civil conflict that everyone's been long expecting."

"Let's hope that day is postponed for many years," I said.

"I'm an old man, Morpheús," he said. "There's nothing much I—or any of the rest of us—can do at this point. If Evetéria survives for a while longer, thereby giving Princess Karlyna time to learn what she needs to know, then the situation may stabilize again. At least we can hope so."

I sighed. Then I thanked him for agreeing to meet me, and wished him the best. I went back to the woods where Scooter was waiting, and transited back to Barstölný.

CHAPTER FIFTY-SIX
"WHAT KIND OF NAME IS THAT?"

When I returned home, I immediately called the others together to relate what I'd learned.

"I know very little about the new Heir," I told them. "I've never met her, and I don't think she was ever at court while I was there. I believe that she's the only surviving grandchild or great-grandchild of Princess Anastasia, the Queen's great-aunt, and was raised by her ward in the provinces. Her immediate relatives have all died, I think. She came of age last year."

"Why did Evetéria pick her, Sir?" Hawk asked.

"She probably felt that there was less chance of civil war if an unmarried girl was the candidate. Several of the other possibilities, including Duke Zoltán and Count Istiál, are as closely related as she, all through female heirs; only Prince Zacharias is descended from a direct-male line, but more distantly.

"If one of the suitors for her hand prevails, or receives the nod from the present monarch, the other pretenders will coalesce against him—and her. Only if Princess Karlyna marries someone with no possibility of making a claim on his own behalf does she have a chance of surviving. But that's not our concern right now.

"In the meantime, let's get this house open again, and hire some staff. Shah'rah and I will go to town in the morning, and see who might be available. Hawk, you and I will transit to Paltyrrha this afternoon, and get you reestablished in your studio."

"We need to settle accounts with the families of my men, Sir," he said.

"Yes, and I'll ask you to provide a list of their real names and situations. I want to pay for a memorial honoring their service."

"What about me, Sir?" the boy Chuchaqué asked in Tyrosian.

"You first need to learn enough of the local tongue to communicate with other folks," I said. "I can lend you some of the language directly, but afterwards I'll have to hire a tutor to teach you advanced Latin and Greek grammar and diction.

"Also, your birth name is difficult for the natives here to pronounce. You'll need to pick something that'll fit in better. Scooter knows Tyrosian, so if you have problems communicating with Shah'rah, please use the wherret as a temporary translator."

"Yes, Sir. I'll do my best, Sir."

"I know you will." I then told Hawk and Shah'rah what I'd said to the boy.

"He'll do fine, Sir," the Sergeant said. "He has more gumption than I did at that age."

"Let's get you settled," I said, and we used my private transit-mirror this time. There was no point in hiding anymore.

We emerged from the main public alcove located near his establishment, and began walking the four blocks there. The weather was sunny but crisp, with a light breeze blowing through the city streets. A few trees were just beginning to sprout.

"I do love this time of year," I said. "I suppose I should begin calling you Strook again. What's your Christian name, Sergeant?"

"Sôpén," he whispered.

"What kind of name is that?"

"The kind of name that they have in western Polonia, where I was born. That's why I don't use it, Sir."

"I understand," I said. Then we came to the soldier's studio, and were greeted by Pervicax, whom Hawk had made co-owner and manager before he left.

"You're back!" the man shouted, embracing his former

comrade-in-arms. "I'd almost given up hope. But where are our friends?"

"Gone, every one," the Sergeant said. "They fought honorably."

"The luck of the dice," the manager said, bowing his head. "None of us beat those odds in the end."

"How's business?" Strook asked.

"Booming, Sir," Pervicax said. "With things as unsettled as they are, everyone wants to beef up their skills. I had to rent the building next door—I hope that was OK."

"Of course." Then Strook turned to me. "I've got a lot to do here, Sir. If you'll call within a few days, I'll get you that list of names."

I handed the man a pouch stuffed with gold.

He hefted it and said: "This is way too much, Sir."

"No," I said, "it's what you earned—that, and my eternal gratitude. Maybe we can do this again one day."

He smiled briefly. "Perhaps so, Sir. Perhaps so." He reached out his right hand. I shook it, gratefully, and we parted friends.

While strolling the avenue on the way back to the public transit-station, I saw a street vendor off to one side, and was just about to pass him by, when something about him stirred a moment of recognition, and I stopped and faced him.

"Ya wants to buy some of my goods, Sir?" he said.

"*You!* You were the one who sold me the Eggs in Julianople!" I said.

"What eggs, Sir? I dunno nothin' about any eggs. I sells junk, pure and simple."

I looked over his array of offerings, and sure enough, there was nothing there worth a second examination. It was all routine cast-offs harvested from local garbage heaps.

"But I was sure…," I mumbled.

"Ya always gots to look before ye leaps, Sir," he said, squinting at me while he grinned.

I shook my head, and walked away, fooled once again. But then I heard his voice behind me say, "And just how did them eggs work out for ye, Sir?" I swiftly swiveled around, but the man and his cart were gone—as if they'd never existed. I'd seen many strange things these last years and months, but nothing so strange as that curious little junkman and his push-vehicle.

I told Shah'rah about him that evening at dinner, while Scooter translated my words to the boy.

"I would have liked to have seen him, Sir," Chuchaqué said.

"Have you picked a name, son?" I asked.

"While you were gone, Sir, Scooter and I looked at a book that listed such things, and I liked Voltairos."

"That's a good, strong name, and it suits you," I said. "So—Voltairos it shall be from now on."

He smiled at my approbation.

After supper, we went out into the much-reduced garden, and walked the curved pathways amidst the overgrown weeds and surviving plants. The periodic bulbs were just starting to sprout. I brushed off a stone bench nearby, and sat there with my new family—my lovely wife, my foster son, and my wherret—enjoying with them the cool evening. Soon it would be summer again, and I was looking forward to having this place to ourselves once more, and finding some peace and solitude for a change. Tomorrow might bring war or chaos or adventure, but *this* day, at least, was filled with joy and love and a sense of completion.

I sighed. I had one more thing yet to do, one more task that I'd promised myself to accomplish before I rested. And it was the hardest one of all.

CHAPTER FIFTY-SEVEN
"BUT THAT'S ANOTHER STORY"

A few days later, while our new cleaning and gardening crew set to work on bringing our abode back to livable standards, the four of us transited to the city of Zmyrna, on the west coast of Asia Minor. This ancient Greek seafaring colony had existed for several thousand years, nestled at the head of a long, protected inlet.

I thought I knew my way around town, despite the decades that had passed since my last visit here, but I quickly became lost, and with that stubbornness that sometimes infuses the male animal, refused to ask for directions, until we'd wandered the back streets of the city for several hours.

Before we left, I'd infused the basic elements of the Greekish tongue in both my wife and foster child, so they could communicate with those around them.

"We're lost, husband," Shah'rah said simply.

"We're lost, Sir," Voltairos agreed.

"We're definitely lost, Master," Scooter added.

I sighed loudly at the lack of patience of my betters, but finally stopped a mounted patrolman, and asked the location of Marankós Street.

"Oh, Sir, that's a half-mile or more east o' here. You take Zarzaváti Avenue till you come to Rháptis Way, and you follow that one to the right till it crosses Marankós. That'll get you there."

I thanked the man, and led the way with greater determination than ever. I thought I heard a few stifled smirks behind me, but I wouldn't give the others the satisfaction of acknowledging them.

Finally we came to territory that I recognized, but when we reached the old, worn-out house where I'd grown up, some other family was living there.

I pounded on the entrance, but had to repeat my action a second time to gain anyone's attention; I asked the woman who finally responded if she knew what had happened to Selíni Vassiliádis, who had once dwelt there.

"Nah," she said, "don't know nobody by that name. Don't want to buy nothin' neither"—and slammed the door almost into my nose.

Then I went to several of the neighbors, and none of them could help either. I was beginning to get that kind of empty feeling in the heart that comes with the despair of knowing that an old connection has been permanently severed. It didn't help matters to realize that I was the one who'd been responsible for the lack of communication with my family—because I was too busy, too self-centered, too ashamed of my humble origins.

"It's all right," Shah'rah said softly, putting her hand over mine. She knew how I felt.

I'd about decided to try some other avenues, when an old man who was lounging on his upstairs window balcony shouted down to me, "You related to Selíni?"

I looked up at him, and vaguely remembered a name to go with a much younger face: "Christos?" I said.

"Ay. Who be you, then?" he asked.

"Oridión Vassiliádis," I said.

"'Ridión? I remember you. You was always a sassy little brat."

"Still am," I said, grinning up at him.

"Your ma's with your sister, Thítis, o'er on Xóma Street. She be glad to see you, for sure," the old man said.

"Thank you," I said, and tossed him a copper bit.

He smiled when he caught it. "No, thank *you*, Sir."

Xóma, I remembered, was three blocks over and four blocks down, and I could hardly contain my excitement when I entered the narrow way. Christos had told me that they lived in the fourth house down from the end, on the left-hand side of the street. We came to the appropriate place, an unpretentious but neatly kept dwelling crammed up against its neighbors, in the style of the Old City. I tentatively rapped on the front door.

"Yes," came a female voice through the look-hole.

"Is this the house where Selíni Vassiliádis lives?" I asked.

"Yes. Who wishes to know?"

"Her son."

There was a long pause, and then I heard the bolt being drawn back. The door cracked open just slightly, and I saw an eye peering out.

"Which son?" came the tentative query.

"The eldest—Oridión."

"That's impossible. He's dead," the middle-aged woman said. "We were told by the Brothers of Saint Bronisláv of the Æthereal Light that he'd gone off somewhere into the void, and never returned."

"He did indeed venture into the Otherworlds," I said, "but he lived to tell the tale, and now he's returned."

"But...." She opened the door fully, and looked me up and down. "Yes, you could be him, except you...you haven't changed much. I don't remember him very well, because I was so young when he left home. Tell me something that only my brother would know."

"If you're Thítis, you were six when I was taken for training—and I was a decade older. The day before I left, you came to me and told me that I shouldn't go, because if I did, I wouldn't come back for a long, long time, and I'd experience much sorrow and pain. You had some of the same talent for foretelling as I, little sister.

"So I gave you a crystal, and I put some of myself into it, even though I had very little technique at the time; and I told you that whenever you missed me, to take it in your hand, and it would glow—and you would know that I still lived, and would return to you one day. Do you remember?"

Then she started weeping, and pulled from beneath the neck of her dress a chain, and hanging from the bottom of the silver links was a crystal stone, now clasped in a demure setting of its own. She put it to her lips, and it began to radiate a warm, golden light.

"You see?" I said. "I still live, dear one."

"'Ridión!" she said, and came into my arms. "And who are these folks?"

"My wife, Shah'rah," I said, "My fosterling, Voltairos, whom I found in the void, and my familiar, Scooter."

"Mother!" she screamed, turning her head back into the interior. "Mother! Look who's here!"

She pulled us into the common room, and led me to a great-chair in which an old woman sat.

"Who's there?" she asked.

"It's 'Ridión, Ma," I replied. "It's 'Ridión."

"I always knew you'd come home again, despite what they said. I knew you weren't dead, my boy. I knew it in my heart!"

Of course, she insisted that Shah'rah and I be remarried in the church, and that I adopt Voltairos as my own, and that the dirty wherret remain outside, and not litter the rug with its fur.

But that's another story.

AFTERWORD
"PEELING THE LAST ELEPHANT'S EGG"

According to my notes, I penned the first few pages of this novel on March 24, 2006. I was intrigued with the idea of a long-distance romance, of creating the story of an impossible liaison between two individuals separated by an enormous void that was nearly unbridgeable.

Now, there have been many such tales in the literature, stories of star-crossed love spanning the bounds of time and space, and I'd already read many of the classics, including such works as Richard Matheson's *Bid Time Return*. I knew all the conventions, and I wanted to do something different with them.

So I started with two words, "Help me!"—and went on from there. As I recall, I either wrote the entire first chapter or the first two pages thereof—and then set the story aside, until I had more time to develop it.

That time didn't arrive for more than two years.

I wrote the actual book in three stints spread over another two years—two weeks in July, 2008, just over four months beginning January 1, 2009, and from December 18, 2009 through May 7, 2010. By then the text had accumulated almost 600 pages and just under 200,000 words—and, strangely enough, I found myself continuing the thread of the tale in a kind of sequel set back in Nova Europa, right *after* Morpheús and crew have returned from the æther; and this went on for several more chapters before I realized (with some horror) exactly what I was doing. I was just having too much fun with the characters to want to abandon them. I'd never had this happen before.

So, I shut things down immediately, capped off the narrative with an appropriate ending, and sent off part of the first section of the manuscript. My then-agent said that she liked the beginning chapters, but that the book was too long to market as is.

A month later, I retired permanently from Cal State SB, and moved into full-time editing and writing, something that I'd wanted to do all my life. But *The Fourth Elephant's Egg*, as I was calling it, just sat there gathering literary motes. What to do with it was the problem—but that problem applied generally to all of my creative writing.

Of course, this wasn't my first fantasy of Nova Europa. I'd previously published three other long novels set in roughly the same *milieu* (but at different times and in different places) through a small California house, Ariadne Press. They'd made very little impression, although several had garnered excellent reviews from Tom Easton at *Analog*—and from a few others as well.

It was my dear wife, Mary, who suggested that all of my long fictions needed to be divided into trilogies to make them more palatable and salable to present-day readers. We started the process with *Invasion!* (this one had actually been penned as three separate books, although it had only been issued in omnibus form), and then turned to the unpublished fantasy, *Elephant's Egg*, which just a few individuals had then seen.

This novel, it turned out, also had potential breaking points at the one-third and two-third marks in the narrative, and was relatively easy to fracture. So I divided the manuscript into roughly equal sections, re-edited the text, and added the appropriate Prologues and Epilogues, as well as some small pieces of additional copy. I renamed the three parts as: *The Cracks in the Æther*, *The Pachyderms' Lament*, and *The Fourth Elephant's Egg*. And that's what I offer to you now.

* * * * * * *

Once Morpheús left Pachydermia, he had to find a way of connecting with the humanity—and alienness—surrounding him in the strange environs of the Fifth and Sixth Circles of the Æthersphere. Because, as both his ancestor and the Pachyderm spokesman had pointed out to him, without such ties the mage would have no chance of putting things to right again. The winding down of Life, the Universe, and Everything was all about people at its core, and the necessity of restoring some balance to the cosmos; and the mage could never accomplish those tasks without some real feeling for sentient beings.

And so I created Festuca, the grain world, whose name in its Latin original also refers to the rod of manumission freeing bound slaves. The humans of this planet had been growing foodstuffs to supply the Overseer-controlled worlds in their sector of the Fifth Circle. In essence, the Festucans had become economic servants to the Overworld.

And then an experiment to increase Festuca's crop yields had gone terribly wrong, causing an ecological disaster—and the Overseers chose to abandon their task-bound farmers to their fate—which inevitably led to mass starvation and disease among the indigenous population. The main transit-station on the planet was shut down, locked tight, and left vacant. Millions perished in the aftermath.

Morpheús and his people had visited this world briefly on their way to the Fifth Circle, but had decided that the cold, cloud-enshrouded planet was devoid of larger life forms, and had left almost immediately. Now, when they seek sudden refuge there again, they realize that a small number of survivors of the original population are still maintaining themselves through scavenging.

And the mage suddenly understands, with his "wife"'s helpful prodding, that *he* must assume responsibility for setting things to right again. It doesn't matter who caused the problem; if there's a possibility of fixing it, he has to find a way.

All writers distance themselves to some degree from the

people around them. They have to do this in order to notice, to observe, to relate the details about how individuals interact with each other. One of the unfortunate results of being a perpetual "observer" is that often there's not enough time to be a "participator" as well. The truths that authors glean from their observations are rarely applied very appropriately to themselves or to their own behavior. Morpheús's blind spot is also the blind spot of his creator.

So, this series of scenes was, at least for me, a key turning point in the mage's development as a man. It was important that he understand the why of things as well as the how.

* * * * * * *

I had an enormous amount of fun writing these books. The characters spoke to me in a way that few ever have. Although I took more time with these three novels than I have with any of my other fiction, I was always able to pick up the narrative again immediately upon returning to the text.

As I mentioned above, when I came to the obvious end of the story, I just kept on going for another couple of chapters. A small part of the first supplemental chapter was salvaged for the beginning section of Chapter Fifty-Five in this book—but the rest was put aside for a future date. The main difference in the narration was that Queen Evetéria had already died in the new piece, and had been succeeded by her designated heir—and things were seriously beginning to fall apart politically in Kórynthia. Obviously, Morpheús would now have had to step forward and do something about that.

But, as I said at the end of *this* novel, that's another story, and if I live long enough to write it—and to pen other tales of Nova Europa—welladay. In the meantime, I hope you enjoy this new trilogy. I certainly had a blast writing it!

—Robert Reginald, 15 May 2011

ABOUT THE AUTHOR

ROBERT REGINALD was born in Japan, and lived in Turkey as a youth. He starting writing as a child, and penned his first book during his senior year in college. He settled in Southern California in 1969, where he served as an academic librarian for forty years. He currently edits the Borgo Press Imprint of Wildside Press, and has also penned more than 125 books and 13,000 short pieces. His recent works of fiction include twelve Nova Europa historical fantasies (2004-11); six science fiction novels: The War of Two Worlds Trilogy: *Invasion!*, *Operation: Crimson Storm*, and *The Martians Strike Back!* (2007/2011); two Human-Knacker War SF novels: *Knack' Attack* (2010) and *"A Glorious Death"* (2011); and *Academentia: A Future Dystopia* (2011); two Phantom Detective period mysteries: *The Phantom's Phantom* (2007) and *The Nasty Gnomes* (2008); a comic mystery, *The Paperback Show Murders* (2011); a horror novel, *Hell's Belles* (forthcoming); and four story collections: *Katydid & Other Critters: Tales of Fantasy and Mystery* (2001), *The Elder of Days: Tales of the Elders* (2010), *The Judgment of the Gods and Other Verdicts of History* (2011), *Dead Librarians and Other Shades from Academe* (2011). He has also edited the SF anthologies, *Yondering* (2011), *To the Stars and Beyond* (2011), *Once Upon a Future* (2011), and the mystery anthologies, *Whodunit?* (2011) and *More Whodunits* (2011). You can find him at:

www.millefleurs.tv

And watch for the other
volumes in *The Hypatomancer's Tale Trilogy*:

THE CRACKS IN THE ÆTHER (Book One)

THE PACHYDERMS' LAMENT (Book Two)

www.ingramcontent.com/pod-product-compliance
Lightning Source LLC
Chambersburg PA
CBHW050411260626
47156CB00003B/963